No Tan Lines

No Tan Lines

KATE ANGELL

KENSINGTON PUBLISHING CORP.
www.kensingtonbooks.com

KENSINGTON BOOKS are published by

Kensington Publishing Corp.
119 West 40th Street
New York, NY 10018

All Kensington titles, imprints, and distributed lines are available at special quantity discounts for bulk purchases for sales promotions, premiums, fund-raising, educational, or institutional use.

Special book excerpts or customized printings can also be created to fit specific needs. For details, write or phone the office of the Kensington special sales manager: Kensington Publishing Corp., 119 West 40th Street, New York, NY 10018, attn: Special Sales Department; phone: 1-800-221-2647.

KENSINGTON and the k logo are Reg. U.S. Pat. & TM Off.

ISBN-13: 978-0-7582-6919-5
ISBN-10: 0-7582-6919-6

First Kensington Trade Paperback Printing: June 2012

10 9 8 7 6 5 4 3 2 1

Printed in the United States of America

ACKNOWLEDGMENTS

Friends and family are so very important: Debbie and Ted Roome, Sue-Ellen Welfonder, Jina Bacarr and the Browns—I appreciate you.

The doctors and staff at Mission Hills Veterinary Clinic, Naples, Florida: Dr. Angela Butts, Dr. Amelia Foster, Cincy, Eddie, Lauren, Shannon, Tracy—you are amazing!

My editor, Alicia Condon: thanks for everything.

Prologue

"We've got customers." Kai elbowed Shaye Cates in the side. Their summer job placed them behind the candy counter of the Snack Shack on the Barefoot William Pier.

Tonight's outdoor movie, *Babe,* was being shown on the outer wooden wall of the concession stand. The family film flickered through the open window above the popcorn machine as a pink pig raised by sheepdogs learned to herd sheep with the help of Farmer Hoggett.

Shaye straightened from her slump behind the counter. She brushed her hair out of her eyes, then tugged down the hem on a T-shirt that had started life five years ago a much brighter shade of blue. Her jeans were bleached white. She was barefoot, and her pomegranate nail polish was in need of a fresh coat.

She'd been stocking oversized boxes of Jujyfruits, red licorice whips, and Sno Caps when Trace Saunders, the hot boy with the cool name, walked in. He carried two navy vinyl beach chairs under his arm, as moviegoers were required to supply their own seats.

His date trailed behind him. Crystal Smith was sixteen going on twenty. She appeared relaxed, whereas Trace looked restless and bored by the ten o'clock feature. He apparently wasn't into talking farm animals.

Shaye despised him. Her dislike surpassed her hatred of cooked cabbage, alarm clocks, cold weather, and shoes. Trace was an ass.

What did she expect from a hotshot jock? He was the star of a rival high school team. He was a sophomore who played varsity. He'd gone through a growth spurt and now stood six feet tall, all lanky and smug. He was big enough to play in Major League Baseball. If he ever did, that was one bubble gum baseball card she'd trash. And fast.

That very afternoon Shaye had sat on the bleachers at Gulf Field and watched Trace hit a line drive between the shortstop and the second baseman in the top of the fifth. His team was already ahead by four runs, yet Trace had rounded the bases as if his hit would win the game.

The boy could sprint, long strides, pumping arms. Not that she noticed. She was more interested in her cousin Kai, who played catcher. He'd crouched low for a throw from the center fielder as Trace slid home. Trace's shoulder caught Kai in the chest and sent the catcher flying. Kai sailed several yards, slamming into a metal post. He'd bruised his spine.

Trace's fan club applauded his run. Ten clueless teenage girls bounced on the bleachers like pogo sticks with boobs.

Shaye was a tomboy and broke the school rule of non-players on the field. She'd climbed the chain-link fence and raced straight for Kai. She dropped to her knees and asked, "You okay?"

Kai fought to catch his breath. "Wind knocked out of me."

She placed a comforting hand on his shoulder, then looked at Trace. The boy dusted off his uniform pants, all smiles and puffed chest. Shaye *despised* his cocky smile and wanted to wipe it off his face. He'd hurt Kai. The incident was unforgivable, and she let him know it with a dirty look. Which Trace ignored.

Trace topped Kai's shit list as well. Kai had always been the athletic superstar until Trace moved to town, coming from a private boarding school. Trace was Kai's chief competitor in both sports and dating. Trace had gone as far as to steal Kai's girlfriend, which was unacceptable to Shaye. Crystal belonged with Kai.

Shaye's hatred of Trace was bone deep. He was a Saunders, and she was a Cates. Their century-old feud killed all pleasantries between them.

Over a hundred years had passed since her great-great-great-grandfather William Cates left Frostbite, Minnesota. He'd been a farmer broken by poor crops and a harsh, early winter. He'd sold his farm and equipment, then hand cranked his Model-T and driven south. The trip was long and hard, yet he pushed on until the Florida sunshine thawed him out.

On a long stretch of uninhabited beach, William rolled up his pant legs and shucked his socks and work boots. Once he experienced the warm sand between his toes, he vowed never to wear shoes again.

He put down roots, married, and named the fishing village Barefoot William. The town expanded slowly, as family and longtime friends moved to the Gulf Coast. Even after he was elected mayor, William walked barefoot through city hall, as did the other town officials. Back then, life existed on a man's word and a solid handshake. For two decades, the village remained small and laid-back.

Until the day Evan Saunders disrupted the peace. He was a capitalist with big-city blood. He wore three-piece suits, a bowler hat, and polished brown oxfords. It was rumored the man never broke a sweat even in summer.

Evan set his sights on real estate. He contacted Northern investors, and, within six months, the Saunders Group began to buy up land. Evan wanted to citify the small town. He sought to turn Barefoot William into a wealthy winter resort.

William Cates and Evan Saunders sparred for sixty years. William battled zoning and expansion. He was comfortable with the short boardwalk and long fishing pier. He valued friendships and a sense of community, whereas Saunders was a developer. Evan built his own boardwalk and yacht harbor and snubbed the barefoot mayor.

Hostility flared between the two men, and Barefoot William became a town divided. On an overcast day with thunderheads roiling, the conservative and the capitalist drew a line in the sand, which neither crossed during the remainder of their lifetimes. The line later became Center Street, the midpoint between Barefoot William and Saunders Shores.

The Cateses' northern cement boardwalk linked to a wooden pier that catered to fishermen, sun worshippers, water sports enthusiasts, and tourists who didn't wear a watch on vacation.

Amusement arcades and carnival rides drew large crowds to the Barefoot William boardwalk. The specialty shops sold everything from Florida T-shirts, ice cream, sunglasses, sharks' teeth, and shells to hula hoops.

A century-old carousel whirled within a weatherproof enclosure. Its wall of windows overlooked the Gulf. The whirr of the Ferris wheel was soothing, while the swing ride that whipped out and over the waves sent pulses racing.

Barefoot William was as honky-tonk as Saunders Shores was high-end. Couture, gourmet dining, and a five-star hotel claimed the southern boundaries. Waterfront mansions welcomed the rich and retired. Yachts the size of cruise ships lined the waterways. Private airstrips replaced commercial travel. The wealthy were a community unto themselves.

In Shaye's mind, Trace Saunders didn't belong on the

Barefoot William Pier. Not tonight. Not ever. He was like gritty sand rubbing against her skin. She wanted to wash him off.

She leaned her elbows on the candy counter and gave him a hard stare to let him know where she stood. "You're trespassing."

Trace crossed the wide wooden planks of the candy shack and came to stand before her. Her breath caught. He was tall. "I'm slumming." His boy's voice was manly deep, a baritone that gave her goose bumps.

She looked him over with careless indifference. His hair was short, black, and spiky. His eyes were blue-gray and as pale as the crest of a wave. Movie night was casual—tank tops, T-shirts, shorts—yet Trace wore a white button-down and dark slacks. She wanted to kick sand onto his polished loafers. No doubt he'd kick it back.

She felt Kai tense as Crystal joined Trace. She wore a pink sundress with a narrow turquoise necklace strap. Shaye tried not to stare. Crystal was all girly and hot, everything Shaye was not. From the corner of her eye, Crystal glanced at Kai for all of two seconds. Kai, on the other hand, glared a hole through her.

The two had a history. They'd grown up together. Crystal had claimed Kai as her boyfriend in the third grade. She'd pulled his hair on the playground until he agreed. They'd hung tight for seven years, up until her six-teenth birthday, when Crystal decided she looked too much like a kid and wanted to appear more adult.

The Scissorhands Salon in Barefoot William no longer suited her. She'd called the stylists juvenile and silly. Crystal crossed to the dark side and booked an appointment at Zsuzsy, an exclusive day spa in Saunders Shores. The spa achieved the desired effect. The girl entered through its mint-green and gold double doors and emerged a young woman. Shaye and Kai hardly recognized her.

Crystal had cut her long brown hair, dyed her eyelashes, then gone on to purchase a wardrobe from Eclipz, a new teen designer.

Kai had made the mistake of saying he missed Crystal's ponytail. Crystal had yet to forgive him. Shaye kept silent when it came to Crystal's lashes, which were so sooty and thick, her brown eyes appeared black.

Trace Saunders was the only one to compliment Crystal's haircut, a style as geometrically sharp as her tongue when she later dumped Kai.

Kai still suffered a broken heart. It was painful for him to see Trace and Crystal together now. Shaye needed to move them along.

She tapped the top of the candy counter. The colors on her mood ring shifted from calm blue to midnight dark. She loved retro jewelry and shopped the local flea market every Saturday.

"Buy something or say good-bye." She was being rude to Trace but didn't care. He never gave her one good reason to be nice to him, so why start now?

Trace raised an eyebrow. Tonight he looked more amused than affronted. He was used to her behavior. She constantly blew him off and, on occasion, openly cheered when he struck out at baseball, missed a hoop in basketball, or came in second at a track meet.

He wasn't crazy about her either. His girlfriends had boobs and hips. Shaye was an A-cup and all legs. Trace had called her Toothpick for as long as she could remember. She hated the nickname.

"I'd like cotton candy," Crystal announced.

"We're sold out, and the machine's being cleaned," Shaye took pleasure in telling her.

"A bag of popcorn, then," was Crystal's second choice.

"All that's left is unpopped kernels," Shaye said. "You could chip a tooth."

"Hot dog?" Crystal tried a third time.

"Steamer's turned off."

Crystal pouted until Trace suggested, "Candy bar?"

His date perked up. "We can play Sweet Treat," she was quick to say. "Shaye created the game. She asks a question, and if you answer it correctly, the candy's free."

"Free sounds good," Trace agreed.

Shaye preferred that he pay. Her family owned the Snack Shack, and any item given away cut into their profits. Even something as small as a candy bar. She was annoyed that Crystal had shared a game played only by close friends. Trace was her enemy. She must never forget that.

"I'll go first," Crystal said.

Shaye had always liked Crystal, until the girl dumped Kai. Crystal was an average student, more into appearances than schoolwork. She often got confused by the wording of a question. "How is cotton candy made?" Shaye asked.

"In a cotton candy machine."

Shaye shook her head. "Sorry, wrong answer. I was looking for either corn syrup or granulated sugar."

Crystal's shoulders slumped.

Trace frowned and took his date's side. "Technically her response was correct." He gave Shaye a disapproving look that made her uncomfortable. "If you'd wanted ingredients, you should have said so."

"I was certain she'd say the candy was made from cotton," Kai muttered from behind Shaye.

"She deserves another chance," said Trace.

Shaye didn't like where this was going. Obviously, Trace was determined to see how far he could push her. She didn't like being pushed.

"I want to go again," Crystal pleaded.

Shaye debated. Second questions weren't part of her game. Still, whatever she asked, chances were good Crystal would botch the answer. "Superman's other identity. Name the candy bar," she said.

"Jimmy Olsen."

Shaye didn't look at Crystal; she met Trace's gaze instead. She was surprised by the sympathy that darkened his eyes. He seemed embarrassed for his date. If it was anybody else, she would have admired that in him. Not Trace. His expression sought Shaye's help to ease the situation.

She scrunched her nose. This boy was a Saunders; she owed him nothing. But because of his genuine concern for Crystal, she gave him something. "Clark Bar. Clark Kent was Superman. Both Kent and Olsen were reporters at the *Daily Planet*. You were close, Crystal."

Crystal sighed. "Close is good."

"Correct would've been better," said Kai.

Shaye removed a pack of gum from a shelf beneath the counter. "Bubble Yum Cotton Candy?" she offered the girl. It was her favorite flavor.

Crystal opened the pack and removed four pieces. She unwrapped each one and popped them into her mouth. Her cheeks bulged as she started to chew. "I can blow a bubble as big as my face," she bragged.

Trace leaned left. "What if it pops?"

"Have fun getting the gum out of her hair." Kai was aware of the consequences.

Crystal ignored her ex-boyfriend. She blew a small practice bubble and sucked it back into her mouth. "It's Trace's turn to play Sweet Treat."

Shaye shook her head. She was done for the night. She'd wasted two good questions on Crystal. She wanted Trace and his bubble-blowing date to move on. "We don't have time."

"Make time." Trace reached into the back pocket of his slacks and removed his wallet, then a twenty-dollar bill.

He set the money on the counter. "I'm buying five minutes."

Shaye bristled. Did he think she was that hard up for a sale? Even if she was, she'd never admit it to him. Still, she debated taking the bill.

Kai, on the other hand, had no such qualms. He snatched the twenty and put it into the cash box, a box with five singles and a handful of change.

Business was slow. Too slow to give Trace back his money. Kai had polished off six hot dogs, eating the profits as he shut down the steamer. Bored herself, she'd eaten a bucket of cheddar cheese popcorn.

Shaye had several tough questions she could ask Trace. She'd love to stump him. She went with the one that caused most people to draw a blank. "Name the colors of candy corn, base to tip."

"Candy corn." He rocked heel to toe, his stance tense and competitive. "Give me a minute. I'm thinking."

Shaye rolled her eyes. Trace was such a dork. He didn't have an answer, yet he drew out the game. Was that a hint of a smile? No, she was imagining things.

The silence within the shack grew as hot and heavy as the humidity on the pier. A full minute passed. Sweat gathered on Kai's forehead and at the crease of his neck. Moisture slicked Shaye's palms. She rubbed the flat of her hands down her blue-jeaned thighs, then curled her fingers into fists.

She soon nudged Trace. "Your answer?"

"Candy corn celebrates a lot of holidays," he slowly said. "Which seasonal colors do you want? There's gingerbread, candy cane peppermint, reindeer, patriotic raspberry lemonade, Indian corn, and eggnog to name a few."

Shaye's jaw dropped. No player had ever named *flavors*. Put to the test, she herself couldn't name the colored stripes on holiday corn. Trace Saunders was either a candy connoisseur or a bullshitter. She clamped her mouth closed, growing uneasy. "Your basic corn," she said.

"Yellow, orange, white."

Damn. Her stomach sank. She was dealing with a candy corn fanatic. What else would he try to put over on her?

Crystal giggled. "Isn't he amazing?"

Amazing wasn't the word Shaye would've chosen. *Asshole* fit him better. She eyed him with suspicion. "You know a lot about candy corn."

He shrugged, then admitted, "Jelly beans and holiday corn are my two favorite candies."

"Trace gave me a box of gourmet jelly beans last week for my birthday," Crystal bragged. "You could eat the jelly beans individually or toss an assortment into your mouth and mix the flavors. Jelly beans are the new birthday cake."

"I'd rather have cake and ice cream," Kai said.

"And candles." Shaye hadn't meant to speak her thought aloud. Birthday candles sounded childish. Not that she cared what Trace thought of her.

Behind her, Kai yawned and scratched his stomach. His camouflage T-shirt was as wrinkled as his khaki shorts. It was getting late.

Shaye tapped a finger on the countertop, avoiding looking at Trace. "Pick your free treat," she said.

"Select one for me."

She went for Lemonheads, only to change her mind. A solution came to her, and she dipped her head so he wouldn't see her smile. She had no conscience where this boy was concerned, so she grabbed a box of Skittles from the lower shelf instead. She passed it to him.

He accepted the candy. "We'll play again, Toothpick."

She hated the humor in his eyes and the fact that he teased her. "Not on my pier, we won't."

"You don't want to get even?" he called over his shoulder as Crystal took his hand and tugged him out the door. The girl was so possessive.

Shaye grinned now. He'd soon realize she'd gotten him back already. He just didn't know it yet. The Skittles were a year old, left over from the previous summer. They'd be stale, hard as rocks. She'd only kept the box around as a reminder to order a new case.

Taste the rainbow, Trace Saunders.

One

"Skittles?" Kai offered Shaye a handful of candy as they walked the length of the boardwalk. The majority of kiosks and colorful wooden storefronts stood open to the public, but customers were few and far between.

She shook her head. "I can't stomach them."

Fifteen years had passed, yet Skittles still reminded her of Trace Saunders. The man was on her mind today. They were scheduled to meet for lunch. A meal she dreaded.

He was now CEO of Saunders Shores, and she presided over Barefoot William Enterprises. Trace had only recently taken on his position. He'd previously worked from New York City, where he oversaw his family's real estate holdings.

It was rumored the Saunders family owned a block of skyscrapers and several hotels as well as held stock in companies that owned national landmarks. Future stock in the Empire State Building was on their acquisition list.

Trace had returned home following his father's unexpected fall from a ladder. Brandt Saunders's attempt at replacing a shutter on a window had landed him flat on his back. He'd dislocated his shoulder and broken his hip. He was homebound for six months.

Gossip had spread with Trace's return. He went on to

surprise everyone by staying on after his dad's recovery. He sold his summer house in the Hamptons and closed his eyes to the bright lights of Times Square. He left the rapid pulse of the city for the slow-changing tides of the Gulf. He'd been home two years now.

Shaye had never left southwest Florida. She couldn't imagine living anywhere else. As a kid, she'd followed her grandfather and father around town, learning the business from the moment she could walk. Her very first steps had been on the pier. Her heart belonged to Barefoot William.

She was the youngest in a family with four older brothers who had all left town for college and never returned. They'd gone on to play professional sports or started businesses in big cities.

Shaye had never wanted to leave. She lived on a land-docked houseboat once owned by her grandfather. Despite their age difference, Frank Cates was both a friend and an ally. He'd given her the houseboat, which was no longer seaworthy, as a gift when she graduated from high school and wanted to move out of her parents' house. It was quite large and her mother and father traveled a great deal, and Shaye wanted her own place, something smaller, cozy and comfortable. The houseboat was perfect. It held wonderful memories. The past had been good to her.

Today, however, looked bad. She and Trace had business to discuss. A proposed professional/amateur beach volleyball tournament required his approval. Trace still straddled the fence.

Her dozen phone calls and countless e-mails hadn't changed his mind. Trace remained noncommittal in sharing *his* beach with her for the event. What was wrong with the man? The tour players would draw a huge crowd and boost slow summer sales for everyone.

That very morning he'd requested a meeting at his office, no doubt surrounded by a bunch of suits. She'd declined. Her idea of an office was sitting under a shady umbrella on the sand with her cell phone and laptop.

They'd argued for thirty minutes about a location. He'd finally agreed to lunch at Molly Malone's. The diner was located on the north side of Center Street, on *her* side of the beach.

Shaye's aunt owned the restaurant, which was known for its home cooking. Molly was as round as a hamburger bun and happy with her shape. She relished food and life and offered a free slice of pie with each luncheon special. Shaye hoped coconut cream was on the menu today. It was her favorite.

Kai adjusted his black baseball cap with *Hook It, Cook It* scripted on the bill, an advertisement for two of his shops. Hook It sold bait and tackle, and Cook It stood next door, a small chef's kitchen where fishermen could have their daily catch cleaned and filleted for a small fee, then baked or fried for lunch or dinner. A salad, hush puppies, and fries came on the side. The tourists found it a novelty to eat their meals fresh from the Gulf.

When times were slow, Kai worked as a handyman. He remodeled the boardwalk shops when they changed hands among the family. He'd worn a tool belt much of the spring.

Beside her now, he shifted his stance. "When does Dune expect an answer on the event?" he asked.

Dune was her older brother. He'd played professional beach volleyball for seventeen years. He was a dominant force and a major voice in the sport. He planned to use his popularity to draw players south for a weekend.

Volleyball had very loyal fans. This wouldn't be a sanctioned tournament, but with media coverage, Barefoot William could turn a profit. This was exactly what she needed to keep the family businesses in the black after a slow start to the summer season.

"Time has run out. Trace needs to make up his mind today." She cleared her throat, swallowing her guilt. She was not looking forward to this meeting. "I, on the other hand, have already made up mine. I called Dune late last night, and we set dates. The players will be in town over the Fourth of July. He will guarantee top seeds from both the women's and men's tour. He'll send a list of names for promotion."

Kai rolled his eyes. "You make crazy look sane."

She had crossed the line, and she knew it. She'd set the date without Trace's consent. She hated the fact that she desperately needed him. All she required was two hundred feet of his beach to set up the final volleyball net, concessions, and bleachers.

Saunders Shores would benefit as much from the competition as Barefoot William. However, her southern neighbors weren't as financially strapped as her own family's businesses. Her side of the street was sucking summer air.

She hated dealing with difficult men. Trace was a royal pain in her ass. He rated no more than a blink of an eye in her book, if that. She released an expansive sigh. "He has to agree."

Kai wasn't so sure. "There's a lot of planning around an event this size. Saunders is formidable. He could ax the tournament out of spite."

Kai was right, as always. It was no secret she and Trace barely tolerated each other. Ill will slapped between them like high tide against cement pilings. She'd cross a street or take to an alley to avoid the man. He rubbed her the wrong way.

She stood as still as her thoughts until a light breeze blew her hair across her cheek. She tucked the curls behind her ear. Overhead, seagulls squawked, circled, and dived for fish. The sun's climb was slow, lazy. The Gulf waters were as pure a blue as the cloudless sky.

High humidity stuck her red tank top to her back. The cement beneath her bare feet grew hot. Shaye hopped to a spot of shade near the entrance to the carousel.

The hand-carved purple and white horses were motionless while the workers wiped them down. Each mount had jeweled amber eyes and a gold saddle. Their legs were bent, ready to race. The wooden platform was polished, the driving mechanism oiled. The ride opened at noon. The calliope music would soon echo across town.

She waved to Oliver Ray, who managed the merry-go-round. Oli was replacing lights along the outer rim of the orange scalloped top. He nodded from his ladder, a thin, gray-haired man of few words. His mechanic's overalls never showed a sign of dirt or grease. Only the heels on his steel-toed boots were scuffed. Pushing sixty, he'd never missed a day of work.

Shaye wished her younger employees had Oliver's work ethic. They unfortunately did not. A midnight beer bash or beach bonfire had someone calling in sick every other day and Shaye scrambling to replace him.

The day before yesterday, she'd helped out her uncle at Hooper's Hoops. The kiosk sold hula hoops in a variety of colors from hot pink and sand tan to metallic silver.

Shaye had entertained a few prospective buyers. She'd twirled a fiery orange hoop until her hips got sore. She swore her waist had a permanent indentation from six hours of twisting.

But despite the sometimes unusual demands of the job, she knew she was fortunate to work with her immediate and extended family. The Cateses owned every shop, arcade amusement, and carnival ride along the boardwalk and down the full length of the pier. Barefoot William needed to stay in the black. A volleyball tournament would save the summer. And her sanity.

The only problem with the event was that it involved Trace Saunders. A fact she couldn't change. She hoped their meeting wouldn't be filled with awkward silences or, worse yet, angry words.

She racked her brain. She needed some assurance that having lunch with him wouldn't turn out to be a bust.

She looked down on her mood ring, now a dark gray. The color reflected her tension and stress. She needed to relax, loosen up. Take charge.

Next to her, Kai leaned his forearms against the bright blue pipe railing that separated the boardwalk from the beach. He looked out over the surf. "Trace is a challenge. What's your plan of attack?" he asked.

"I'll charm the man."

Kai couldn't help himself. He laughed, as she'd known he would. "Good luck. You're sarcastic as hell and always snub him."

"Not always."

"Name a time you've been nice to him."

One moment came to mind, which she'd never shared with Kai. It had been late January, and she and Trace were at city hall for a beach erosion meeting. They'd collided in the doorway of the conference room, as she was going in and he was coming out. She'd bumped his chest with her shoulder. He'd been all starched white shirt and solid muscle. He'd loomed over her, a big man with a bigger presence.

His cologne was subtle yet masculine. The scent reminded her of early mornings down by the pier when the air was fresh and the sand was free of footprints.

Neither of them had moved until the chairman of the committee arrived. Trace took a polite step back then, allowing her to pass. She'd forgotten the snide comment she was going to make about his crowding her. She'd let their closeness slide. That one time.

"You need to change your tactics," Kai suggested, breaking into her thoughts. "Find his weakness, and exploit it. A pretty woman is the best weapon against an unsuspecting man."

She frowned. "Trace is always suspicious. He never lets his guard down."

"Neither do you," Kai said. "Saunders likes the ladies. You clean up nice, Shaye. Distraction could work in your favor. Show up in something besides a T-shirt and cutoffs. Wear shoes. Flirt a little."

She blew raspberries. "Bad idea. He'd see right through me. I'm not that good an actress."

"You may dislike the man, but you need him," Kai reminded her. "Both your signatures are required on the recreational permit. You can't forge his name."

He nudged her with his shoulder. "You're doing this for family. We love you for it. None of us wants to close up shop."

Kai was her voice of reason when she was being unreasonable. Her parents, siblings, and relatives meant everything to her. Without the proper paperwork, Trace could bust her for trespassing. He wouldn't think twice about pressing charges. Once behind bars, she'd be out of his hair.

The sun beat down, and her shadow grew short. She looked down at her toes, freshly polished a Peruvian-orchid-pink. Her pedicure would be wasted by wearing shoes, although flip-flops might work.

Flirting, however, was out of the question.

She couldn't force what she didn't feel.

Over the last year, newspapers and magazines had profiled Saunders with curvy brunettes. Shaye's high metabolism kept her thin. Her hair was white-blond.

She wasn't Trace's type. Neither was he hers. She preferred bare-chested men in board shorts, whereas he wore tailored shirts and trousers.

He was all business, and she was all beach.

She scrunched her nose. There had to be another way to force his hand, beyond breaking his fingers.

Trace Saunders cracked his knuckles. He sat in a black leather booth at Molly Malone's and exhaled the pressures of his busy morning. It felt good to get out of his office, even for a short time. Saunders Shores was thriving under his expert hand. He was his father's son and proud of all he'd achieved. Every hotel room at The Sandcastle was reserved. The restaurants and nightclubs were booked solid. Even the boutique sales reflected the strong tourist trade. His financial projections for summer were right on target. The profit margin would be high.

All was well in his world—until Shaye Cates had introduced the volleyball tournament.

She didn't fit any known corporate image with her laid-back style and off-the-wall business tactics. She was a thorn in his side. She disrupted his life.

He refused to look like a fool around this woman. Everyone in Barefoot William thought him an ass for not committing to the event. They found him disrespectful to one of their own. Shaye's family saw her as sweet and lovable, whereas he found her too shrewd and unpredictable.

He'd never forgotten the stale box of Skittles she'd dumped on him back in high school. She'd cost him a chipped tooth and a trip to the dentist. He wondered what game she would play today.

Through the diner's wide front windows he had a clear view of the Barefoot William boardwalk. He'd purposely arrived early to judge his reception.

The PLEASE BE SEATED sign freed him from waiting for a hostess. The atmosphere was casual and bustling, yet the crowd was cool toward him. Those having lunch had eyed his progress to the corner booth. Suspicion sat down with him. Disapproval surrounded him. His waitress ignored him.

He was as welcome as a mouse in the kitchen.

Those related to the Cates family found him more intruder than customer. Apparently Shaye hadn't mentioned their lunch date to her aunt.

It wasn't exactly a *date,* he revised. It was likely to be more of a debate. Narrowed eyes and raised voices characterized each of their encounters, as neither cared to compromise.

His stomach growled. He was hungry. He'd traded his usual breakfast cheese omelette for morning sex with Nicole Archer. He hadn't had time for both.

But she'd killed his mood by sneaking her request for a favor between the sheets just as she straddled him.

Nicole wanted retail space for her costume jewelry, and she seemed more interested in doing business than doing him. He'd seen several of her signature pieces. Her collection was inexpensive and would sell far better from a touristy beachfront shop than in the luxury boutiques at Saunders Shores.

He'd already known they were nearing the end of their relationship. He almost always parted amicably with the women he dated. Nicole proved no exception. She had entrepreneurial aspirations. He'd agreed to set her up so she could concentrate more on her business and less on him. They'd both be happy. The only thing wrong with the picture was that his promise to Nicole was putting him in a precarious position with another female.

Shaye Cates.

He ran one hand down his face, then realized he needed a shave. Shaye wouldn't care if he was clean shaven or grew a full beard. Asking her for a storefront would be the first time a Saunders had ever asked a favor from a Cates. He would approach the topic at the end of their meal, after she'd hit bended knee and begged for the volleyball event. Once he gave his approval, she would owe him something in return. He would then claim a Barefoot William shop for Nicole.

He loosened his black-and-white-striped tie and unhooked the top button on his dark gray shirt. Leaning back, he stretched his arms along the edge of the low booth and forced himself to relax.

He scanned the diner, quickly noting that locals crowded the tables, counter stools, and doorway. He knew everyone by name, and they all recognized him. They stared, but no one spoke or smiled. He got the cold shoulder.

No doubt he'd get a similar reception from Shaye.

He was used to such treatment on this side of the street. The Saunders and Cates families didn't mesh. Where was Shaye, anyway? It had already been a long day, and she had yet to arrive. The woman could make a minute seem like an hour.

The music from the carousel entered with the next customer. Trace glanced out the window and caught the first turn of the merry-go-round. As a kid, he'd snuck onto the pier and ridden the rides more times than he could count. He was now thirty-two, yet the carnival atmosphere still brought out the boy in him.

Barefoot William was all about fun.

Saunders Shores honored refinement.

There was no middle ground.

Same with Shaye. Their family histories stood between them. They were at each other's throats, or they didn't speak.

He closed his eyes for a second and breathed in the scent

of fried onions, garlic, and . . . Dove soap. The soft, clean fragrance startled him.

He cracked one eyelid and found his nemesis standing over him. She'd recently showered. Her hair was slightly damp, the ends brushing her shoulders. A black satin hair band contrasted with her sun-white curls. Two sets of gold hoops pierced each ear. The retro mood ring on her index finger shone bright orange, a daring, challenging color.

A lacy, stretchy, off-the-shoulder turquoise top showed some cleavage. He'd swear she was wearing a push-up bra but couldn't be certain. No tan lines, he noted. Her shoulders and the high curve of her breasts were smooth and evenly bronzed. She must sunbathe topless. He wondered if she had a full-body tan. Front and back.

He lowered his gaze farther. Her short denim skirt bared a lot of leg. Two zippers curved over each hip on her skirt. Fashionable, he supposed, and sexy.

There was something different about her today. She wore a sensuality that had nothing to do with her wardrobe. The transformation made him instantly wary. At first glance, she looked pretty and pleasant, yet he knew better. Clothes couldn't hide her pride. She was one stubborn woman.

He'd expected her to show up in her *Fudgin' It* T-shirt and ripped jeans. *Fudgin' It* advertised the best fudge shop in southwest Florida. Her grandmother Maxine made the fudge from a century-old recipe. Maxine was known to be as sweet as her confections.

Too bad Shaye hadn't inherited her grandmother's sugar. Agile and athletic, she'd grown up a tomboy. She remained slim but was no longer a toothpick. She definitely had a shape now. He'd heard that she dated but never long-term. She was dedicated to her family. Business always came first. No man wanted to come in second.

Trace liked women who dressed for him. A low-cut baby-doll in the bedroom, a skimpy bikini on the beach, and a black dress cut thigh-high for cocktails.

That profile didn't fit Shaye. She'd had an ulterior motive when she'd put on this miniskirt. She was dressing to seal the volleyball deal. She was out to distract him. For some reason, that irritated him, a whole hell of a lot.

It was high noon, and their gazes now locked. He caught the faint yet manipulative flicker in her dark brown eyes. Earthy eyes, he'd always thought. One of her eyebrows was raised at an aggravating angle; the tilt of her chin was aggressive. She stood beside the booth while he sat. She purposely looked down on him, the position of power.

The lady was out to control their meeting.

Trace couldn't allow that to happen. He needed to shake her confidence. He chose the unexpected and disarmed her. He met her man to woman and undressed her with his eyes.

His once-over was slow and thorough, even though he'd never taken an interest in her prior to that moment. His sudden attention brought color to her cheeks. Surprise parted her lips. Confusion lifted her chest, and her stomach sucked in. Goose bumps rose on her forearms.

Her mood ring turned red.

He'd hit a sexual nerve.

Satisfaction set his smile—until her scent rolled back on him. Dove soap, along with a steamy image of her naked in the shower, suddenly tempted and aroused. His dick shot up hard against his stomach. He shifted on the seat. He hadn't expected that.

The booth closed in. He felt trapped.

It was bad news all around. His plan had backfired. He'd toyed with her, and she'd turned him on. She made him feel like a high school jock, horny and with no girl to score.

Could it get any worse? She was a Cates.

Her last name should have rendered him impotent.

Shaye quickly recovered from his scrutiny, now a woman fully composed. The color of her mood ring softened to a clover green. The lady was calm while he sat on edge. He needed to make an adjustment.

She didn't give him time to do so. She slid into the booth across from him, *accidentally* kicking him in the shin. The sole on her flip-flop left dust on the leg of his black slacks. His pain shifted from his groin to his calf. She dipped her head. He swore her hooded eyes smiled.

The back of her bare legs stuck to the leather seat as she scooted to the middle of the table. She tugged down her short skirt and retrieved an orange flip-flop that had slipped off as she settled in.

Over the years he'd seen her relax with relatives, friends, and close business associates. She had deep dimples and sexy lips. Her frowns were reserved for him. The lady could scowl.

Her features were once again set, her shoulders squared. Her intensity poked him in the chest like a finger. She was all business.

Trace willed his erection away. He concentrated on Shaye's proposition instead. The sports weekend interested him, but he'd been slow to respond. He knew how much she hated depending on anyone but herself, yet today she needed him. His decision would make or break the tournament. For his own purpose, he wanted her to squirm a little longer, though it wasn't easy on him. It took more discipline than he knew he possessed to keep his mind on business and off his cock.

The menacing flick of her fingers across the prongs on

her metal fork told him she was ready for battle. They hadn't exchanged a word, yet she looked ready to wound him. She bit her lip. And stared.

More amused than threatened, he reciprocated. He ran his index finger along the dull blade of his knife, then palmed it. He waited for her reaction. She drew back. Barely. She continued staring at him, her expression telling him she could not have been more eager to play a mental game of jab and stab.

He laid the knife flat on the table, and she folded her hands in her lap. The score was even, for now.

"Shaye." It killed him to speak first, but manners forced him to.

"Trace," she returned.

As soon as the formalities were out of the way, a waitress approached with red vinyl menus and glasses of ice water. The server looked from him to Shaye, her expression curious. She'd probably expected dinner forks at twenty paces.

Shaye cleared her throat. "Trace, my cousin Violet," she stiffly introduced.

Violet handed Shaye a menu, then slammed one down like a gauntlet before Trace. He frowned. He imagined whatever he ordered would be laced with Tabasco sauce.

"The volleyball tournament?" Violet asked, not looking at him.

"Still under consideration," Shaye said.

Trace wasn't surprised that Violet knew the reason for their meeting. The Cateses were tight-knit. Family worked for family, and all Barefoot William stood under one umbrella.

"Would you like to eat now or later?" Violet asked.

"I'd like a few minutes," said Trace.

"Now is fine." Shaye was either hungry or out to provoke. He figured she'd counter anything he said.

Violet sided with her cousin. She offered the two lunch specials. "Fish sandwich or a basket of clams."

"I'd like——" Shaye started.

"To study the menu." Trace put his foot down.

He refused to be rushed by either woman. He'd never eaten at Molly Malone's prior to today, yet the waiting line now forming at the door was a testament to the woman's cooking. People stood six deep. He might as well enjoy the food, since that was most likely the only thing he'd enjoy during this meeting.

"There's coconut cream pie," he overheard Violet whisper to Shaye.

Shaye's expression softened. One corner of her mouth lifted, and Trace swore she sighed. Apparently pie did it for her.

He returned to the menu, and Shaye took to tapping her fingers on the Formica tabletop. Her nails were just long enough to be annoying.

Her attempt to hurry him failed. He ignored her.

She wanted to talk volleyball.

He forced her to wait, only glancing up to ask her, "Your recommendation?"

"Everything is good."

"What are you having?"

"Cobb salad and coconut cream pie."

He settled on a roast beef sub. "I'm ready to order."

Shaye motioned to Violet. The waitress refilled cups of coffee at a four-top before crossing to their booth. She quickly jotted down their orders. "Drinks?" she asked.

"Water's fine," he and Shaye simultaneously said.

They had one thing in common, Trace noted. Water. Not much to go on. He reminded himself he wasn't there to form a friendship. They simply had business between them.

Shaye hit him with a hard look the moment Violet left

to turn in their order. She got right to the point. "It's decision time."

He admired her tenacity. In his experience, people who beat around the bush had little to say. Shaye ran Barefoot William Enterprises. She pushed as hard as any CEO of his acquaintance. Sometimes even harder.

He held her gaze. He took a mild interest in the contrast of her dark brown eyes and pale blond hair. Her lips were lush and pink. She was pretty, but her attitude sucked.

He worked his jaw, cut a glance around the diner. He knew the majority of customers were keeping an eye on him. Most of them strained to hear their conversation. All would jump to Shaye's defense if he raised his voice to her.

He leaned forward, rested his forearms on the table, and kept his voice low. "I've given your request a great deal of thought," he said. "You need two hundred feet of my sand over the Fourth of July weekend."

She nodded. "We'll draw a holiday crowd."

"The event will be loud. Rowdy."

"Fans cheer and party."

"They'll drink on my beach."

"Hot day, cold beer—it's all part of the game."

"The gathering could get out of hand."

"A city permit guarantees police for crowd control, along with additional lifeguards," she pointed out. "The profit margin will still be high."

He shrugged. "Saunders Shores doesn't need the revenue." A cheap shot. Could he stoop any lower?

Her lips pinched, ever so slightly. "We could run the tournament without you. Work on a smaller scale."

Less space would cut into her returns. Good. He'd hit her where it hurt, in the pocketbook. She needed him more than he needed her.

He could call her bluff, or not. Every document she'd

faxed was well researched, from the concession stands, sponsors' tents, to the price of tickets. She'd gone big, and she needed his sand. Downsizing wasn't an option for her.

"Our split?" Which he already knew. He'd only asked to irritate her.

"Seventy-thirty."

Not good enough. "Fifty-fifty."

"I'm doing all the work." Her mood ring darkened to brown. The lady was reactive.

"Sixty-forty, then. I'm renting you beachfront."

"Rent it cheaper." Her ring went black.

Hell, no. If their situations were reversed, she'd rob him blind. She wouldn't rent her beach for cheap. He wasn't about to either.

Their meals arrived. The sandwich Violet set before him could've fed two men. He faced down an oven-warm, foot-long hoagie stacked with roast beef and smothered in Swiss cheese. Shaye's Cobb salad pushed the rim on her plate. He was surprised she didn't dive right in. Instead, she openly stared as he cut his sandwich in thirds and took his first bite.

She was on a tear. She didn't lighten up, didn't give him time to chew. "Your answer, Trace?"

He covered his mouth with one hand, his words slightly mumbled. "I'll tell you once we've eaten."

"You're dragging this out for no apparent reason," she accused.

"My stomach doesn't think so."

"Skip breakfast this morning?" she asked.

He swallowed. "A meeting." Business in bed had re-placed great sex.

"Blonde or brunette?"

"No one you'd know."

She tapped her fork against her plate but didn't take a bite. "I'm waiting."

"And I'm still eating." His hunger pains subsided with his second bite.

Shaye's stomach tightened. She was hungry but wasn't certain she could manage to eat. Trace Saunders made her nervous. *Very* nervous. He was a formidable presence in the small booth with his broad shoulders that no expensive tailoring could hide. He was always well dressed. He looked rich and competent. And way too complacent.

She, on the other hand, grew fidgety. His procrastination gave her pause. She shifted her weight in the booth, slipped off her flip-flops. She pressed her toes into the old linoleum. The floor felt cool and familiar amid the dozens of scuff marks.

She released a breath she hadn't realized she'd been holding. Her nerves were getting the better of her. Barefoot William had a grapevine for news. She'd told Dune not to announce the tournament prematurely. She would spread the word once Trace gave his approval. Dune, however, played by his own rules. She hoped her brother had abided by her decision this one time.

Trace would be one angry man if he discovered she'd already set the wheels into motion. Shit would hit the fan.

She studied him now as he ate. He wore his hair longer than he had as a kid, and a little less spiky. His angular bone structure carved lean hollows in his cheeks. He had a strong jaw, heavy with stubble. She would get whisker burn if he kissed her.

Kissed her? She dropped her fork, and it rattled onto the tabletop. She picked it up quickly before he noticed her clumsiness. Such a ridiculous thought and one that would never have crossed her mind had Trace not given her the once-over on her arrival. Her outfit had done the trick, just as Kai had said it would. Yet no one fooled Trace for long.

He'd seen through her ploy and countered her pretty woman with male pursuit. He'd humped her with his eyes. A far different reaction from what she'd expected. Amusement, maybe. Excitement, a little. But a visual seduction, not in this lifetime.

She'd been as shaken by his look as by the tent in his pants. The teeth on his zipper had grinned at her. A full-out jack-o'-lantern smile.

He'd crossed their line in the sand.

Enemies fought.

They didn't attract.

She hated the fact that she couldn't take her eyes off him. She needed to speed things up. "You finished?" she asked.

He looked down at his plate. "Does it look like I'm done?" He had two-thirds of his sandwich to go.

He was taking his sweet time, while her stomach turned sour. He was one aggravating man.

She spooned lemony chive dressing from a side bowl onto her salad. Molly's signature salad dressing was tart yet tasty. Shaye took several small bites before setting down her fork. She wasn't hungry anymore. She'd have a piece of pie later, once Trace consented to the event.

Molly Malone soon appeared at their booth. The owner had made the rounds, spoken to all her customers. She wore kitchen whites and a broad smile. "I chatted with your grandfather this morning right after he'd spoken to Dune." She pumped one chubby arm in victory. "Volley-ball! Sign me up for a concession tent on the beach."

Shaye winced, wishing herself invisible. *Damn.* The cat was out of the bag. The whole boardwalk was depending on a deal that *wasn't* a deal. Yet. She was a fraud. And had no immediate way to right the situation.

Across from her, Trace slowly set his hoagie on his plate

and wiped his mouth with a paper napkin. All the customers turned and stared at their booth, awaiting Shaye's confirmation. No one seemed to breathe.

Her chest squeezed painfully.

She'd stretched the truth.

Trace was about to call her on it.

Her family would lose faith in her ability to run Barefoot William Enterprises. She'd worked so hard for them. She fought down all emotion, refusing to let her fear show. Failure wasn't an option.

"Shaye?" Kai pushed through the diner door, all sweaty and out of breath. He hurriedly crossed to their booth. He curved his hand over her shoulder, digging his fingers deeply in a warning that came far too late. "I've talked to your grandfather—"

"Who's spoken to Dune," she said softly. Now there could be no question in Trace's mind as to what she'd done.

"The news is out?" asked her cousin.

"Oh, yeah."

"Ah, shit." Kai was sympathetic.

The silence grew oppressive and weighty. Those in the restaurant waited for Shaye's thumbs-up. She now clutched her hands so tightly, her fingers were numb.

Trace sat still, his face stone-cut. His eyes had turned a gunmetal-gray, dark and questioning. She wondered what he was thinking. She was certain they weren't good thoughts. He was about to condemn her.

He took a sip of water, then cleared his throat. "Shaye negotiated the tournament to my satisfaction," he finally said. "We've agreed on all terms. It's a go."

Trace had made her a hero.

Stunned, she sagged deeply into the booth as applause erupted all around her. Violet jumped up and down. Molly offered free blackberry lemonade to every customer.

Family and friends rushed Shaye's table. She mumbled a few words but nothing that made sense. The men shook her hand, and the women hugged her. Trace remained detached. He received only the briefest of nods.

Her conscience scolded her. The glorious moment was diminished by her scheming. She'd treated Trace poorly. She hadn't finessed the deal; she'd outright cheated. She knew it, and he knew it. She owed him a great deal. He would not take her deception lightly.

He told her with no more than a narrowing of his eyes that he had something up his sleeve he wasn't yet telling her. He would get even, sooner rather than later. She would suffer. Paybacks were hell.

Trace left her to her thoughts of what he might or might not do. He slid across the booth and stood, a man of intimidating stature and cool indifference.

He reached into his pants pocket and pulled out a money clip. He dropped two twenties onto the table. It was twice the price of the meal. Violet would appreciate the big tip.

Nevertheless, Shaye tried to return his money. "Lunch is on me."

His fists closed against her offer. "Next time you can buy, on my side of the street."

She shivered. She didn't want to have lunch with him again. Ever. He gave her a final hard look, then angled through the crowd. He never looked back.

Panic pushed her to follow him. Shaye motioned to Violet. "Pack up the coconut cream pie." She slipped on her flip-flops and scooted off the seat. Vi met her at the door. With the take-out box in hand, Shaye hit the sidewalk. The slap of her flip-flops betrayed her hurried pace.

The celebration in the diner would continue without her. She'd made everyone happy but Trace. And he was one angry man. That bothered her down to her orchid-pink toes. She didn't care if he liked her. She did, however, need to make amends, however she could.

Pie always made her smile, especially coconut cream. However bad her day, a slice turned things around for the better. She hoped a piece would appease him too. Doubtful, but worth a try.

Shaye moved swiftly down the boardwalk. Saunders Shores differed greatly from Barefoot William. The walkway shifted from cracked cement to cocoa-brown brick. Here, there were no in-line skaters, unicyclists, street singers, portrait painters, magicians, or vendors hawking their wares. There were no rickshaw pedicabs. No one wore swimsuits or ran around barefoot.

Those shopping the main city blocks were dignified and well dressed. Everyone wore shoes. No one browsed; everyone bought. Customers carried designer boxes and bags. The boutique owners flourished.

The Saunders corporate offices stood three stories high, one block off the beach. Bronze-tinted windows shone gold in the early-afternoon sun. The glass allowed those within to look out, but those outside couldn't see in.

Shaye wondered if Trace saw her coming.

She entered through an old-fashioned revolving door. Wide-open space and high ceilings greeted her. Pale blue walls and vivid artwork surrounded navy leather chairs and short sofas. Arrangements of yellow snapdragons, sunflowers, and blue periwinkle splashed color throughout the lobby. Artsy but dignified.

The gray floor tiles shone with a mirror polish. Shaye caught her reflection. Her hair looked untamed and wild, and her short denim skirt was wrinkled. Her orange flip-flops appeared out of place in this well-heeled world.

Directly behind her, the door again spun slowly. A brunette breezed in, tall and buxom. Sophisticated and feline. She slid her black cat's-eye sunglasses onto her head and let her eyes adjust from the sun's glare to the soft lobby light.

The woman's plain white shift provided a perfect backdrop for her jewelry, Shaye noted. She jingled with her first step. Elaborate gold hoops hung at her ears, ones designed with silver beads and tiny gold bells. The thin metal chains on her three-tiered necklace sparkled with lavender rhinestones and reflective mirror disks. Bangles of charms looped her wrist. A thick, hammered-silver bracelet curved near her right elbow. A triple gold ring with three pearls arched from her index finger to her fourth.

Shaye was in awe of the brunette's wide leather belt embellished with amber. An assortment of charms decorated the brown satin ties on her wedge sandals. But what made Shaye smile wide was the color of the woman's toenail polish. Stylish and elegant.

"Glazed Almond," the new arrival supplied when she saw Shaye looking at her feet. That surprised Shaye, as she hadn't expected that an uptown woman would even notice her.

She shifted the take-out box beneath her left arm. An uncomfortable vibe rattled her confidence and made her feel out of place. The woman looked cool and collected, while she perspired from her power walk.

Where was the ladies' room? Shaye needed to splash cold water on her face before locating Trace. With her luck, she'd need to know a secret password to enter the restroom.

"Going up?" The brunette motioned toward the elevator near the security desk.

Shaye shook her head. "Not right this minute, but thanks."

The tinkle of bells followed the woman into the elevator. She waved to Shaye as the doors closed.

Shaye left the pie box at the security desk, then scanned

the lobby for her destination. A short walk down a hall-way, and she entered the ladies' room.

To her relief, no one asked her to leave.

Soft tea rose wallpaper and a burgundy brocade fainting couch made the room feminine and pretty. She glanced into the mirror above a pink marble sink and cringed. Her cheeks were red, her bangs plastered to her brow. Her lips looked dry. She hadn't brought her purse, which meant no hairbrush or lip gloss. All she could do was straighten her hair band.

She dampened a paper towel and pressed it to her fore-head. A welcome coolness soothed her. She immediately felt less harried.

She went on to wash her hands, then proceeded to ad-just her clothing. She pulled her turquoise blouse higher on her shoulders and smoothed her skirt. She looked down and wiggled her toes in her flip-flops. Why did her orchid-pink toenails suddenly seem so unfashionable?

She was procrastinating. As her mind wandered, she moved more slowly by the second. She pulled herself to-gether.

She hated the fact she'd soon be admitting she was wrong to a man who believed he was always right. He'd rub her face in her mistake. Most likely in her coconut cream pie.

She glanced at her watch and noticed that twenty min-utes had elapsed. She needed to pull herself together and move on.

She retrieved her take-out box from security, then en-tered the elevator. The smooth ride up did little to soothe her nerves. Too smooth, like everything else on this side of town.

She reached the third floor, and apprehension swamped her. She'd been to Trace's office once before, and his administrative assistant had announced her. Not so today. It appeared Martin Carson was at lunch. Just her luck.

She moved down the hallway. Trace's door stood open a foot. Her knock pushed the door even wider. A step inside, and she stopped short and did a double take.

Before her now, Trace and the jewelry lady were getting it on. He leaned back against the edge of his desk, the brunette pasted to him. Their kisses were open-mouthed, hungry. The intimacy branded them as lovers.

She should've retreated, but her feet failed her. Her flipflops sank deeper into the thick carpet. She swore her toenails blushed a deep purple. She looked high and low and away from the couple headed for a nooner.

She cleared her throat, attempting to draw their attention off each other and on to her. *Awkward* didn't begin to describe her feelings as she stood there like a voyeur. Worse yet, a slow burn hit low in her belly, then spread beneath the waistband of her panties.

Trace was first to notice her. He narrowed his gaze but never broke the kiss. Lazy arrogance arched one of his eyebrows, a sexual taunt.

Damn him. He knew he was turning her on but did nothing to ease her discomfort. He probed even deeper.

He dared Shaye to look away.

She found she could not.

Payback time.

Ten feet separated them, yet she felt surrounded by the man. She was conscious of only him. He had a way of making her feel as if *she* was the woman in his arms, and he made her want more. A lot more. She knew his lips would be firm, his breath hot, the slide of his tongue practiced.

The sensation was surreal.

The familiarity scared her silly.

Sensations stroked like sins. Her breasts prickled, and her nipples puckered. Her nerves stretched thin. Arousal slid up her thighs like a man's hands. Goose bumps scored her skin. Her pulse quickened.

Her shiver broke the trance, and she let out the breath she'd been holding.

Reality was restored.

Stepping back, Shaye forced a calm she didn't feel. She hoped Trace hadn't seen how the kiss had affected her. One look at him, and she knew otherwise. He looked her up and down as if he'd just stripped her naked. She felt the need to cover herself.

Victory flashed in his eyes. He was all smirk and superiority as he set the brunette gently aside.

The woman looked at Shaye but didn't seem to see her. Her eyes were dilated, her lips parted. No trace of embarrassment. Once focused, she managed an apology. "Sorry, I didn't hear you arrive."

Trace was less repentant. Satisfaction cut the corners of his mouth as he introduced the two women. "Nicole Archer, meet Shaye Cates, your new landlord."

Landlord? Misgiving sank deep. Concern surfaced as Shaye waited for an explanation.

Nicole was quick to clarify. "I'm a jewelry designer," she said. "I've searched for months for a shop to rent. Today was my lucky day. Trace took you to lunch, and you told him you had a boardwalk storefront available. I can move in shortly."

Shaye's breath stalled. The man had crossed the line. She went so stiff, she crushed the take-out box against her left side. The lid popped, and the scent of coconut cream escaped.

Damn Trace Saunders. He knew that no one outside the Cates family could rent space on the Barefoot William boardwalk. That she had the final say on all agreements. Yet he'd gone ahead and stolen a prime location from her. *Retaliation.* She could barely digest the word. She'd started the dispute by agreeing to the volleyball tournament without his consent. He'd ended their argument by renting real estate without her permission.

She set her back teeth. Coconut cream pie would never have settled their differences. They went deeper than that, *way* deeper. The two of them faced off with century-old baggage.

She was a barefoot kid at heart who loved homemade pie.

He was a corporate suit with back-stabbing finesse.

Their differences were as wide as the Gulf of Mexico.

She was so angry, she couldn't speak. She pressed the pie box to her hip with such force, the meringue exploded on her denim skirt.

Nicole jumped back, avoiding the bits of shaved coconut and graham cracker crust that flew through the air, then rained down on Shaye's toes. She pointed at Shaye's leg. "The pie tin is stuck to your thigh. Wait here. I'll grab a towel from the wet bar in the conference room."

Then she was gone.

Stuck and sticky, Shaye noted. Gooey globs of pie filling clung from the side zipper on her skirt to her bare knee. Any movement, and she'd stain the carpet. It would be costly to clean the thick pile. So she held still.

Trace took an intimidating step toward her. He wore the smirk of bad news. She waited for him to blurt out that the volleyball deal was off and he never wanted her to mess up his life or carpet again.

He did not.

Instead he circled her. His gaze darkened with curiosity,

lingering on her butt, then taking a long, leisurely look at her bare legs. He stopped before her.

He inhaled slowly.

She exhaled sharply.

They breathed the same air.

He touched her without warning.

She nearly came out of her skin.

Deliberately slow, he scooped cream filling off her hip with two fingers and sampled the pie. "You taste good . . . for a Cates."

Two

Trace Saunders enjoyed the coconut cream pie as well as Shaye's unease. Lady was nervous. He continued to eat off her hip. The pie was the best he'd ever tasted. Molly Malone could bake. Small chunks of fresh coconut enhanced the filling, while shredded bits were baked into the pie crust. The pie was creamy yet had a hint of tropical crunch.

He was scraping the last bit of filling from the side zipper on Shaye's skirt when Nicole returned with a moist bar towel in hand.

Nicole raised an eyebrow. "I see you were hungry. Didn't you eat your lunch?"

He stepped back. "It was cut short."

"Can I order you a sandwich from the Garden Café? They deliver," Nicole offered.

He shook his head. "I'll survive until dinner." Unless Shaye killed him first.

Her temper was lit. She wished to lay him low. Unfortunately for her, he was flying high. He could live with the volleyball tournament. It would only last two days, not all summer. He had planned to agree to the event once he'd finished his roast beef sandwich. Yet she hadn't given him time to fall in with her plans.

Molly Malone had unwittingly spilled the family beans.

Shaye's conniving had caught up with her, and Molly's announcement had turned the tables in his favor.

He smiled to himself. Shaye's expression at that moment would stay with him forever. She'd wanted the diner floor to open up and swallow her whole. It had not. She'd been forced to sit and face the consequences of her actions. She'd believed he'd take her down, hard and fast and unforgiving.

He'd let her slide, for the moment. In the aftermath, he gained retail space for Nicole. And eaten pie off Shaye's denim hip. It was a win-win for him.

Shaye, however, didn't like losing, even if the loss was justified. She'd come back fighting.

Trace crossed to his clear acrylic desk and took to his chair. A chair that had been specially molded to his spine. His desk was pure science fiction made to order. There were only six such desks available. The transparent frame with its thin glass top gave the illusion that his computer and files floated in thin air. It was designed for both function and the future.

The taupe carpet was new. Sunlight bounced off windows that were recently washed. Grape gourmet jelly beans and patriotic raspberry-lemonade candy corn filled two glass dishes to satisfy his sweet tooth.

He watched as Shaye cleaned her skirt with Nicole's assistance. Shaye twisted left to get the last of the pie crust off her thigh. She caught him watching her and curled her lip. She looked ready to bite his head off.

He felt no shame in having secured the storefront for Nicole. He hardly needed to ask Shaye's permission after she'd sabotaged him.

He'd left the diner and headed back to his office, phoning Nicole on the way. She'd been in the vicinity shopping and had rushed to Saunders Square.

His ex-lover had flash. She nearly blinded him with her jewelry. Her appreciation at gaining the boardwalk shop she'd wanted had been expressed in a deep French kiss and an unspoken offer of sex.

Trace had passed on the sex. He'd assist in getting her business off the ground and planned to be a regular customer, in order to keep her solvent. After twelve months, Nicole should be able to support herself fully. Or so he hoped.

He liked Nicole; he just didn't love her. He always made an attempt to remain friends with the women of his past. Some stayed close, seeking his business advice. Others sent the occasional Christmas card. Only one had flipped him off, Crystal Smith from high school.

She'd wanted an engagement ring for graduation. The ring had meant more to her than he did. She'd liked his status as a Saunders, yet during their time together, Crystal had talked nonstop about Kai Cates. Trace had gotten tired of her increasingly intense attempts to make Kai jealous.

Twenty-four hours after Crystal tossed her tasseled cap into the air, she took off for Milan. Fashion was her passion, and she apprenticed at the Instituto di Torrisi. According to his twenty-four-year-old sister, Sophie, Crystal was doing exceptionally well for herself. She'd established Crystalline, her own line of luxury undergarments, and had a selective international clientele.

Shy, studious, somewhat klutzy Sophie loved the glossy fashion magazines. Sophie swore that Crystal's sheer chiffon teddy was as intimate as skin. Her handmade corsets were works of art. No man could ignore cleavage so prettily revealed by the bejeweled neckline of her signature camisole.

Trace shrugged off Crystal's memory. He had more than

lingerie to deal with today. He scanned a stack of paper-work in need of his attention, then looked at the two women. Their cleanup was completed. Nicole now held the aluminum tin. Shaye's skirt was damp but free of pie.

They were opposites, he noted. And their differences went well beyond hair color.

Nicole was just starting a business, whereas Shaye had run Barefoot William Enterprises for six years. Her grand-father had appointed her president when her father retired. The old man trusted her. Her entire family backed her. There was no dissension among the Cateses. Ever.

Many of the Cates women were powerhouses. Most were known to be active, innovative, and smart. To those traits Shaye added sneaky.

She'd worked every shop and carnival ride on the boardwalk. She knew the businesses inside and out. Trace knew because over the years he'd occasionally discarded his suit to check out the competition.

He used a disguise to do so. He crossed Center Street wearing a baseball cap, mirrored Oakley's, a Miami Dol-phins jersey, ripped jeans, and athletic shoes. No one stopped or questioned him. He'd trod the boardwalk, end to end.

Sitting on a bench, and always from a distance, he'd watched Shaye work her ass off. Day after day, she breathed life into her family's enterprises. She walked the pier and handed out two-for-one coupons for the arcade games. She scooped ice cream cones and deep-fried Oreos. She tossed toy seagull boomerangs out over the water and caught their return. She wore tank tops advertising Three Shirts to the Wind and modeled henna surfer tattoos from Waves. She rode a unicycle when she got tired of walk-ing. The lady had incredible balance.

A month earlier, he'd caught her on hands and knees re-pairing a broken-down bumper car. Later that same day, his heart had nearly stopped when she and an employee scaled the roller coaster ramp to check the track.

Shaye was independent, daring, and worked at least a sixty-hour week. But she was a Cates, so his compliments only went so far.

Before him now, Nicole stood poised and sophisticated. Her skin was flawless and pale. She avoided the sun.

Shaye lived for sunshine. She wore T-shirts and shorts and so often went barefoot, her toes were always sandy.

Nicole had a standing appointment at the Zsuzsy Salon. She never had a hair out of place.

Shaye's curls were untamed. Her hair band barely contained her bangs.

Nicole dabbed expensive cologne at every pulse point. Shaye's scent was Dove soap.

Nicole was rational and, most times, cooperative. She had, however, blindsided him that very morning during sex with her business proposal. All the same, Nicole wasn't nearly as cagey as Shaye.

Shaye had sneaky down to a science. He was glad her plan had backfired and he'd benefited from her takedown.

Across his desk, both women watched him watch them.

One smiled warmly.

The other scowled deeply.

Nicole was first to speak. "Can we see the shop today? I want to sign the rental agreement as soon as possible." She unknowingly rubbed salt into Shaye's wound.

Why not? Trace wanted to enjoy Shaye's discomfort a while longer. His paperwork could wait. He wouldn't be gone long. He rose and joined the women near the door.

He cornered Shaye. "We have time now."

Nicole deferred to her landlord. "Does this work for you, too?" she asked.

"Of course it does." Trace spoke for Shaye. "She's happy to accommodate a new renter. You may want to expand the shelving and counter space. Renovations come with the agreement."

"You're mistaken," Shaye was quick to say. "Overhauls are paid by the renter."

"Not in this case," said Trace. "Construction costs fall to the Cateses."

"To be continued," she said.

"Finalized," Trace shot back.

"This day couldn't get any better," Nicole gushed.

Shaye Cates disagreed. This was the worst day of her life. She bit her tongue. She had no bargaining strength. The volleyball tournament came first. Then she would revise the rental agreement. In her favor.

Shaye had two storefronts available. All the shops had adjoining walls and multicolored doors. The one with the hot-pink entry was wide and deep, situated at the corner of two busy streets. The store with the soft lime and avocado door was tiny and in the middle of the block.

Shaye's eighteen-year-old niece had graduated from high school that spring. College wasn't in her future. Eden wanted to bring Old Tyme Portraits to the boardwalk. Customers could stand behind life-size cardboard cutouts, their faces showing above vintage swimwear.

Eden had already purchased several cutouts and an expensive Nikon. She'd begged for the store with the hot-pink door. Shaye hated to disappoint family.

Kai was in the process of rewiring the electrical fixtures and updating the plumbing in the smaller second shop. The store was old and no longer up to code. He'd be working there now.

Shaye wished she had time to forewarn Kai of their arrival. Fortunately she and her cousin were close. He always read between the lines.

"I have a shop in the middle of the block," she told

Nicole as they left Trace's office and headed toward the elevator. The designer's jewelry jingled to the smack of Shaye's flip-flops on the hardwood floors.

Trace followed them closely. Shaye could feel him breathing down her neck. The man had hot breath.

The elevator doors soon opened, and the three rode down. It was the longest ride of her life. Trace stood to her left, his height intimidating. His overwhelming presence seemed to take up enough space for two men. Shaye felt his gaze on her, evaluating and direct. He bumped her once, then twice, as he shifted his stance. She swore he did it on purpose.

They reached the lobby with its wide entry and crossed to the revolving door. Nicole slipped into the first rotating wing, and Trace slid in behind Shaye with the next opening. The toes of his leather loafers bumped her bare heels. The man was tailgating her. Again. And she didn't like it.

Outside, heavy gray clouds had gathered. It was rainy season. An afternoon thunderstorm was forecast.

"Can we make it to the shop before the downpour?" Nicole asked, hopeful.

"Depends how fast you can walk," Shaye said.

Nicole looked at her wedge sandals. "Not that fast, I'm afraid. My shoes are built for show, not speed. I'd sprain an ankle hurrying."

Shaye had a solution. "Once we reach Barefoot William, I can hail a pedicab. You can ride to the shop."

The covered, three-wheeled rickshaws shielded passengers from both sun and rain. The friendly drivers pointed out landmarks and entertained passengers with local lore. People waited in long lines to take a bike taxi along the boardwalk and pier. It was all part of the Barefoot William experience.

Trace made his own offer. "We could head to the parking lot and get my car. I'm fine with driving the short distance."

"It's only a few blocks," Nicole braved. "I can manage the walk."

They'd gone one block when it started to sprinkle. Trace took Nicole by the elbow, and they picked up their pace. Shaye couldn't help admiring Nicole. She was a team player. She didn't complain, even after the drizzle turned to big, fat drops.

They darted across Center Street, and Shaye hailed a pedicab. One person was already on board. The elderly woman moved over, offering Nicole half the seat.

"Crabby Abby's General Store," Shaye told the driver. "It's next to the rental shop," she added for Nicole's benefit. "Wait for us there. We'll meet you shortly." The bike taxi took off.

Trace set his jaw. "We're walking?" Raindrops glistened on his dark hair, which he slicked back with his fingers. His lashes were spiky. His gaze was liquid dark.

"*I'm* walking," she said. "Feel free to duck into a store and wait out the storm." She expected him to do so.

She removed her flip-flops and pressed on. What few customers there were had cleared the boardwalk. Shaye felt safe. There was no lightning or thunder. The steady pelting was warm, like a shower. She loved storms. She enjoyed every footstep.

Four blocks farther, the sun pushed through the clouds and struggled to shine. The rain fizzled to a sun shower. Each drop sizzled off the hot cement. Steam rose like a sauna. The humidity shot high. The sun winked and disappeared a second time. It was again overcast.

Shaye slowed, scanning the beach. Frothy waves crested the rain-soaked sand. One surfer braved the breakers. She ran one hand down her face. Her hair was damp, and her cheeks were moist. Her stretchy lace blouse and denim skirt were soaked. She didn't care, not until Trace cast his shadow over her.

She'd hoped to shake him, but there he stood. He, too, was wet. His dress shirt clung to his wide shoulders and flattened against his abdomen. The cotton dented at his navel. The front of his slacks defined what made him a man. A very big man. No shrinkage there.

Shaye scrunched her nose. "You're as crazy as me" slipped out before she could stop herself.

"Not nearly as crazy," he said. "I thought you'd melt in the rain."

Like the Wicked Witch of the East. She didn't take kindly to his reference but let it slide. She spread her arms wide. "Sorry to disappoint you. Nothing dissolved."

He took in her breasts, which were still an A-cup. If there'd been melting, she would have been as flat as a boy.

His gaze lowered, and her stomach quivered. He showed great interest in her skirt. A skirt that seemed to have shrunk in the rain. The denim wedged between her thighs and creased into her crotch. An arrow to her sex.

Heat chased through her body. Shaye tugged at the hem, yet the denim stuck to her like a second skin. She needed to change her clothes. Immediately.

Three Shirts to the Wind allowed her to do so. She entered through a tangerine door. Trace tailgated once again. She glared over her shoulder, expressing her displeasure.

He ignored her, moving even closer. She'd need an air bag if he bumped her again. The store was packed with customers who preferred retail therapy over walking in the rain. The shop specialized in shirts: plain white cotton to brightly colored polos. Some tees had caricatures, while others had decorative designs. A few naughty logos raised eyebrows. Most sayings were funny and silly. All sold well.

Shaye hugged her third cousin and shop owner Jenna

Cates. Jenna was petite with short dark blond hair. She looked smart in her round Ralph Lauren glasses.

Jenna homed in on Trace from behind the counter as he moved off to the side, avoiding the crush of the crowd. Her voice was low, flat, firm. "No welcome mat for that man."

"No need," Shaye whispered back. "He won't be around long. After the volleyball tournament, you can put a sign in your window that reads: No Shirt. No Shoes. No Saunders."

Jenna grinned. "I like that."

So did Shaye.

Jenna turned and snagged two purple beach towels from a shelf behind her. "No dripping either—the tile floors will get slippery. Dry your wet selves off."

A puddle had already formed at Shaye's feet. She requested a third towel for them to stand on, which she dropped onto the floor. Trace sidestepped onto one end of the terry cloth. His leather loafers squished water.

Shaye patted her face and arms.

Trace dried his hair and the back of his neck.

Jenna fanned her face. It was getting warm in the shop, Shaye noted. Those browsing stood four deep around the circular T-shirt racks. With each opening of the door, humidity snuck in. Shaye grew sticky, too.

Jenna undid the third button on her yellow polo. *Been there. Done that. Got the T-shirt* was scripted in navy over her breast pocket. "How about a change of clothes?" she offered.

"Would be appreciated," said Shaye.

Jenna slipped her two decorative plastic bags with the store logo on them. "For your wet clothes," she said. "There's plenty of T-shirts, but I'm running low on shorts and swim trunks. My weekly shipment has yet to arrive.

There's still a few pair on the sale rack by the dressing rooms. You wear a small," she said to Shaye. She glanced at Trace. "A large?"

"Extra large," Shaye said without thinking.

"Board shorts or Speedo?"

Shaye nearly choked. "Board shorts." There wasn't a Speedo made to fit a man his size.

Trace now moved around the shop as if he owned it. He looked polished, even after getting caught in the downpour. His dark good looks and strong presence had him standing head and shoulders above everyone in the store.

Men stepped aside, and women eased closer. The fact that he was wet didn't seem to matter. His scent was clean rain and damp cotton. And very male.

A redhead tugged on the towel he'd slung around his neck, offering to dry him off further. Trace smiled but passed on her offer. The woman flirted a little longer, only to frown when he focused on the shirts hanging from numerous clotheslines strung across the rafters of the ceiling.

Shaye felt an odd sense of relief. A relief she refused to evaluate too closely. She'd seen better-looking men, yet she was hard pressed to come up with their names. She hated making comparisons.

Jenna bumped against her. "You're staring a hole through the man."

"I'm making sure he doesn't shoplift."

"I plan to charge him double."

"Why not triple? He's a Saunders. He can afford it."

Jenna bit down on her bottom lip. "I hate that you have to partner with him for two hundred feet of sand."

"It was a business decision," Shaye said. "It's only for three weeks."

"You're the boss."

Being in charge wasn't always easy. Today had certainly proved difficult, Shaye thought. Nicole Archer came to mind. The jewelry designer was waiting for them at Crabby Abby's. Nicole was about to rent a Cates store.

Shaye would soon have to explain Nicole's presence. No one but family had shops on the Barefoot William boardwalk. She had to find a way for the new rental to work in her favor. She didn't want the family to question her judgment. Neither did she want to field their concerned questions.

Her acceptance of the volleyball tournament prior to Trace's approval had started this fiasco. She was the instigator. There was no way around it. She was paying heavily now.

She needed to bring things full circle without further mishap. Trace was the wild card. She had no control over him. The one thing she did know was that he'd take advantage of her as often as he could.

Sunshine soon beckoned through the front display window. The customers were quick to grab their purchases and return to the beach.

Jenna pointed to the dressing rooms at the back of the store. "One just opened up. Grab a couple tees. I'll get your shorts."

Shaye crossed to a circular rack of shirts. From the corner of her eye, she caught Trace in profile as he removed two T-shirts from one of the clotheslines. The man could stretch. Jenna used a step stool or the chrome pole garment hook to lower a shirt for a customer. Trace used neither. The man had reach.

His own cotton button-down pulled from the waistband of his slacks. Shaye couldn't help staring. His abdomen was lean and buff. His hip bone was sharply arched. A shadowed gap drew her gaze even lower. Down his happy trail. There was no visible sign of a tan line.

She should've looked away. Needed to look away, but she could not. Curiosity got the better of her.

He rolled to the balls of his feet a second time. Twisted right. His shirt bunched over muscle, and his pants tightened over his ass. She blinked. No jockey or boxer line. Interesting. His boys had freedom.

A shift of his weight, and his pants again flattened against his stomach. The untucked tail of his dress shirt now lay against his thigh.

Shaye blinked, breathed again.

Trace held up two shirts for her inspection. "Which one?" he asked. "I want to advertise volleyball."

His chest would make a great billboard, she thought. Thick, wide, toned. Either shirt would work for him. She was certain whichever one she chose, he'd pick the opposite.

She went with the tan T-shirt with *Volleyball* printed over a tattoo tribal design. It was very masculine. The white polo with *Got Sand?* would be a constant reminder that she was forced to rent two hundred feet of his beach.

Trace was surprisingly agreeable to her choice. He reset *Got Sand?* on the clothesline, then leaned his forearms on the rim of a circular rack, a relaxed stance.

"We should get T-shirts made up for the tournament," he said. "They'd make great souvenirs."

Oh, crap. "They're, ah, already on order," she was forced to admit.

"I missed the memo."

"I didn't consult you." She experienced a hint of guilt but not enough to make her feel bad. "I've worked with the same silk-screening company for years. To get the T-shirts in time, they had to be ordered yesterday."

She'd placed the order last week but wasn't about to tell him so. A day or two shouldn't matter in the grand scheme of the event.

The irritated tic along his jaw told her she'd jumped the gun. Once again. He pushed off the clothes rack and came to stand beside her. "How many did you order?"

"Five thousand."

"On credit?"

She nodded. Every store in Barefoot William extended their credit line over the summer months, when tourism in Florida slowed to a snail's pace. Money was tight. They didn't have the cash flow to pay outright.

He pinned her with a look. "That's a hell of a lot of shirts to store in your garage had I not gone along with the tournament."

She shrugged. "You did agree. We're working together now."

She'd been confident when she purchased the shirts that the event would move forward, with or without Trace's beach. Just on a smaller scale. They were going big now, and she wished she'd ordered ten thousand.

He pinched the bridge of his nose between his thumb and forefinger. "You're a difficult woman."

"You're not easy to like either." He was a Saunders.

"I did agree to your event," he reminded her.

"The pro/am benefits you, too."

"There will be perks," he said with annoying assurance.

She thought of Nicole Archer. "*One* perk only." There would be no more. Ever.

"Ground rules," he went on to say. "I want full disclosure from now on. No more moves behind my back. We discuss before you initiate. Understood?"

He wasn't the boss of her. She'd never worked with a partner. But she would agree for the time being. She shrugged and said, "Sure. No problem."

She adjusted her hair band, then scuffed her bare toes across the floor tile. She had more to confess, but it would only piss him off further. She needed his signature on the recreational permit. She would downplay whatever decisions she'd already made as they arose.

She smiled to herself. She wasn't his keeper. She had no idea where he would be each second of every day. If a snap judgment was needed, she'd pretend she couldn't locate him. She was perfectly capable of moving forward on her own.

Trace Saunders studied Shaye. She hadn't come clean. He was certain she had more to share but wasn't giving it up. He hated surprises, especially in business. The volleyball tournament was a huge undertaking. They had only three weeks to pull it all together.

Instead of talking to him, she ran her fingers through her rain-tangled curls. Each movement drew her sagging top farther off her shoulders. The swell of her small breasts became evident. Her nipples pointed at him through the stretched-out lace. No bra for Shaye Cates.

He watched her now as she'd watched him earlier. He'd felt her earthy brown gaze as he'd taken the T-shirts off the clothesline. She'd eyeballed his groin as his wet pants slipped nearly to his short hairs. He was damn lucky his cock hadn't waved back at her.

He'd gone for distraction and recited the alphabet backward, *Z, Y, X, W, V, U.* A habit he'd formed in high school when he was hot and horny and sitting in English class.

She hissed her annoyance when she caught him looking down her top. She immediately tugged it higher. The lace was resistant. It stuck to her teacup breasts, outlining her curves and hint of cleavage.

She blushed, right before she blindly snatched six shirts from a circular rack without paying attention to size or logo. Men's large. The top shirt in the cluster read *Orgasm Donor.*

"A dressing room just cleared," she said. "I'm changing first."

She stomped on his foot as she passed him, a purposeful crunch to his toes. Slender and athletic, she had the muscle to come down hard. He curled his toes inside his wet loafers. Fortunately nothing was broken.

Trace waited patiently, quietly, for his chance at the dressing room. During that time, he reflected on their day. Shaye was an unpredictable pain in his ass. She'd shown up at the diner all sexy, enticing, and seeking the upper hand.

He had seen through her scheme. He took her as advertised and gave her the once-over. She went from turned on to ticked in two minutes flat. She didn't give ground gracefully.

She'd tricked him into the tournament.

He'd swindled rental space for Nicole Archer.

She'd placed an order for five thousand T-shirts.

What was next? He needed to keep a sharp eye on her at all times. A supreme undertaking. Never had he imagined spending three weeks in her company. Shaye came with an extended family. He'd be knee-deep in Cateses. And not overjoyed by the prospect.

"Another dressing room has opened." Jenna walked up the center aisle to him, a pair of Hawaiian board shorts in hand. Her expression was challenging. There was laughter in her eyes.

Trace blinked against the neon colors. Lime and orange surfboards flashed on the hot-pink shorts.

Clown shorts. No wonder they were on the sale rack. No one in his right mind would wear such loud colors. The shorts would scare off sharks.

"Not my style," he said slowly. This had to be a joke. He took pride in his appearance. Boardroom *GQ* fit him better than glow-in-the-dark trunks.

"This is my only extra large." Jenna tossed him the shorts. "Unless you go Speedo."

No Speedo. The tight-fitting swim briefs reminded him of women's panties. A Speedo left little to the imagination. His package would be peeking out. His only other option was to remain in his wet pants. The damp fabric was already rubbing his boys the wrong way. There would be chafing.

He took the neon board shorts from Jenna. He'd never worn pink in his life or dressed so brightly. People would see him coming from a mile away.

He tucked the clothes under his arm and continued down the side aisle to the dressing room. It took him ten minutes to fully towel off and change. His leather loafers leaked water. He hoped they weren't ruined. They were his favorite pair.

Barefoot, he stepped from the dressing room. He immediately spotted Shaye moving toward the women's T-shirt rack. The lady was in a hurry. The men's large she presently wore hung almost to her knees. Her shorts beneath were well-hidden. The brown color washed out her tan. Her shoulders looked lumpy. She was on a mission for a smaller size.

He stopped her in her tracks. "No way in hell. If I have to wear neon shorts, you're keeping the shirt."

She turned to him then, and he read the motto: *Save a Tree, Eat a Beaver.* He fought a smile. Lost. "Works for me."

Shaye pulled a face. "It's meant for a man."

"Too bad." He felt no sympathy for her. "I'm not going to be the only one on the boardwalk collecting stares."

She glared, ready to square off.

He raised his hand and silenced her. "Your cousin brought me these shorts. A joke on me. You grabbed the Beaver shirt. A joke on you. We're even. We wear what we've got on."

Shaye tossed him a store bag for his wet clothes. She looked at his feet. "Flip-flops or barefoot?" she asked.

He shoved his shirt, slacks, and loafers into the bag. "Flip-flops," he decided.

Jenna had anticipated his request. Humor curved her lips as she passed him a pair of black flip-flops with *I Love Barefoot William* highlighted in white on the two bands that separated the big toe and the second. He saw Shaye cover her own smile with the back of her hand. These women were playing him. He was the butt of their joke.

He scanned the wall where an assortment of flip-flops hung on wire hooks. Some had rhinestones, others plastic flowers. A few came with colorful, interchangeable bands. Every single pair bore the same logo.

No way in hell would he promote Barefoot William. He felt no love for the town. Nor did he care for Shaye Cates. Going barefoot was preferable to the flip-flops.

He returned them to Jenna. "I'll pass."

"The boardwalk cement gets hot this time of day," Shaye warned.

His stubbornness set in. He'd suffer second-degree burns before he'd advertise anything Cates. If worse came to worst, he'd hop off the boardwalk and walk in the sand.

"Nicole is waiting for us," he said. He crossed to the cash register. "How much do I owe you?" he asked Jenna.

Jenna snagged scissors off the counter and cut the price tags off his clothes. She rubbed the tags between her thumb and forefinger. "Sixty dollars," she said, straight-faced.

Jenna was all Cates and out to take advantage of him. By his calculations, she was charging him triple. He could argue, but he knew he wouldn't win. He was being screwed and not enjoying it. Shaye stood off to the side. Her lips twitched as she took in the transaction.

Two could play this game. He'd pay now, and Shaye would pay later. He'd collect more than sixty dollars from her.

He slipped his hand into the plastic bag and withdrew

his money clip from the back pocket of his slacks. The bills were soggy and wrinkled. He laid three twenties on the counter to dry.

He moved to the front door, then swung it wide. Jenna quickly snipped the tags off Shaye's shirt and shorts, then gave her cousin a hug. Shaye left the store ahead of him. The sun was so bright, it made him pause. He wished he had his mirrored Oakley's, but he refused to buy a pair from a Cates. Damn, the pavement was hot.

Shaye walked briskly. She shot ten feet in front of him, quickly extending her lead to another couple yards. Her body shifted beneath the baggy brown T-shirt. Her slender curves were nicely defined.

Save a Tree, Eat a Beaver drew a lot of attention. Every male tourist on the boardwalk openly stared. Some smirked. Others made buck-toothed faces.

Trace took his own hits. One woman put on her sunglasses against the glare of his neon board shorts. A hot chick in a bikini asked if all his other clothes were in the laundry. A man in a lemon yellow Speedo winked at him.

He picked up his pace. The soles of his feet felt on fire. The cement hissed like hot coals. He caught up to Shaye at the door to the Denim Dolphin, a children's store.

She cast a look over her shoulder but didn't acknowledge him fully. The boardwalk was her domain. She *allowed* him to walk with her.

They reached the general store, where everything from fresh fruit, toothpaste, pots and pans to sunscreen was sold. Nicole Archer stood just inside the door. Her eyes widened when she saw them. Her uncertainty showed.

"You've changed clothes," she managed. "Interesting choices. I've not seen this side of you before, Trace."

"Shaye likes walking in the rain," he said. He didn't add the fact that he'd been afraid he would lose her if he hadn't walked, too.

Trace knew that Shaye hated renting to anyone other than a Cates. She could've darted off in any direction to avoid showing Nicole the shop. He'd dogged her steps and gotten drenched for just that reason.

"We stopped in Three Shirts for something dry," he added. He'd paid an outrageous price for his outfit.

Nicole reluctantly eyed the beaver on Shaye's shirt. She fingered her multichain necklace, completely at a loss for words.

"Roomy." Shaye pulled out the sides. The men's large could have fit two of her easily. "The design is all about saving the ecosystem."

"I see that now." Nicole was always polite.

Trace moved things along. "Are you ready to see your new shop?" he asked. The sooner he could get out of these board shorts, the better. The web lining scratched his balls.

"The store is two doors down, next to Madame Aleta the Fortune Teller," Shaye said.

"Is she any good?" Nicole asked.

"She has *the sight*." Shaye used air quotes.

"I'd love to get a reading."

Trace took Nicole by the arm. "Save it for another day. Focus on your shop."

They reached their destination in a matter of seconds. Shaye's cousin was already on the premises. Kai leaned against the doorjamb, his arms crossed over his chest.

Kai welcomed Shaye with a raised eyebrow and tight smile. Trace saw the look the two exchanged. He was certain Shaye was silently requesting that Kai neither judge nor comment, that she would explain later when they were alone.

Shaye then introduced Nicole. "Nicole Archer, my cousin Kai Cates."

Nicole offered her hand, but Kai was slow to take it.

Nicole withdrew first. She dusted off her hands, looking out of place in her stark white shift.

Kai stood stiffly. There were wood shavings on the shoulders of his olive-green T-shirt, the knees of his jeans, and the steel toes of his work boots. He wore his tool belt low, like the holster of a gunslinger. Kai looked ready to draw on Trace. The men had never been friends.

Nicole wasn't shy. She inspected every inch of the shop. Trace leaned against a wobbly wooden display case. He looked on as Kai and Shaye lowered their voices. Trace had exceptional hearing, so he eavesdropped.

"You're here because . . . ?" Kai asked.

"Nicole is a jewelry designer," Shaye explained. Stress drew white lines at the corners of her mouth. Trace caught the rapid rise and fall of her chest beneath her baggy T-shirt. "She's been looking for a shop to rent."

Her cousin curved the fingers of his right hand around the handle of a hammer. His knuckles turned white. "You brought her to *our* boardwalk?"

"We have space available." Shaye's mood ring glowed with multicolored stripes. The lady was conflicted.

Space, available? Trace looked around. The shop was being gutted. Torn Sheetrock hung off bare studs. The entire room was no bigger than a bread box. He hoped Nicole would have adequate space for her custom creations. There was no alternative.

He heard Shaye sigh. "It was a trade-off," she softly confessed to her cousin. "I got the volleyball tournament if he got a shop for his girlfriend."

"His girlfriend?" Kai balked. "That's the same as renting to a Saunders."

"Let's hope they don't marry anytime soon."

Trace saved the fact that he and Nicole were no longer

involved for another day. He let Kai and Shaye sweat it out.

"How long will she be here?" asked Kai.

"A short time, no longer than a month, maybe two," Shaye whispered.

"How much is she paying?"

"We haven't settled on a price."

Trace took that moment to join them. He spoke directly to Shaye. "The rental agreement will run a full year." He was emphatic. "Nicole won't be charged a dime."

"You're bullying me."

"And you blindsided me."

She shook her head. "This isn't fair."

Trace looked down at his T-shirt and board shorts. "What wasn't fair was your cousin Jenna charging me sixty bucks for these clothes. Paybacks are a bastard. You'll eat the rent and pay for the remodeling. Twelve months will establish Nicole in business."

"Jackass," muttered Shaye.

"Beave," said Trace.

"You two argue like an old married couple," Nicole commented as she approached them.

Trace's throat tightened.

He swore he heard Shaye gag.

Married. The word would never extend to a Cates and a Saunders.

"The shop is perfect." Nicole touched his arm in an appreciative gesture. "I can envision the renovation."

"Envision it small," Kai said darkly.

Trace had never seen Nicole glare at anyone as she now did at Kai. She had fire and fight in her eyes. And a backbone. Kai's jaw jutted at a don't-mess-with-me angle.

Battle lines were now drawn between the jewelry designer and the handyman. Trace hoped it wouldn't escalate into an all-out war.

He had his own problems with Shaye.

She would try to double-deal him down the road.

He had to expect the unexpected.

Three

Shaye Cates expected Nicole and Trace to depart shortly after viewing the shop. But there was no hurrying them. They pushed an hour into ninety minutes. Nicole shared her vision of the store with Trace while Shaye and Kai stood by the door.

Twice Kai held the door open.

Twice the two ignored his hint that they leave.

They'd stuck around forever.

An apprehensive lump formed in Shaye's throat, one she couldn't swallow. Kai was ticked at her, as he had a right to be. Anger poured off him in waves. His aversion to Trace went back years. However, his immediate dislike of Nicole Archer proved puzzling.

Kai was laid-back and never judged anyone, yet Nicole seemed to hit a nerve from the get-go. Perhaps it was because she was Trace's lover. Kai saw them as a team. Both of them were trespassing on Cates property.

Shaye rolled her shoulders to loosen the tension. The knots only tightened. She might have gotten off easier had Nicole paid rent. A total freebie wouldn't sit well with her family. Not well at all.

The designer's free pass would force other shop owners to cover her rent so the boardwalk remained solvent.

Business was slow, and everyone was struggling. Nicole would add to their burden.

Shaye glanced at the couple as they moved toward the door. Could they walk any slower? She scrunched her nose. *If* she were objective, she'd have to admit, the two looked good together. Handsome men and beautiful women were drawn to each other. Trace and Nicole were no exception. They complemented one another, even amid the gutted shop.

Wood shavings now speckled the satin ankle ties on Nicole's wedge sandals. Dirt smeared her white shift. But she had the polish and poise to pull it off. Her jewelry dazzled amid the dust.

Then there was Trace. His *Volleyball* T-shirt accented his chest, the tribal tattoo a stamp to his masculinity. His board shorts hitched low on his hips. Pink wasn't his color, but neither did the neon detract from his long, muscular legs. Barefoot, he watched for discarded nails and picture-frame hooks. He looked more like a tourist than the heir to a town.

He listened attentively to Nicole, then made a few suggestions of his own. His lover took them all in, nodding her approval.

Nodding was not good, Shaye realized. Each agreement raised the cost of the renovation. The Cateses would be laying out a fortune. Kai would do the work. Maybe he could cut a few corners.

"What shop was here most recently?" Nicole asked. "There are picture hooks all over the floor."

"Behind the Lens," Shaye said. "My Uncle Dave was a professional photographer. He restored historical photos of the town and its earliest residents. He also made scenic postcards and amusement-park videos. Tourists flocked to the memorabilia. He retired this spring."

Shaye still had dozens of Uncle Dave's photographs safely stored away. Her favorite was one of her great-great-great-grandfather William standing on the shore at twilight. His pant legs were rolled to his knees. Waves splashed his ankles. He held a fishing pole. A bucket of bait was submerged in the sand. He appeared as free as the breeze that mussed his white hair.

There was something or someone down the beach from where William stood. It appeared no more than a black dot. No matter the magnification, it was unrecognizable. Shaye thought it might be either a seagull or a sand castle. Perhaps a piece of driftwood. Maybe a fellow fisherman.

She had yet to decide where to display Uncle Dave's historic collection. The photos were her heritage. The past was a huge part of her present.

Nicole had her own plans for the photos. "You could continue to hang them here," she offered. "I design vintage jewelry from sea glass. I could drape necklaces over the frames. The photographs would enhance my signature pieces."

"A possibility," Shaye was slow to say.

"Not likely," Kai decided more quickly.

Nicole was not to be discouraged. "I'm ready to sign the agreement."

"The paperwork isn't ready," Shaye hedged. "We can finalize the details tomorrow."

"You're stalling," Trace said. "We'll follow you to your office."

Her office. Most days she worked from the beach. She set up near the pier, needing no more than a sand chair, sunscreen, sunglasses, an umbrella, cell phone, and wireless laptop. Her work wardrobe consisted of three swimsuits and two cover-ups. The sunshine and fresh air cleared her head. The splash of the waves soothed her.

Shaye stood firm. "My office is closed for the day."

Trace glanced at his watch, his look hard. "It's barely four o'clock."

"I'm on Barefoot William time."

"I like the way you do business," Nicole said, surprising Shaye. "I can set my own shop hours, too. Barefoot William won't be as strict as Saunders Shores."

The two towns were nothing alike.

Saunders Shores was as stuffy and starched as its board of directors. Discriminating tourists reserved stretches of shoreline for private parties and sunbathing. A cabana boy raked the sugar sand. General beachgoers were fined for trespassing. At the end of the day, exclusive nightclubs opened their doors to members only.

Barefoot William was casual and carefree, and vacationers could cut loose. The boardwalk and beach were open to the public. The sand was scuffed and scattered and welcomed footprints. Flashing neon lights lit the night sky like fireworks. Music echoed from the shops. Shaye had danced down the boardwalk more than once. She didn't need a partner.

The party atmosphere was endless and unbroken. The town was an eclectic mix of singles and families, toddlers and grandparents. The air stirred with perpetual motion, as if something new and exciting was just around the corner. It usually was.

Nicole smiled tentatively. "Anyone up for dinner?" she asked. "My treat. How about Slip Twelve at the yacht harbor?"

Shaye was familiar with the five-star seafood restaurant. The menu was pricey, the view, spectacular. Reservations were made six weeks in advance. No problem there, though; Nicole was dating a Saunders. A table would be available for Trace at a moment's notice.

A silence held for several beats. It didn't take Shaye long

to realize that Nicole was new to the area. She wasn't yet aware of their families' dispute. The line their forefathers once drew in the sand had endured one hundred years. It could last another century. Easily.

Shaye appreciated Nicole's generosity, but dinner was out of the question. She'd had lunch with Trace, and that was one meal too many. She still smelled like coconut cream pie. She refused to face off with the man a second time. They had nothing in common. Fine dining stretched on for hours. Their table conversation would be stilted or nonexistent.

Kai saved her. "Shaye and I have plans," he announced.

Nicole's smile slipped. "Another time, perhaps."

"Another lifetime," Kai said under his breath.

"Where shall we meet in the morning?" Nicole asked Shaye. The woman was trying to smooth things over.

Under other circumstances, Shaye might have liked her. As it stood now, they'd never be friends. Their situation was too awkward. The designer was Trace's lover. He'd forced Nicole on her. After the volleyball tournament, Shaye would show Nicole the door. She'd find a loophole, however small.

She looked at Trace and found him eyeing her. Heat crept up her neck, and her stomach gave a strange little flutter. Her reaction was unwanted. His woman stood at his side. Trace should be looking at Nicole, not at her.

Shaye swallowed, her throat dry. "I'll meet you west of the pier, near the shoreline, at sunrise."

Nicole blinked. Twice. She appeared stunned by the early hour. Shaye assumed she slept late. Nicole appeared pampered, a woman who preferred brunch to breakfast.

"I won't keep you waiting," Nicole promised. "I'm temporarily staying at The Sandcastle until I can find my own place. I'll request a wake-up call."

The Sandcastle was a Saunders hotel.

Trace treated his woman to the finest accommodations. "You won't sleep a wink," he teased Nicole. "You'll pull out your sketchbook and lay out your shop, then make a long list of renovations."

"You know me too well," Nicole said.

"You also need to unwind." Trace went on to massage the tension from the back of Nicole's neck.

Shaye stared, transfixed by each slow, circular motion. Nicole momentarily closed her eyes. Pleasure softened her features. She released a slow, appreciative breath, then licked her lips moist.

Shaye blew out her own breath. Her sigh was embarrassing. How could she get so lost in Trace when he touched another woman? Yet she had. She'd felt as if he was stroking her rather than Nicole. She didn't like the sensation one bit.

He sensed his effect on her. It was evident in the banked heat of his gaze. His look alone was a sexual burn. He was toying with her for no apparent reason other than to get under her skin. Her nerves frayed.

Kai nudged her shoulder. "We should get to the ballpark. I need to open the concession stand and set the scoreboard. Several lightbulbs need to be replaced before tonight's game. The kids always show up early."

Parks and Recreation ran two sandlot leagues for nine-to twelve-year-old boys. Barefoot William and Saunders Shores each supported four teams. They played on separate ball fields for most of the summer, but on the third weekend in July the two top teams faced off in the all-star game. Both towns turned out in force. The rivalry was fierce.

Saunders Shores' brand-new recreational facility had locker rooms, a raked infield, and a mowed outfield. Their uniforms were new and dry-cleaned after every game. They would host the play-off game this year.

The Barefoot William teams practiced every night and played a rotating schedule. The players' T-shirts sported logos for Pinscher's Crab Shack, Saltwater Sharkey's, Goody Gumdrops, and Crabby Abby's. Some shirts had been worn several years in a row. Hand-me-downs were an athletic ritual.

Players on the Barefoot William teams had to toss rocks from the baselines before each game, and after nine innings every fielder had sand in his sneakers.

Pinscher's Crab Shack's team would play Saltwater Sharkey's at twilight. Most of the town would turn out for the game. Play would be close. Both teams had strong hitters and base-stealers.

Shaye needed to find a home plate umpire to fill in for her Uncle Paul, who owned a charter fishing boat. Red snapper were running near Key West. A group of Chicago stockbrokers had hired her uncle to take them out to catch their limit.

Without Paul, there was no one to call balls and strikes. Her uncle had a great eye for runner and catcher disputes at home base. He instinctively knew who was safe, who was out. He was fair and was respected by the players.

Shaye had crouched behind home plate more times than she could count. She was up, down, up, down with each pitch. The next day her legs were so sore, she could barely walk. Stiffness was not her friend.

"Off to the park," she finally said.

Nicole perked up. "I haven't seen a kids' game in years. It might be fun." She smiled at Trace. "Take me out to the ball game?"

Shaye's stomach sank all the way to her toes. Nicole could have an intimate dinner with Trace at Slip Twelve.

Why in the world would she want to sit on splintered bleachers in the late heat of the day? She didn't know the name of one child on either team. This was family night for the Cateses. Was Nicole that hard up for entertainment? Surely Trace could find something else for them to do.

Apparently he could not. Amusement lightened his eyes. One corner of his mouth tipped. He knew his attendance at the park would needle her. "Hot dogs, popcorn— I'm game."

Nicole glowed.

Kai growled.

Trace grinned.

Shaye felt grumpy. Trace was taking advantage of her. His approval of the volleyball tournament was his ticket to all Barefoot William events. No Cates would be rude or openly disapprove of his presence. Her family and relatives would tolerate Trace for three weeks. Only after the event would her life return to normal. Then Center Street would once again separate Barefoot William and Saunders Shores.

She couldn't stop him from attending the ball game. Or could she? An idea formed, took hold. She tried not to smile. "Don't waste your time." She waved them off. "My Uncle Paul is in the Keys. No home plate umpire, no game. We may have to reschedule."

The game would go on, with Shaye behind home, but there was no need to share that information. Let them believe play would be suspended.

Nicole looked disappointed. "No one can sub for Paul?"

"We have a strict sandlot rule: parents aren't allowed to umpire if they have kids on the field. Everyone attending the game is related to the players. We don't have instant replay. No one wants to make a bad call. Paul's a bachelor and unbiased. He's our best bet."

Nicole was thoughtful. "What about Trace?"

"What about him?" Shaye's heart slowed. She was instantly suspicious.

"He knows a little about baseball," Nicole said. "He has no ties to the Cateses, other than his friendship with you."

"Trace and I aren't terribly close," Shaye was quick to say. "We're doing one business deal together, and that's it. There won't be another. Ever. Besides, I wouldn't want to interfere with his plans for the evening."

"I've got nothing going on," Trace said easily. "Ask me. I might do you a favor."

His goodwill would cost her dearly, she suspected. She'd be forced to repay him in due time. Trace had played baseball all his life. He'd been an All-American shortstop and played in the college World Series. He'd been good enough to turn pro.

Major League Baseball was not his destiny, however. After college, his father insisted Trace head Saunders New York, the headquarters for their international holdings. Trace had left Florida State to sit on the board of directors. He was the youngest chairman in the history of the firm. His father supported his every initiative.

Shaye scrunched her nose. Trace was all about big business, not sandlot ball. "But if you umpire, Nicole will have to sit in the stands alone," she pointed out.

"Kai can keep her company," said Trace.

Kai stiffened. "I work the concession stand."

"I can sell popcorn," Nicole was quick to say. "I've worked trade shows. I can bring out the best in a product."

"It's popcorn," Kai snorted. "It sells itself."

"Do you want our help or not?" asked Trace.

Shaye debated. She needed an umpire and could also use another worker in concession. Desperate times called for desperate measures. She looked from Trace to Nicole and forced herself to be civil. "If you can help out, it would be appreciated."

"What time?" asked Trace.

"Be at the park at seven. Game starts at seven-thirty," Shaye said.

"Equipment?" Trace asked.

"Mask, chest protector, and shin guards are stored on-site." She paused, and her cheeks warmed. "Wear a—"

"Cup," he finished for her.

"There could be a wild pitch."

"Thanks for the warning."

Shaye was relieved. The game would go off without a hitch. She had her home plate umpire, whether she wanted him or not.

"Dress down," she told Nicole. "We supply an apron, but the snow cones can be messy."

"I have the perfect outfit." The woman was excited.

Shaye took a step toward the door. She couldn't afford to waste any more time. "Any questions?" she wrapped up.

Trace cut her a glance. "How much does it pay?"

Pay? He didn't need the money. "Twenty dollars."

He nodded. "Let's do it."

Nicole left first and Shaye second. Trace fell in behind her. His breath was once again hot on her neck. The man knew no boundaries. Kai locked up the store.

"All mine." Nicole took a final look at the storefront. "I want to paint the door a brilliant emerald green, like a gemstone. Lime and avocado are too fruity."

Trace looked pointedly at Shaye. "I'm sure that can be arranged."

Shaye refused to commit. Dollar signs danced in her head. Costs were adding up fast. "Something to consider" was all she could say.

Nicole took Trace by the arm, then waved to Shaye and Kai. "See you tonight."

"Can't wait." In truth, Shaye wished she could stop time, cancel the baseball game, and forget Trace Saunders existed. From the corner of her eye, she watched the couple move down the boardwalk.

Trace had the athletic stride of a jock, and Nicole took two smaller steps to his every one. His neon board shorts could be seen a block away. He remained barefoot.

He stopped twice on the boardwalk, once to listen to a guitarist strumming for tips. Trace tossed money into the man's guitar case. A half block farther, he added a few dollars to the daily earnings of a young girl who danced on stilts.

His generosity to her relatives surprised Shaye. At that moment he looked nothing like a Saunders. He wore surfside, sand-in-the-crack beachwear, a far cry from designer casual. Dressing less straight and stuffy made him *almost* human, but he could never fully pull off beach bum.

He would become an eyesore the moment he crossed Center Street. Saunders Shores was all about pricey fashion. Shoppers kept to the redbrick sidewalks—sidewalks swept clean of sand. The trash receptacles were emptied hourly.

She released a long-suffering breath. They would endure the volleyball tournament. Then get on with their lives.

Kai's cell phone rang. He took the call. "I'm walking your way now," he told the caller. "Be there in ten." He disconnected.

"Aunt Molly's dishwasher is stuck on the rinse cycle," he said. "I need to stop by the diner on our way to the ball park. All her equipment is old. I fixed her grill yesterday, and the fryer the day before that."

Shaye was well aware of the deteriorating diner. "Her kitchen needs a major overhaul."

Kai hooked his thumbs inside his tool belt. "Molly's not going to spend money on new appliances. Her spare change goes to feeding those who can't afford a meal. Her diner's become a soup kitchen for many. Molly never turns anyone away. She runs a long tab."

Shaye tucked her clothes bag under her arm, then crossed her fingers. "Let's hope the tournament increases cash flow." The boardwalk hadn't been in the black for a very long time, but she believed better days were ahead.

They struck out at a fast pace. "Explain your deal with Nicole Archer," Kai said as they dodged a juggler, then a unicyclist.

She gave him the abridged version, ending with, "I took advantage of Trace, and he got back at me."

Kai slowed. "He used Nicole against you?"

"I owed him," she said wearily. "I don't know their history. Trace did, however, appear relieved to find her a store."

"On *our* boardwalk." Kai was ticked.

"All the boutiques at Saunders Shores are filled."

"So he says."

They soon reached the corner, and Molly Malone met them at the door to her diner. Her round face was red and damp with perspiration. The front of her apron was grease-streaked. "I tried to fix the dishwasher," she huffed. "I wasn't successful."

Kai headed for the kitchen. Molly directed Shaye to a table. "Lemonade? Iced tea? Coconut cream pie?" her aunt offered.

Shaye agreed to a glass of raspberry iced tea but passed on the pie. Coconut cream would now forever remind her of Trace. He'd eaten the filling off her hip, as if he were tasting her. The image made her stomach twist.

Molly went for her drink, and Shaye located an empty

table. She pulled out a chair and sat down heavily. She set her bag of wet clothes on the floor by her feet. It had already been a long day. And it wasn't over yet.

Molly returned and stood over her. "What's with the T-shirt?" she asked.

"I got caught in the rain and stopped at Three Shirts to change." Shaye kept it short.

"You chose the Beaver?"

"I grabbed the shirt without paying attention." And Trace hadn't let her switch designs. "It wasn't what I wanted."

You should've seen Trace, she wanted to say. Oh, well. Eventually word would trickle back to her aunt. More than one Cates had seen Trace barefoot and wearing neon-pink board shorts. He'd been hard to miss. Everyone would have a good laugh.

"I have a question," Molly said, keeping one eye on her customers. "People have been asking all day where you're setting up shop for the tournament. We know you work at the beach, but you'll need an office for the event, a central contact point."

There was so much to do. And so little time. She needed to get organized fast. That meant working closely with Trace. The very thought of having the man in her life twenty-four/seven nearly stopped her heart. He made her nervous.

Shaye ran through her options for an office. Her niece Eden was already setting up Old Tyme Portraits. Eden would open for business at the end of the month. Kai would be starting renovations for Nicole Archer tomorrow. There were no more empty spaces.

Trace had office space; she was sure of it. But she refused to set up the headquarters in Saunders Shores. It was too damn ritzy. She'd be forced to wear shoes.

NO TAN LINES   77

"I'll let you know as soon as I'm situated," she promised Molly. "Give me a day or two."

Molly glanced at her watch. "I need to batter the grouper for the fish fry tonight. Can I fix you a take-out?"

Shaye shook her head. Food was the last thing on her mind. She'd grab a bag of popcorn at the ballpark.

Her aunt took off for the kitchen, and Kai joined Shaye moments later. Sweat dampened his brow, and his shirt was wet. "Dishwasher sprayed like a fire hose," he said. "It's fixed for the moment."

She pushed off her chair. "I need to change clothes. I'll meet you at the park."

He snagged a napkin from a nearby table and wiped off his forehead. His jaw shifted, locked. "I could've worked the concession stand alone tonight," he said. "Nicole will only get in my way. If she accidentally gets squirted with ketchup . . ." He left the sentence hanging.

"You're thirty, not ten. No condiment fights." She didn't need a blowup. Not with Trace behind home plate. She could only handle one situation at a time.

A dozen people made demands on Trace Saunders all at once. He'd yet to change clothes and now sat at his desk in his volleyball T-shirt and neon-pink board shorts. His administrative assistant, Martin Carson, tried to herd people back out the door, but his staff stood three deep with no plans to leave. He was the final answer to their questions.

He ran one hand down his face, exhaling his day away. Shaye Cates complicated his life. Molehills turned into mountains. And now the two of them would be joined at the hip for the next three weeks.

She was a sexy beach chick with surprising business sense. She was also opinionated and annoying as hell. Sneaky, too.

He had three hours until the sandlot game. Whatever had possessed him to umpire? His knee-jerk agreement would have him crouching behind home plate. He'd never been an umpire, but he understood fairness. He'd call the game to the best of his ability.

Ninety minutes of paperwork, and Trace showed everyone to the door. He motioned to Martin to remain. Martin slid onto a translucent chair. He appeared to be sitting on air.

Trace had always shown remarkable forethought. It served him well now. He'd faced a lot of challenges in his life and knew when to stack the deck in his favor. The volleyball tournament was bigger than the rivalry between him and Shaye. They had little time to set up the event. Success depended on having the right people in place.

In his opinion, sharp as she was, Shaye was too small-town to handle the event. If all went as expected, Barefoot William and Saunders Shores would be overrun by tourists, traffic, and volleyball fans. His survival instinct kicked in.

He looked across his desk at Martin. "Contact Event Planners in Miami. Ask for Marlene Mason. Explain the circumstances of the pro/am, and agree to whatever she charges. I want her here tomorrow."

"What if she's booked, sir?"

"She'll show." Of that he was certain. He and Marlene were old friends. He'd known her at Florida State. He'd given her the seed money for her event-planning business.

Marlene was in demand. She organized political, corporate, and sports events. She would put together a top-of-the-line tournament and turn a profit in the process.

She had promised him a favor, whenever he chose to collect. The time was now.

"I'll introduce Marlene as my secretary," Trace said, feeling that was best. "I'd prefer her identity be kept secret."

Martin clucked his tongue, then spoke his mind. "Shaye Cates won't be happy, sir. This is her tournament. You're going behind her back. She's a proud woman. Her family will be involved. Her brother Dune is the major draw."

Trace felt a twinge of guilt, but not enough to change his mind. Shaye ran Barefoot William Enterprises. Her boardwalk and pier were rapidly heading toward bankruptcy.

Without professional direction, the event could prove a disaster. He was afraid that, left to her own devices, Shaye would lose her shirt. He couldn't take that chance. Not if he was going to be involved.

Shaye didn't like him now.

She'd hate his guts when she discovered his duplicity.

But when all was said and done, her town would be in the black. That's what mattered most to her. He could then walk away, even if she threw darts at his back.

Martin cleared his throat. "Will you be working late? Should I have dinner sent over from Barconi's?"

The bistro's rigatoni often helped Trace burn the midnight oil. But tonight he had no plans to work late. He had a baseball game to umpire. He rose and headed out. "I'll grab a hot dog at the park."

He never got to eat. Shaye met him in the parking lot. She barely gave him time to grab his athletic bag from the passenger seat of his Porsche before hustling him to the storage facility. She seemed anxious and not all that glad to see him. He eyed her slender backside as she walked several feet ahead of him. She wore a gray *Gulf Field* T-shirt, black jeans, and red Keds.

He smiled to himself. Apparently athletic events warranted shoes.

The storage facility smelled like a locker room. It was small, barely big enough for one person to turn around in, but he and Shaye somehow fit inside. He dropped his bag on the floor. He'd packed a towel and a fresh shirt for after the game.

One dim bulb shed minimal light. She fumbled twice with the combination lock on a paint-chipped locker but finally was able to retrieve his mask, chest protector, and shin guards.

Equipment in hand, she pivoted on her heel and bumped him hard. Her arm scraped across his chest. Lady had sharp elbows.

She scrunched her nose as she looked at his light blue dress shirt, navy slacks, and black athletic shoes.

"I dressed by the rule book," he told her.

"So you did," she muttered. She handed him the gear, then raised an eyebrow. "Need help with the clips?"

She stood so close, her breath warmed his skin above the top button on his shirt. The scent of Dove soap surrounded her. A freshly showered woman appealed to him, especially one standing this near. Her chest rose, and his chest fell. Less than an inch separated their hip bones and thighs. His athletic shoes bracketed her keds.

She lifted her hand in an attempt to put space between them. Her palm firmly pressed his abdomen. Her expression was standoffish, yet her mood ring flashed the vivid pink of arousal.

She had no idea the ring gave her away. Had she known, she would've gone screaming into the sunset. Their situation was as grave as it was humorous. She was a Cates, and, for him, that closed the door on seduction.

He'd never been attracted to slender, opinionated, sneaky women. Then why did his body harden with their contact? It was a mystery he didn't care to solve.

"I can dress myself," he finally said. "I'll need some room."

"I'm gone." She scooted around him, a very tight squeeze. Her wild blond curls bounced off his chin. Her silver headband was as shiny as a fishing lure in the pale light. Her lip gloss left a print on his shirtsleeve. Her breasts grazed his side, and her butt pushed into his groin.

He was glad he'd worn his cup.

The second she was out the door, he reached for his shin guards. He put them on first, followed by his chest protector. One closure clip was missing on the left side. He carried his mask at his side.

Shaye was waiting for him when he emerged. He found her leaning against the storage shed, tapping her fingers against the metal siding. Her uneasiness was even more evident now.

"This would be a good time to put on your mask," she said.

"I'm not behind home plate."

"It's a short walk."

She snatched the mask right out of his hand, went up on tiptoe, and slipped it over his head. Something was up. She wanted his face covered.

He squinted, then asked, "What the hell, Shaye?"

She was all innocence. "You should be ready to play the moment you step onto the field."

Not good enough. He tipped back the mask and stared at her so intently, she squirmed. Realization hit, and he wasn't certain whether he should laugh or leave her where she stood.

"Your family doesn't know I'm umpiring the game, do they?" he asked.

She swallowed hard, then said, "Not exactly. I couldn't let the kids down. Will you keep my secret?"

"Kai knows," he reminded her.

"He won't tell a soul. He's busy dealing with Nicole at concession."

"The home plate umpire runs the game," he stated. "People in the stands will soon realize I'm not Paul Cates."

Shaye looked him over. "You and Paul both have dark hair. You're close to the same height. You're wider in the shoulders, so hunch over a little. The mask covers most of your face."

"What about our voices?" he asked.

"Paul's voice is higher." She pursed her lips. "Can you raise yours an octave?"

"Not on your life."

She went to Plan B. "Very well, then, I'll spread the word that Paul has a cold. Could you cough a little, make it sound like deep congestion?"

"No coughing," Trace refused. "Deception will bite you in the ass," he warned, conveniently ignoring his own planned deceit.

She rubbed her left butt cheek. "As long as it doesn't take too big a bite, I'll take my chances."

"You'll owe me, right?"

Her eyes went wide, and her chin came up. "You *volunteered* to umpire."

"Nicole offered me up."

His lover had done just that. "But you accepted," she argued.

"I saw a further exchange of favors in our future."

She exhaled sharply. "What more do you want? I'm paying you twenty dollars."

"Nothing comes to mind, but I'll let you know once I decide."

"I'm sure you will," she said, then nodded toward the field. "Ready to play ball?"

He eased his mask into place, then nodded.

"There's one other umpire on the field, Daniel Malone, Molly's husband," she said. "He's positioned behind second. Daniel will handle any outfield disputes. He doesn't have any kids playing in the game tonight."

That suited Trace just fine. "Where will you be during

the game?" He needed to know where she'd be sitting and whether she'd cause him further aggravation.

"I sit on a stool behind the fence to the left of home plate," she said. "I can see the bag perfectly. If you make a bad call, you'll hear about it."

He heard about it six times in the first three innings, but Trace ignored her. He got into the swing of the game, and each call was made with respect and fairness.

Of all the voices cheering and commenting on the game, Shaye's reached him the loudest. He kept his cool when she shouted he was *blind as a bat*. No one else in the stands contradicted his calls. Only Shaye.

He refused to reverse his "out," even when she stood at the fence and argued her case for a home run. Through it all, he kept his back to her. He had the plate advantage. He saw every hit and slide firsthand, whereas she strained to see around him.

He debated gagging her or going as far as to evict her from the park. That would rile those in the stands. He wondered if she razzed Paul Cates but doubted she'd be so hard on a relative.

That was the catch. Paul was not only the regular umpire, he was also family. Trace was a substitute. And a Saunders.

While the Cates appreciated his involvement with the volleyball tournament, he might not receive the same welcome on the diamond. He'd yet to lift his mask to make a call. He hoped the remainder of the game would be as clear-cut as the initial innings.

Despite his misgivings, Trace enjoyed the game. The young athletes had confidence and strut. They chewed gum and spat sunflower seeds. Supported each other like brothers.

This was no organized Little League contest. It was pure sandlot. Equipment was shared between the two teams. The plastic batting helmets were dented and cracked. The leather on the outfielders' gloves was well-worn. A middle finger poked out on occasion.

Holey T-shirts were tucked into torn jeans. Crab claws bracketed the logo for Pinscher's Crab Shack. *Saltwater Sharkey's* appeared inside a shark's fin on the opposing team's shirts. Sneakers were scuffed. Many parents had purchased tennis shoes with room to grow.

Beneath the lights, the cheers grew louder. Praise puffed the boys' chests. Humbleness came with three strikes or a dropped ball.

Through it all, Trace felt the love of a big, boisterous community. The Cateses were the definition of family. Win or lose, every boy would leave the field with a parent's hug or slap on the back, no matter how he played.

An announcement over the PA system called for the seventh-inning stretch. The score was five to three. The Pinschers were ahead by two runs, yet the Sharkeys would bat last.

The bleachers emptied. Everyone headed to the concession stand. Trace hoped Nicole wouldn't be overwhelmed by the stampede of customers. Kai didn't seem the type to show her the ropes. He didn't have the patience. It was evident he didn't like her.

Trace sought a quiet spot along the fence, just beyond third base. He rolled his shoulders, only to have them stiffen again when Shaye showed up.

"Fierce Grape Gatorade?" she asked, offering him a tall plastic cup. "I added a straw so you could sip through the wires."

"How thoughtful." He wanted to remove the mask and scratch his head. Wipe the sweat from his brow. It would have to wait. He could stand the mask another thirty minutes or so. There was a distinct possibility she'd owe him a further favor by the end of the game.

Beside him now, Shaye fidgeted while he sipped his

Gatorade. Her unease seemed to increase as she said, "My ten-year-old cousin Jeff bats second in the bottom of the ninth. He's number sixteen. I need you to—"

"What?" He prodded when she paused.

"—cut him some slack."

"How much slack?" he asked, frowning. "Surely you're not asking me to throw the game."

"No, not throw, just show compassion," she was quick to say. "Jeff has scoliosis. He's always played ball and never missed a rotation. He gets one at-bat per game. That's all he can handle. He tires easily.

"Jeff has trouble squaring his shoulders and swinging the bat. He's never gotten a hit," she added. "He runs with a limp. If there should be a tie at home, give him the benefit of the doubt."

Trace frowned. "Despite his condition, you're not helping the kid by handing him a home run. My call will be fair—that's all I can promise."

She wasn't satisfied. "Promise more."

"I can't." He took a final sip of Gatorade and passed her the empty plastic cup. He left her standing by the third-base fence, wishing she'd plant her ass there for the rest of the game.

She didn't. Shaye returned to her spot on the stool. She was the head cheerleader for both teams. She encouraged each player, only to censure Trace's next three calls. All were strikes, but she saw them as balls.

He rubbed his hands together. He was one second away from turning on her. He'd love to see her expression if he faced the stands and whipped off his umpire mask.

But that would defeat his purpose.

He wanted her to owe him another favor. Such a favor would extend far beyond a ninety-minute sandlot game.

The next innings passed quickly, and it was soon the

bottom of the ninth. The score remained 5–3, in favor of the Pinschers.

The first batter for the Sharkeys hit a double. Next up was number sixteen, Shaye's cousin Jeff.

Excitement rolled off his skinny shoulders. The boy's blond hair stuck out in tufts beneath his batting helmet. His cheeks were red, and his breathing was rapid.

Jeff nodded to Trace but didn't look beyond the mask. None of the players had noticed he wasn't Paul Cates. All their concentration had been on the game.

Jeff attempted a practice swing. Failed. The curvature of his spine prevented him from taking a proper batting stance. He faced the pitcher, as if he was going to bunt.

The boy's hand-eye coordination was slow. The pitcher compensated by throwing underhand, instead of a straight fastball. The infield backed up, as if anticipating a solid hit. Their silent encouragement wasn't lost on Trace. Both offense and defense wanted Jeff to get a hit.

"Strike one," Trace called with the first pitch. It had been a perfect throw.

The pitcher narrowed his gaze and concentrated even harder. His second attempt cut Jeff hip high and straight down the middle of the plate.

Jeff pushed the bat instead of swinging and nearly landed facedown in the dirt. He could barely catch his breath.

"Strike two," came from Trace.

Silence struck the ballpark, the deafening quiet of a funeral. Trace watched Jeff swallow and saw the determination written on the boy's face.

Trace debated, then decided on a time-out. He pulled Jeff aside. He wasn't a doctor, but he'd played enough ball to get the kid on base. He gave Jeff a few pointers. "Go for the bunt," he instructed. "Square up your body toward the pitcher. Don't clutch the bat; hold it loosely in front of the plate. Push out, punch the ball."

Jeff stared at him now, suddenly more interested in who Trace was than the advice being given. "You're not Uncle Paul."

"Take it up with Shaye after the game."

Jeff looked from Trace back to the field. "You honestly think I can get a hit?"

"How do you usually get on base?"

"Four balls."

"You've already got two strikes."

"You're tough."

"Life isn't always easy."

Jeff frowned. "I'm not very good."

"You've got as much heart as any kid on the team," Trace said. "The pitcher's throwing underhand like he would for girls' softball."

Jeff got huffy. "You callin' me a girl?"

"Not unless you plan to hang up your Nikes for a pair of ballet slippers."

The kid actually smiled.

The game resumed. Collective breaths were held. Cheering was nonexistent. Not even a sound from Shaye.

No one had a clue what *Uncle Paul* had said to Jeff. They assumed he'd given the kid a pep talk, even with two strikes against him.

Trace again hunkered low behind the catcher and awaited the pitch. "Ball one." The throw was wide.

Jeff planted his feet and took the stance Trace had recommended. He winced slightly when his hips wouldn't fully turn. He clenched his jaw so tightly that Trace feared he'd crack a tooth.

He took the kid to full count, three balls and two strikes. He wasn't cutting Jeff any slack. He wanted the kid to perform to the best of his ability.

Jeff was so nervous, he was shaking. So was the pitcher. The final throw was wobbly, off center, and a total stretch for even the best of ballplayers.

Trace was ready to call ball four and let the kid take his base. There'd be no shame in his walk to first. Jeff, however, surprised not only him but everyone in the stands. He swung.

The connection of ball and bat was a soft pop. The ball rolled no more than four feet. That didn't stop Jeff from taking off. He dropped the bat and limped fast down the baseline.

The catcher was as stunned as Trace. It took the kid several seconds to retrieve the ball and fire it to first. Jeff pushed himself so hard, Trace was certain the kid would pull a muscle. Jeff made it to the bag a true split second ahead of the ball. The infield umpire called him safe.

The runner at second advanced to third. There was a chance for the Sharkeys to tie or even win the game.

The crowd went crazy. Clapping erupted, along with loud whoops. Trace swore he heard a happy sob, no doubt from Jeff's mother.

The third batter was a burly kid, big for his age. It was no surprise that the boy took the first pitch and powered it over the fence.

The runner at third came home.

Jeff crossed the plate next, tying the score.

The big kid jogged around the bases. The Sharkeys won by one run.

All the players gathered on the field, giving high fives and rehashing the game. Jeff stood at the center of attention, being praised for his first hit.

Trace took to the exit before he was recognized. Quickly, he crossed the grass to the storage facility. Once inside, he flipped the light switch and immediately pulled off his mask. He unzipped his athletic bag and located his towel. He wiped sweat from his brow and neck. He jammed his fingers into his hair and scratched his itchy head. He exhaled. Game over.

His Porsche was parked in a far corner of the lot. He would make his escape as soon as he removed his gear. No one besides Shaye, Kai, Nicole, and Jeff would ever know he was here. He would be the Houdini of Gulf Field and disappear. They would all keep his secret.

He unlocked the clips on his chest protector, then shrugged it off. His shin pads came next. He unbuttoned and discarded his blue button-down, then went on to swipe the towel over his bare chest.

His back was to the door when it creaked open and Shaye Cates slipped in. She dragged two burlap bags filled with baseball equipment and dropped them by the short row of lockers.

She turned to stare at him, her gaze curious and lingering. "Should I come back?" she asked.

"No need." He allowed her a few more seconds but grew uneasy when her gaze lowered to his zipper. He wasn't interested in her, but his body seemed to like her just fine. His cock was close to requesting an introduction.

He reached down, snagged a lightweight navy polo from his bag, and slipped it on. He waited to see what she wanted.

She came to him, taking up half his space. He would've stepped back had there been room. She'd never been nice to him. She was a hard person to read.

They continued to stare at each other, neither one willing or able to look away. Her brown eyes shone brightly. Her expression was soft. Her bottom lip was slightly purple from the Fierce Grape Gatorade. Her scent touched him, all warm and womanly. And earthy, he thought.

She was a woman of twilight and a fan of the ballpark. If her family was happy, then she was happy.

Tonight her spirits soared, and her guard was down. Her breathing deepened.

So did his.

The sudden pull between them was poignant and strong. This wasn't a moment he would have expected or predicted, yet Shaye got to him. He found her sexy, in a slender, sneaky sort of way. That concerned him greatly.

Keep your friends close and your enemies closer.

Time spent with her confused him. She was as fascinating as she was frustrating. Her passion for life would extend to the bedroom. He'd bet she'd be one hell of a lover, on top and dominant until he tumbled her beneath him.

He couldn't stand there much longer and not be affected by her closeness. His body was ready to make a move on her.

A kiss was tempting. Sex, insane. He had no intention of being the first Saunders to get involved with a Cates. It was too damn risky. His family would never forgive him.

He'd thought umpiring the sandlot game would be a breeze, yet nothing about Shaye was simple or easy. She'd screwed with his head and complicated his life. That brought out the caution in him. He dismissed his wayward thoughts and pulled himself together.

She smiled at him then. "I've never seen Jeff so excited," she said. "His bunt gave him a whole new confidence. You inspired him. Jeff said you'd make a good coach."

Trace looked down at her. At her wild curls, wide eyes, and full mouth. "He can't correct his scoliosis, but he can be taught to compensate in sports."

"He's a special kid." Emotion left her unguarded. Her voice was as soft as the night air. "Family is all-important to me. I appreciate your calling the game."

Her sincerity touched him. He didn't, however, want

her reading more into the situation than was warranted. He'd umpired a sandlot game and been kind to a young boy. He needed to reset the distance between them. "It was a favor."

"I owe you now."

"Yes, you do," he said. "I want you at my office at nine tomorrow morning so we can organize the tournament."

"We can discuss matters at the beach."

He shook his head. "I prefer to plan from behind a desk, not sit in a sandbox. My secretary will attend our meeting. She sunburns easily."

"There's always sunscreen," she said. "I do my best thinking outside."

"Turn your thoughts inside, and don't be late."

He could almost hear her mind searching for an excuse. "Nine is when I have breakfast at Molly Malone's."

"I'll have my assistant, Martin, cater in bagels and muffins."

"I need something more substantial. Bacon, eggs, waffles."

"Difficult woman," he muttered as he hefted his athletic bag, ready to leave. And to think he'd almost kissed her. She would be his worst mistake.

It was time to walk away. "My office in the morning— don't forget," he said on his way out. "Wear shoes."

"Nicole Archer's rental agreement is my first priority of the day," she called after him. "If I'm late, start without me."

The meeting would be pointless without them both in attendance. They were partners. Approval had to come from both sides, whether she liked it or not.

He hoped Nicole's renovations went smoothly. And that Kai Cates was more cooperative than Shaye. Kai's obvious dislike of Nicole puzzled Trace. Kai had made it known she wasn't welcome. He had no right to be so rude.

Trace didn't want Nicole hurt. He'd make a point of checking on her often. She didn't deserve Kai's cold reception.

Four

No man had the right to look *that* hot.

Especially a hunk with his jeans cut so low, Nicole Archer could read the words *Calvin Klein* etched on the rim of his underwear.

She lingered at the doorway to her boardwalk shop, toying with the red pop-it bead necklace around her neck. The layered beads were a retro design and one of her favorites. A slider brooch of plastic cherries clasped the strands together. The brooch was flirty, summery, and one of her best sellers.

The sight of Kai Cates drew her inside. She was unable to take her eyes off him. His hair was dark blond, overly long, and mussed. Sweat glistened on the taut muscles rippling over his stomach. He had a swimmer's body, solid and lean.

He'd yet to look up and acknowledge her presence. She felt invisible, just as she had the previous evening at the concession stand at the ballpark. Kai had worked around her. He'd kept nudging her aside, preferring to do the work of two people instead of showing her what to do.

She'd taught herself how to make snow cones. Scooping ice into cone-shaped wrappers and adding flavors had proved simple enough. Yet no matter how careful she'd been, cherry and blueberry polka dots had patterned her white blouse by the end of the game. Along with a major ketchup stain. The wide red smear was Kai's fault. He'd *accidentally* squirted her.

She licked her lips now and found them dry. Her pineapple lip gloss must have melted from the heat. Even the floor fan blowing a breeze her way didn't cool her off.

She fanned her face and forced herself to look away. Why her sudden interest? The man was a boardwalk handyman. He had a hot body, but he wasn't corporate America.

Big business mattered most to her.

She breathed a little deeper, then sighed. There was something about a man in a pair of work boots. Something rough-and-bedroom-tumble. If he'd shown a little interest, she might have returned his attention. But he wasn't the least bit into her. He'd made that perfectly clear. His rudeness the previous day had hurt her feelings. She wished she had thicker skin. Staring at him now wouldn't get her anywhere.

Kai's negative opinion of Trace had been extended onto her. It was obvious the men had an unpleasant history. Because of her association with Trace, Kai had taken an instant dislike to her as well. He'd judged her without knowing her. That ticked her off the most.

She hoped he wouldn't try to sabotage her renovations. Which was why she'd shown up today to make sure everything went as planned. Nothing must stop her from realizing her dream.

Trace had been of great assistance. She now had what she'd always wanted. A shop of her own. Her passion for jewelry design surpassed her desire for sex.

She'd signed the lease a short time ago. Shaye Cates had been right where she had said she would be, seated on a low sand chair, working on her laptop. Several waterproof file folders were scattered in the sand around her. A cooler banked her chair, and a pale blue beach umbrella provided shade.

Shaye was a natural beauty, Nicole thought. She had a born-to-the-beach look with her white-blond hair and gorgeous tan. She glowed with health and vitality. Her navy one-piece swimsuit was both modest and sexy. Early-morning male joggers sent her admiring glances. Shaye nodded but didn't encourage them. She was at her "office" working.

Shaye's hair band interested Nicole the most. It was a work of art. Translucent petals formed a coral rose at one side of the sky-blue satin-covered band. The design inspired Nicole to create her own line of hair bands and clips, all glitzy with a beach twist.

She was so excited over the new venture that she didn't mind when Shaye cut their meeting short. Shaye's smile had been tight but cordial when she handed Nicole the lease agreement. Nicole penned her signature in turquoise ink.

Nicole was so happy, she didn't mind the sugar sand that trickled into her white ballet shoes as she crossed the wide stretch of beach back to the boardwalk.

Shaye had warned Nicole that Kai's day started early, and he was already working at the shop. Nicole hadn't realized his *working* would include mussed hair and a bare torso. He looked like he'd just rolled out of bed.

She hated the fact that sexy thoughts continued to run through her mind when she looked at him. He was a tool-man fantasy. His belt was slung low, and every time he moved, it inched his jeans down lower.

He finally looked up but didn't speak. He gave her no more than a quick once-over, as if he was inspecting a piece of drywall. He immediately went back to removing cracked, chipped paint off the wall.

The nerve of him, Nicole thought, chewing on a fingernail sparkling with gold Midas Touch polish. She wanted to discuss specifics on the renovation, and Kai needed to listen. Yet he'd tuned her out. She wasn't used to being ignored.

Miffed, she popped the beads off her neck with a loud *snap*. Kai glanced at her with a slow, quizzical look, then went back to dragging the squared-off scraping knife up and down the wall with long strokes. His shoulder muscles rippled, and his biceps bulged.

Nicole frowned. She refused to get sidetracked by him, even if his profile was strong and masculine. And was that a smirk she saw turning up the corners of his mouth?

Like he was enjoying her discomfort?

Nicole snapped the beads back together, then stepped over boards and debris as she crossed to the display case. She traced her fingers over the spidery cracks in the glass. Dust fluttered, and she wished it were fairy dust.

She needed more than magic to get The Jewelry Box open in time to attract the summer crowd rolling into town over the Fourth for the volleyball tournament. She'd chosen the shop name with great care. It came with childhood memories, some hurtful, some happy. She still had the plain walnut box her mother passed down for her jeweled keepsakes.

If only she could wave a wand and the shop would be finished. Kai, on the other hand, seemed in no hurry to get the job done. He slid his hand up and down the wall to check for holes as if he were in slow motion.

She couldn't help staring at the smooth muscles of his back. He knew she was watching him, but he made no effort to put on his T-shirt. It sat in a rumpled heap in a corner.

She cleared her throat loudly.

He squinted in her direction. "Problem?"

He was her problem. She opened her purse and pulled

out a notepad. She'd written down twenty-two concerns. She planned to address each one. Right there, right then.

She started with, "How long will the renovation take?"

He scratched his chin. "A day or two, possibly a week. The more interruptions, the slower my pace."

She had every right to interrupt him. This was her store. A mere few days' work gave her pause. How could he create her dream shop in such a short time? "I don't want shoddy craftsmanship."

He widened his stance, then slowly hooked one thumb inside his tool belt. "I've brought the electric up to code and will fix the plumbing next. You'll get new drywall and a coat of paint. The rest is up to you."

"I feel shortchanged."

"Take your feelings and leave." His tone was low and dismissive.

She dug in her heels. "I'd be happy to assist you." She would watch him closely, be sure he didn't cut corners.

Kai narrowed his gaze on her. "You're wearing white. Not a good color for construction work."

She looked down on her white satin halter and front-pleated walking shorts. A narrow red patent leather belt circled her waist. Sterling silver stars dangled from the buckle. "I don't mind a little dirt," she said. "What can I do to help?"

"You can—" He stopped himself from saying whatever he might have said. His jaw shifted, his temper barely banked. He nodded to where she stood. "Hold down that spot," he said. "I'll holler when I need you."

He went back to work. Had amusement darkened his eyes? She swore he was silently laughing at her.

She stood and stood, then stood some more.

No hollering from the man.

"Did you call?" she finally asked.

His "no" was muffled.

He stripped the last of the drywall, then dragged the broken pieces to the back of the store. He stepped into the restroom, leaving the door cracked open. She heard clanking, banging, and the grinding twist of pipe. Slipping her notebook back into her purse, she hunted him down. She found him crouched by the sink. His back was to her. Once again he ignored her. She hovered in the doorway. Her left foot itched, so she took a moment and shook the sand from her ballet shoe.

"You're making a mess," Kai said.

Mess? He had to be joking. Paint chips littered the floor, along with slices of drywall, bent nails, and picture hooks. The sand barely covered a square inch. She slipped on her shoe and went on to clean up. She swept the sand beneath a loose floorboard with her foot. The toe of her shoe got scuffed.

"You left your spot," he pointed out.

"I thought you called me."

"You heard wrong."

She clenched her fists in frustration. The man had fooled her into standing still for an entire hour. Her cheeks heated. "Not funny." She liked him less and less.

One corner of his mouth turned up before he removed the U-shaped pipe from under the washbasin. He then pushed to his feet. Faced her. "You're in my way."

Yes, she was. She blocked his exit. She stood nose-to-pecs with the man. His scent was masculine heat with a hint of sweat and not the least bit offensive. Her heart fluttered. "New drywall," she forced out. "When will it be delivered?"

"The truck usually arrives within two hours once I place an order."

"You'll make the call today?" she pressed.

"Soon as I can find time."

"Find time now."

He raised his arm, pipe in hand, and she jumped back. She doubted he'd actually strike her. But there was significant threat in his dark brown eyes. "Go back to your spot."

She moved in that general direction but purposely stopped short of where she'd originally stood. Rebellion felt good. From the corner of her eye, she saw him shake his head.

Kai set the pipe on a board between two sawhorses. He pulled his cell phone from the ripped back pocket of his jeans and made the call. A short call; the man wasn't long on words.

He disconnected, then told her, "We need to toss the old drywall into the Dumpster to make room for the new sheets."

We. He'd requested her help! She took Zumba classes and was fairly fit. Any activity was better than "holding down her spot." She was ready to work.

He shoved open the back door and carried out the largest piece. Nicole followed his lead. The cut-up drywall wasn't heavy, but it flaked and separated, and loose particles dusted her halter and shorts. She struggled to keep her balance on the back dock that oversaw the alley. The slabs were broken and uneven. She missed the Dumpster on her first toss. The drywall landed in the dirt, six feet below.

Kai locked his jaw and waved her off. "I'll get it." He climbed down a ladder, then returned within seconds. The man was agile.

Her second attempt was a washout as well. She stumbled into Kai with a corner sheet. The sharp edge stuck him in the ass. He grunted, glared, and took the drywall from her.

Her "sorry" was ignored.

She was quite pleased when she hit the Dumpster with

her third throw. She dusted off her hands and smiled at Kai.

"Major accomplishment," he muttered. "You deserve a bronze medal."

His sarcasm deflated her efforts. She let it pass.

He crossed to a small storage shed that was attached to the back of the building. He fished a key out of his pocket. The rusted hinges creaked when he jerked the door open. He pointed to several five-gallon buckets on the lower shelves.

"Three colors of leftover paint. Make your selection." He snagged one bucket and pried the lid off with a screwdriver. "Army khaki."

She almost gagged.

He returned the bucket and produced a second. "Mustard."

The condiment color was not to her liking. She shook her head.

"Lawn green," he read from the next label.

The color was more crabgrass than freshly mowed yard.

"The paint is fast-drying," he said. "Once the new drywall's up, I can slap on a coat in under an hour."

Slap it on sounded incredibly messy.

She turned on her heel and walked stiffly back into the shop. She heard his heavy footsteps close behind her. She went straight to her purse, flicked the clasp, and found her paint wheel. She held up the desired shade.

"I want antique white," she said. "It's pristine and will make the perfect backdrop for my jewelry designs."

Kai rested a lean hip against the wooden counter, then crossed his arms over his chest. He shook his head. "New paint isn't in the renovation budget."

"Expand the budget."

"It's stretched to the max already," he said. "I'm installing a new glass top for the counter and a set of shelves. Anything further comes out-of-pocket. *Your* pocket."

"You're mistaken," she argued. "Trace specified—"

Kai raised one hand, stopping her. "Doesn't matter what Saunders told you. Your shop is on the Cates boardwalk. I watched Shaye draw up the contract last night. She added an addendum to the customary agreement."

Addendum? Nicole's hand shook as she set the paint wheel on the splintered glass. She retrieved the twice-folded lease agreement from her purse. In her excitement, she'd done no more than scan the contract at the beach. Scanned it far too quickly, it seemed.

She now reviewed it once again, slowly, thoroughly, and, with each word, her chest tightened. There was a paragraph of small print at the bottom that spelled out how all repairs would be made. Barefoot William Enterprises would renovate to the point that the shop was habitable.

In other words, every item outside the basics was hers to provide. That didn't sit well with her.

Her personal finances were running low.

She'd maxed out her line of credit with her latest order of semiprecious stones. She had jewelry to design and needed to keep a large inventory.

She refused to borrow money from Trace, although he'd lend her whatever she needed without question.

She clasped the contract so tightly, it balled within her fist. She shoved the crushed paper back into her purse.

She forced a calm she didn't feel.

She was not one to complain.

She refused to run to Trace.

He'd been generous, overly so. He'd kept his word and found her a shop. That morning she'd hurriedly signed the rental agreement on the beach, the sun in her eyes, her soft white ballet slippers filling with sand. Her own excitement had blinded her.

What had she done? She was no pushover. She was smart. A designer with sophistication. But her eagerness had dumped her into a sand trap.

She was stuck working with a man who would slap any old color paint on a wall and walk away happy. She needed to come up with a solution. She couldn't afford new paint, but she was innovative.

She glanced at Kai and raised the question, "What if we blended the three buckets? What shade would we get?"

He made a rude sound. "Do I look like a color wheel?"

Sarcastic ass was more like it.

Nicole took a moment and mentally mixed the colors. She discarded the green, kept the brown and yellow. If she were lucky, she might get gold. A dark gold. A Vegas gold. That was better than any of the choices before her now. She could always repaint at a later date. Once she established a regular clientele and money rolled in. She remained optimistic.

She didn't ask for his help, but Kai followed her anyway, straight back to the shed. She bent, wrapped her fingers over one bucket handle, and strained to lift the five-gallon weight. The paint bucket was definitely heavy.

She struggled, stumbled sideways, finally dragging it all of an inch. She was more relieved than she let on when Kai slid his big hand over hers.

"It's heavy. I've got it," he grumbled.

His strong grip sent a chill through her, something she wasn't expecting. A slow shiver went up and down her spine.

She stared at him as if mesmerized; then suddenly, realizing his look was equally intense, she let go of the paint. Kai hadn't fully secured his hold, and the bucket rolled toward her foot.

In a flash, he pushed her aside with his free hand. He'd saved her from the bucket but not from his foot. His boot heel came down on her right toes. The thick rubber sole left a black tread mark on her ballet slipper.

She flinched and fell against his bare chest. A very hard chest that flexed with their contact. Her own nipples hardened. She blushed.

She never would have worn a sheer bra if she'd known she'd come into such close contact with Kai Cates. She was now "pointing" right at him.

He didn't seem to notice. He clasped her shoulders and set her aside. "Your foot okay?" he asked.

She curled her toes. Nothing was broken. "I'm fine."

He nodded toward the shop. "Return to your spot. I'll deal with the paint."

The paint was far less difficult than the man, and she wasn't ready to back off. Sidestepping Kai, she searched the buckets in the shed. She found a clean, empty one at the back. She pulled it free. "I want to mix the khaki with the mustard."

"Right now?" He looked pained.

"No, next week," she replied with her own brand of sarcasm.

He glanced at his watch. "We have twenty minutes before the truck arrives with the drywall."

"We can do this in ten."

"Damn, you're pushy."

"You need prodding."

"I get the job done."

"Not fast enough."

A muscle in his jaw ticked. "Ease up."

She forced herself to exhale. She was anxious, her emotions overwrought. She'd grown up poor and had waited her whole life for this opportunity.

She had her own demons, ones that constantly caused

her doubt and threatened to defeat her. She'd been criticized and ostracized from the day she was born.

Sixth grade had been exceptionally tough and had left lifelong bruises. She'd hated recess and being on the playground. Girls had made fun of her thrift-shop clothes and her fingernails broken from doing housework for the neighbors to help put food on the table. The kids had bullied her with words that hurt just as much as blows.

To evade their meanness, she'd sat on the grass and made jewelry out of daisies and paper clips. She'd later molded her own designs in clay and taught herself how to solder wire into interesting shapes. She'd used costume rhinestones to create her own distinct style.

The younger girls had gathered to watch her work. Nicole had made a few friends by giving away the occasional beaded bracelet. The girls would giggle and show off their one-of-a-kind designs.

At the age of twelve, her mother had given her a jewelry box with one large compartment and two tiny drawers. The plain walnut box was her greatest treasure. She knew jewelry was her destiny.

The memory was old, faded, yet always returned when she was stressed. Kai Cates stressed her greatly.

The Jewelry Box was her baby, and no one was going to spoil it.

Not even an aggravating, tool-belt stud.

Her throat was dry. She found it hard to swallow. Heat rose like a mirage on the back loading dock. An iced coffee would cool her down. "Where's the nearest coffee shop?" she asked.

Kai crouched down and began combining the paint. He didn't look up. "What do you want?"

"A tall, iced, skinny-vanilla latte would be nice."

He rolled his eyes but didn't otherwise readily respond. He went on to snag a yardstick from the shed and handed it to her. "You stay and stir, and I'll see to the coffee," he directed.

There was no hustle in the man. He stood off to the side for a good long time, overseeing her smooth circles before quenching her thirst. Once he approved her motion, he took off.

She clutched the measuring stick and put all her muscle into mixing the paint. Stamina eluded her. She grew tired and careless in her stirring. Paint spattered off the stick and onto her white shorts. A blob of dark gold colored the left toe on her ballet slipper.

Her shoulders soon ached, and she was certain her fingers would never straighten again. Her numb hands slid down the yardstick, and her fingertips skimmed the paint with the next turn. At least the paint matched her nail polish. The color wasn't too bad.

She wondered how far Kai had to go for the coffee. Time dragged. It could've been five minutes or fifty before he returned. When he did, he carried a blue thermos in one hand and a metal cup in the other. He poured for her. The coffee steamed, black and strong.

She stopped stirring, leaned the yardstick against the side of the bucket, and slowly straightened. Her back felt tight. "This isn't what I ordered."

"It's what I had on the premises."

He was too lazy to walk down the boardwalk? Or perhaps he didn't trust her here alone. As if she could do any damage. The shop was all naked studs with debris on the floor.

"I only have one cup," he went on to say. "I took my coffee break while you were mixing the paint."

They were to share a cup? Not going to happen. "The coffee is hot, and I wanted cold." She'd also wanted vanilla flavoring and nonfat milk.

"Coffee cools. Blow on it."

There'd be no blowing. "I'll pass."

She went to step around him, but he blocked her path. "Where are you going?" he demanded.

"Out." A breath of fresh air would be nice. A decent cup of iced coffee even better.

Kai Cates couldn't let her go. He'd promised Shaye he'd keep an eye on Nicole Archer. That meant holding her at the shop, not letting her roam the boardwalk. The rest of the family hadn't been informed of her rental. The jewelry designer would raise eyebrows. Shaye would be called on the carpet. She planned to explain Nicole in her own good time.

"How did the colors mix?" he asked, trying to distract her.

She rubbed her right shoulder. "I got tired of stirring."

"I have a battery-powered handheld mixer you could use."

She glared at him. "Now you tell me."

There'd been no reason to offer sooner. The lady wanted to help with the renovations. He'd let her stir her little heart out.

The delivery truck from Cates Hardware and Lumber arrived right on time. It rumbled down the narrow alley. Brakes screeched as the driver parked parallel to the loading dock. Two burly men hopped down from the cab. Both eyed Nicole with male curiosity.

"Butch, Branson." Kai drew his cousins' attention back to him. "Stack the drywall in the middle of the shop."

The men were slow to move. Kai refused to make introductions. Nicole wouldn't be around long enough to make friends.

But damn if she didn't prove friendly. She crossed to the men and held out her hand. "Nicole Archer, jewelry designer."

His cousins found her introduction amusing. "Butch Cates, nuts and bolts," one said.

"Branson Cates, two-by-fours."

The men weren't making fun of Nicole; they'd just followed her lead. And added their own sense of humor.

She half smiled as they all shook hands. She went on to run her palms down her shorts, as if hand-ironing the pleats. Her movements smeared the flecks of gold.

His cousins were on a tight schedule, so they immediately started unloading the truck. That didn't stop them from grinning at Nicole with each load of drywall that went into the shop.

Kai saw what they saw. Although he hated to admit it, Nicole was a beautiful woman. A sleek brunette with arched eyebrows and a magazine-cover shine about her, as if she'd been Photoshopped to perfection. He usually went for surfer chicks with their laid-back style and athletic, bronzed bodies.

Nicole was curvy. She wore designer white. She was out of her element. He'd purposely pushed her buttons, just to see how much crap she would take.

She'd taken a lot. But she was no pushover.

She'd held her spot, then hefted drywall and stirred paint.

Her breasts had swayed with each turn of the yardstick. The visual had hit below his tool belt. He'd gone for his coffee break so she wouldn't catch him stiff.

He shrugged off any attraction he felt for her.

She was *way* out of his league.

He watched her now as she left the loading dock and moved back inside. Kai followed her. She crossed to the broken wooden display case and leaned fully against it. She scanned her surroundings, then sighed. A soft yet long-suffering sigh.

Her face was flushed, her expression flustered. He'd only added to her frustration. He'd been an ass from the moment she'd walked through the door. His behavior had been negative, almost mean. He couldn't help himself.

He'd known she was watching him work; he'd felt her gaze on him from the moment she entered the shop. Her initial look had been one of female interest, which soon turned to irritation the longer they spent together. He'd toyed with her, tried to scare her off.

The lady hadn't left. She'd continued to stare at his chest. If Nicole felt threatened by his sexuality, he figured she'd go running back to where she belonged.

Trouble was, his plan had backfired. *He* was the one who'd gotten hot under the collar, even if he wasn't wearing a shirt. Damn, she made him sweat.

No matter their situation, he refused to be distracted by the enemy. She wasn't officially a Saunders but close enough. According to Shaye, Nicole and Trace were involved. She'd caught them kissing in his office and about to have a nooner, had she not interrupted them.

The thought of Nicole becoming a Saunders twisted his gut. He refused to evaluate the feeling. Instead, he closed his mind to her.

He would finish the renovations, then move on. He didn't buy jewelry, so once she occupied the shop, there would be no reason for them to cross paths.

"Later, Kai, Nicole," Branson called as he and Butch wrapped up their delivery.

Kai blinked. Engrossed by Nicole, he hadn't realized the men had brought in the last sheet of drywall.

His cousins caught his surprise and nudged each other, smiling knowingly. Damn it all. He should have been more cautious.

Word would spread that he had a beautiful woman at the shop he was working on. Everyone would wonder who she was and if they were seriously dating. He wouldn't be able to step out onto the boardwalk without being questioned. Nicole's identity wouldn't sit well with his family. He'd have to leave by the back door.

He shifted his stance and said, "Let's be honest here. You're in my way. I work best alone. Solo, I can renovate your shop in two days. Otherwise we're stepping on each other. You don't need another boot print on your ballerina slippers."

She took her sweet time but finally agreed with him. "I need to browse pawnshops and the local flea market. A second display case is a must, along with a large mirror so customers can admire themselves wearing my jewelry."

Kai was relieved, or so he thought. The fact that he wouldn't see Nicole for a few days crimped his gut. He absently rubbed his stomach. The pain remained.

She went on to gather her purse and, as an afterthought, traced her finger in the dust on the glass top. Her smile was small. Secretive. Pleased.

"It's Wednesday," she said on her departure. "I'll start moving in on Saturday." She paused in the doorway, then surprised him by saying, "Thanks, Kai."

Thanks. Her show of appreciation cut low. He felt a twinge of guilt for being such a bastard all day.

He crossed to where she'd stood and looked down at the cracked glass. The afternoon sun blinked over the words The Jewelry Box. Classy, smart, and apparently the name of her shop.

He rolled his shoulders. It was time to get busy. He mentally organized the remainder of the day and the days yet to come.

He faced long hours. He had a few ideas of his own for the shop. The extra expenses would go beyond the renovation budget.

Shaye wouldn't be happy, but the changes would ease his conscience. A part of him wanted to satisfy Nicole.

Saturday, daybreak. The sun yawned, stretched, but was slow to rise. The night shadows clung to the storefronts. A morning person, Kai Cates took to the boardwalk. He breathed in the pungent scents of dawn: ham and eggs fried at Molly Malone's, coffee perked at Brews Brothers, and oven-fresh doughnuts from the Bakehouse.

The air was clear, and the sounds were amplified. Noisy seagulls dived for fish. The waves rhythmically slapped the shoreline. A few tourists milled about, some eagerly waiting to sunbathe and others heading to the pier to fish.

Kai felt at peace with the day.

He had met his deadline.

He'd worked hard to get Nicole's shop ready on time. In before dawn, out long after the sun went down.

His shoulders and arms had ached from the strain and begged for some TLC. He'd stopped at Molly's for a beer afterward and a look-see at the cute new waitress, but even her dimpled smile didn't do it for him.

Nicole Archer was not an easy woman to forget. He couldn't get her out of his head.

That was why he'd dragged his butt up early this morning and decided to forego his usual coffee run before heading over to the shop. He intended to give it one final inspection before she arrived. He'd spent extra effort cleaning up the store.

Nicole had wanted emerald paint on the front door, but she'd gotten gold, a sparkly welcome. The paint was the color of polished coins.

He wanted to check the interior coat, to make sure it was dry enough for her to start hanging whatever it was she planned to hang.

Nicole Archer might be off-limits, but he had to admit

he was looking forward to seeing her again, if only to inhale her ritzy scent and let his eyes wander where they shouldn't.

A frown wrinkled his brow. *Nicole is the enemy,* he repeated to himself, turning the corner.

His job was done.

He found the front door unlocked. *A thief?* What was there to steal? Oh, yeah. Yesterday UPS had delivered several big boxes addressed to her. He'd signed for them.

Kai was suddenly seized by the insane idea that if a robber was in there, he could bring the man down with his hammer. And ask questions later.

He drew the hammer from his tool belt so fast, it snagged on his gray T-shirt, ripping it straight across. He paid the tear no attention and opened the door carefully, peering inside.

A sound alerted him. Shuffling noises.

Someone *was* in the shop. More than one person, he thought, noting the dark silhouettes along the far wall.

The moment turned dangerous.

Could a gun be pointed at him? Pale sunlight pushed at his back, making him the perfect target.

He shoved open the door with his foot and crouched down low. A woman screamed.

He double blinked.

Nicole.

She sat cross-legged on the floor, surrounded by jewelry pieces. The first glint of daylight made the gemstones shine like buried treasure. Her eyes were round, and she clutched her cell phone to her chest.

"You could have knocked," she said, her voice shaking, "instead of barging in here with your hammer cocked."

"*Shit,*" he cursed under his breath, then lowered his weapon. "I thought the store was being robbed."

"Lucky for you I recognized you by your bed-head and

work boots." Her gaze lingered on his ripped T-shirt. A good bit of his abdomen was bare. "I was ready to call for help."

Kai stiffened. That was all he needed. His uncle the local sheriff would spread the news all over town that someone other than a Cates had rented a shop on the boardwalk. Someone involved with Trace Saunders.

"What are *you* doing here?" he growled, her hard stare unnerving him. "I hadn't expected you to roll out of bed before noon."

A snarky remark, but except for wiggling her pretty nose, she let it pass.

"I wanted to get an early start," she said, "but it was dark when I got here, and when the lights didn't go on, I tripped over a box and dropped the tray of jewelry I brought with me." She let out a big breath. "I've spent the past hour matching up earrings by touch."

Kai mentally kicked himself. When he'd finished the paint job, he'd flipped the circuit breakers to check the wiring. He must have missed one or two when he flipped them back on.

"Who's here with you?" he asked, his eyes adjusting to the darkness.

"I'm by myself."

"I saw a bunch of shadows."

"Not people, only mannequins."

Thank goodness he hadn't gone crazy with the hammer and beheaded the clothing dummies. He would have looked like a fool.

Nicole appeared very much alone on the floor and somewhat disheartened, as if her day had started on the wrong foot. She'd tripped, and the items on her tray had scattered. She had hundreds of mismatched earrings on the floor.

He'd set things right for her. Enemy or not, it was time

to unveil his surprise. After all, it was his fault the lights hadn't worked. He couldn't wait to see her face when he switched the breakers back on. He did so now.

Light filled the store. Flattering, indirect lighting glowed from the tiny spotlights installed on the ceiling. A glossy antique white covered the walls. A petite silver-paddled ceiling fan stirred overhead. The floorboards were buffed and polished. The effect, he had to admit, was as stunning as the woman herself.

Kai held his breath and awaited her response. No words came forth. She pushed to her feet, her legs shaky, and turned in a full circle. Absorbed the magic.

The Jewelry Box looked like a fancy resort boutique, not a funky boardwalk shop. Her lips parted in astonishment. He'd definitely impressed her.

She stood in awe, all curvy and feminine. He couldn't remember when he'd last seen a woman so beautiful so early in the morning. Her skin was fresh and dewy. Her lips, full and glossed. She wore a stark white T-shirt and matching skinny jeans. She'd dressed down to work. He liked her casual.

He couldn't take his eyes off her.

She moved around, stroking the walls, then staring at the tiny spotlights. She drifted toward him but stopped short of actually touching. Her hazel eyes were soft and liquid, her voice, questioning. "You stretched the budget?"

He shrugged. "A few pennies here, a nickel there."

"Why?" she asked.

He didn't have an answer. There was something about Nicole that prompted him to provide and protect. "You need to open your business the way you plan to proceed," he said, sharing advice once given him by his father. "Go big." Although the shop was quite small.

Nicole bit down on her bottom lip. "What about Shaye?"

"She'll come around." Or so he hoped. He'd point out that the shop would be in tip-top shape for the next renter.

She grazed his forearm with the tips of her fingers, a light gesture of gratitude. "The shop is spectacular. Thank you."

He looked down at her hand, so pale and smooth. Silver rings inlaid with turquoise sparkled on her fingers. A twisted copper wire bracelet with multicolored rhinestones circled her wrist. Today her fingernails were painted dark blue. Nicole was an intriguing woman.

So fascinating, in fact, he was forced to shift his stance. His painter's pants stretched tighter across his crotch than when the lights were out. He needed to make an adjustment.

Nicole took a step back, relieving the tension. She went from touching his arm to punching his shoulder. "Don't stand there like a cigar-store Indian. Give me a hand with the earrings."

She had no idea just how wooden his body had become.

He hunkered down next to her on the floor. Sorting out the earrings was like matching puzzle pieces. He scooped up one dangly earring and one button style. He held them up to the light. Pretty, very pretty.

He next picked up a big gold hoop with chunky red beads and a purple feather. He palmed a hammered-sterling ear cuff.

He and Nicole bumped heads as they simultaneously bent forward to search the pile of earrings.

Her sweet breath brushed his cheek.

His whiskered jaw scraped her chin.

They were so close, he could have kissed her. He did not. She belonged to another man.

She eased back. "I found a mate," she said, and she held up two drop earrings with filigree hearts.

After a great deal of looking, he finally found the second gold hoop. Each set of earrings was unique, as if she'd worked months to create the pair. The lady had talent.

Earrings came in pairs, just like people, Kai thought. He'd had only one serious relationship in his life, and that was with Crystal Smith. She'd wanted a bigger world than Barefoot William and had found that with Trace.

The longtime romance had ultimately opened his eyes to women who desired money over love. Crystal had left a serious scar. He still guarded his heart.

A companionable silence settled between them, and he stretched out his time with Nicole. His handyman list was long, and he had a lot to accomplish: replacement shingles at Crabby Abby's General Store, new window treatments at Goody Gumdrops, and the installation of a new hairstylist chair at Scissorhands.

Another ten minutes, and they would part ways. The shop was officially hers now. She was on her own. She would be fine, he assured himself.

She didn't need him looking out for her.

That was Trace Saunders's job.

He watched as Nicole matched a pair of peridot flower earrings. She then dipped her head, and her cheeks pinkened. She looked embarrassed. "Yesterday I had my fortune read by Madame Aleta," she admitted.

His aunt the fortune-teller could read a person's soul. She was quite famous, with an international following. News articles frequently featured her gift, and she'd made several television appearances. She worked with law enforcement to solve local crimes. She could've lived anywhere in the world, yet she'd kept to her roots. Barefoot William remained her home.

Aleta's psyche would've picked up on Nicole's status on the boardwalk. Fortunately, Aleta wasn't prone to gossip.

He hoped his aunt would be discreet and keep the secret until Shaye was ready to make a full disclosure to the family.

"What'd she say?" His curiosity got the better of him.

"She said I had great courage, and, no matter the odds, I'd succeed in business. Within a year I'd be moving to a larger location and expanding to two stores."

She paused, then sighed. "Aleta told me that I'd already met the man I would eventually marry. She saw young boys around me. *Lots* of boys."

She swept her hair behind her ears and rubbed the back of her neck, looking thoughtful and serious. "I never thought about having children. Business was always my top priority."

He understood and was about to tell her so when her cell phone rang, a sexy, jazzy ring tone.

Who could that tone be for? Maybe it was—

She looked at the caller ID. "It's Trace," she said, confirming his suspicion. "I need to take the call."

Jealousy pricked. He should've offered to leave and allowed her privacy for her conversation. Instead, he openly eavesdropped.

Her "hello" sparkled like dry Champagne. Her expression softened when she spoke. "It's all perfect. Exactly like we planned."

There was a significant pause as she listened to him; then she smiled. A very happy smile. "Everything is on schedule. I've ordered flowers, the invitations, talked to the caterer. I can't wait for the big day either."

The big day? Kai pulled back as if he'd been slapped. He didn't want to hear any more. They weren't talking about the shop. It sounded as if they were planning a wedding.

Not acceptable. His cousin Shaye might be able to convince the family to let an outsider rent a shop for a short time, but if Nicole married a Saunders, shit would hit the fan. Big-time.

Nicole ended the call with, "I'll see you for lunch."

Lunch followed by sex, Kai imagined.

He grew tense and irritable and figured it was time to leave. He handed her the final pair of earrings he'd picked from the pile. The cluster of crystals shone like diamonds.

He pushed to his feet. "I've got places to go, people to see."

She looked surprised yet accepting. "How can I ever thank you for all you've done?" she asked.

Don't marry Trace Saunders.

The thought slammed him hard. Then stupidity punched him. He'd only known the woman a few days. Somehow she'd rubbed off on him. He wanted to get to know her but would never have the chance. She belonged to Trace. Kai would never try to steal another man's woman; that was Trace's style.

He looked at her, letting his gaze linger over her stylish brown hair and sophisticated features. "Thank me by making a lot of money and moving to a larger location," he finally managed. The sooner, the better.

That bigger store would be a boutique in Saunders Shores. She should be closer to her future husband and not near him, the Barefoot William handyman.

Their proximity was dangerous.

He didn't trust himself with her.

Not one damn bit.

Five

Trace Saunders was damn mad. He held his anger inside. Three days had passed since he'd requested that Shaye Cates meet him at his office. She had not shown.

Marlene Mason had arrived, an exceptionally beautiful woman with extensive credentials. She'd been ready to work from the moment she stepped off his private plane. The event planner was in demand. She'd contracted with Trace for two weeks—that's all she could give him. Several days were now lost, all due to Shaye's unreasonable behavior.

His time was valuable, too. He hated chasing Shaye Cates down. He'd thought about sending his assistant, Martin. But Martin was polite and accommodating. Shaye would have bowled him over. The woman was beyond tricky. If she thought she could pull off the volleyball tournament without him, she was sadly mistaken. He needed to set her straight.

He knew right where to find her, at the west side of the pier near the shoreline. He stood on the boardwalk now and shaded his eyes against the sun. Shaye was easy to spot. Her "office door" stood open for business. Various family members clustered around her, five deep. It was time to break up their meeting.

He took the wide wooden steps from the boardwalk

down to the beach. He'd come casual, in gray knit shirt and black shorts. He slipped off his Sperry Top-Siders and carried the deck shoes. They were comfortable and well-worn from sailing.

The sand had the cool crunch of early morning, prior to the shuffle of sunbathers. He crossed to her low beach chair. Shaye faced the Gulf and didn't see him coming.

Her relatives noticed his approach and stepped aside. A few nodded, but no one spoke. He was getting used to the silent treatment. They remained cautious. He was a Saunders after all.

Shaye was deeply involved in a lively conversation and going strong. She'd yet to notice him. She spoke quickly, assuredly, a woman in charge. "Committees need to be formed. Uncle Phil's responsible for tent rentals. Aunt Molly is the go-to for catering. Jenna's pushing souvenirs. Kai heads ticket sales. Uncle Paul will handle parking. Anyone know a good hotel for the cocktail party?"

One lonely seagull squawked in response. Until Trace said, "I do. How about The Sandcastle? The fifth floor has a ballroom with a wraparound balcony."

Shaye's shoulders squared, stiffened, as he rounded her chair for their face-to-face. His shadow fell long and wide over the sand, covering her completely. He took his time and checked her out.

Her white-blond curls surrendered to a wide brown beaded hair band. The thin straps on her aqua one-piece crisscrossed in the back. Her skin was glossed with suntan oil. Her scent, coconut and banana. She belonged in an ad for Hawaiian Tropic.

Her cell phone rested in her cleavage. A wireless computer sat on her lap. Her hand fluttered ever so slightly, and he caught the change in color on her mood ring. The soft, peaceful green shifted to a startled rose. He liked her nervous.

"Good morning," he said.

"It *was* good," she muttered.

Sensing discord, the Cateses hovered but didn't interfere. Trace kept his cool. "You're late for our meeting," he said.

"Only by three days."

So she'd counted. He was certain she'd laughed off every second. Her amusement didn't sit well with him.

"My administrative assistant set up a breakfast buffet—"

"Sorry if the muffins got stale."

Her apology fell flat. "I've arranged office space for you at Saunders Square. How soon can you move in?" *Right now would be good.*

"It's Saturday, my day off."

"You were working when I arrived."

"My family came for a social visit."

A visit cut short. Her relatives drifted off, one by one. Apparently they didn't foresee any bodily harm.

He glanced at her computer screen. "Does 'social' include tent rentals and ticket sales?"

She'd structured numerous columns and filled each one. She closed the file, but before the screen went blank, he caught the full depth of her deception. It wasn't pretty.

"Care to share?" he asked. "The tournament is a joint effort. Where's our unified front?"

"I work best alone."

So did he. "We had an agreement."

"Which I'll honor, to a point." She stretched her legs, then slid her laptop into a waterproof case. "Don't crowd me, Trace. The boardwalk is my home. I wouldn't survive on your side of the street."

"We're not that different."

"We've nothing in common."

"There's the volleyball tournament, or do you suffer short-term memory loss?" he asked.

She went inordinately still. He let her sit with her thoughts. She needed to decide if she was with him or against him. He'd bet on the latter.

Cheers and chatter along with music from the carousel carried on the air. The boardwalk was alive with activity. Trace ran one hand down his face. "How can you work with so much noise?" He preferred the quiet of his office.

"Laughter isn't 'noise'—it's happiness," she said. "The turn of the carousel tells me someone has bought a ticket and is enjoying a ride. When was the last time you felt like a kid and raced a purple horse with jeweled amber eyes and a gold saddle?"

Ages ago, he realized. "It's been a while," he told her.

She drew a compact navy backpack from beneath her sand chair. She popped a side snap and pulled out a pair of gray athletic shorts. She then stood, stepped into them, and drew them up her legs. She tied the drawstring at her waist.

He stared way too long. She had slender inner thighs and a sweet ass. He enjoyed the view.

She shouldered her backpack and said, "Back to business. I owe you twenty dollars for umpiring our game last night."

"I'm not about to take your money."

"It's money owed," she insisted. "We Cateses don't shirk on our debts." She extracted a twenty from a coin pocket in the backpack and passed it to him.

Still he refused. "Keep it."

She pursed her lips. "I have an idea."

He couldn't wait to hear it.

"Let's take your cash and spend it on my boardwalk."

"I'll be feeding your economy?"

"We like to eat." Her next words came with a challenge. "We'll ride the carousel, and whoever catches the brass ring decides the remainder of the day. Work or play."

That interested him greatly. "If I grab the ring first, you come to my office at Saunders Square?"

She nodded. "If I win, I return to the beach."

"You're a procrastinator." He hefted her sand chair.

"Yeah, and I'm good at it." She grabbed her laptop.

He sensed that she'd conducted her daily quota of business early and now wanted to play. Trace would play, too. Once he won the brass ring, he'd steer her down the boardwalk, back to Saunders Square.

How hard could it be to grab the ring?

Pretty damn hard, he was soon to discover. She stored her beach chair, laptop, and backpack at the ticket booth, then asked the operator to keep an eye on her items.

Shaye was barefoot, but he preferred shoes. He slipped on his Top-Siders.

He went on to buy two tickets, then checked out the horses. Shaye chose a lavender horse ahead of his dark purple steed, which meant she had first crack at the prize. Lady was both smart and sneaky. Calliope music played as the horses went up, down, and around.

Trace got distracted by Shaye's every attempt. She pushed up in the stirrups, all tanned and toned and driving him crazy. She leaned toward the ring stand yet missed each time. Her laughter mixed with the music.

The lady was competitive. She looked over her shoulder with each pass to be sure he hadn't captured the prize. He hadn't come close. Snagging the ring was harder than it looked.

After a dozen passes, he swore the carousel was rigged. With each circle, Shaye's horse rode high as it neared the ring stand, while his dipped low. He had to reach twice as far to connect with the brass ring. He refused to lose his balance and topple off his horse.

Shaye's enthusiasm was contagious. He found himself grinning. She was a woman who threw her head back and let the sunshine play over her face. She looked happy and free. She'd never grow old, he thought. She always allowed her inner child out to play. The boardwalk was the perfect place to be twelve.

She wanted the ring, and eventually she captured it. His heart kicked when she stood in the stirrups, hung on to the pole with one hand, and stretched precariously, appearing suspended by air. Her daring earned her the brass ring.

She whooped and held the ring high. She was the winner, which meant she got to choose how they spent the rest of the day. So much for getting her to Saunders Square.

The carousel slowed, stopped, and they dismounted. He moved to the entrance, waiting while Shaye reset the ring. Her eyes were bright, her smile broad, when she crossed to him. "Back to the beach for me," she said.

"Two out of three," he surprised himself by saying.

"You like getting beat?" she challenged.

"I lose only once."

Her expression told him that he would go down a second time. "Bumper cars and baseball caps. Whoever bumps off the other person's hat wins."

He'd never played, but it sounded easy enough. They walked a block down the boardwalk. Summer tourists invaded the hula hoop kiosk, and several tried on sunglasses at The Rising Sun. The boomerang seagulls proved a popular novelty. Trace watched two young boys toss the curved plastic out and over the Gulf. The seagulls' airfoil wings took an elliptical path and returned. They were well-built toys.

He bought them each a baseball cap at Heads Up, where all manner of headgear, from straw hats to visors, decorated six outdoor hat stands. It was a small business with a big draw.

Shaye chose a mesh baseball cap with *Beach It* on the

bill. She slipped it on backward, over her hair band. The cap was tight, and the rim pinched her forehead. "To hold down my curls," she clarified.

She dipped her head, but not before he caught her smile. A sly smile, indicating she was about to pull one over on him. Son of a bitch. Not again.

He selected a cap with the *Tampa Bay Bucks* sports logo. It fit comfortably on his head. They donned their caps and proceeded to Water Wings.

The kiosk sold dozens of toys for the beach, from water guns and sand castle kits to Frisbees. Shaye pointed to two bright blue water noodles, explaining that they would need them for their next contest. The five-foot-long flotation devices were made of soft foam.

"Flexibility counts," Shaye said once he'd purchased the blue noodles. She poked him once, right in the stomach, with one. The noodle bent easily; he barely felt her jab. He retaliated by bopping her on the shoulder with his.

A short distance farther, they reached the bumper cars. A big sign said NO HARD BUMPING at the entrance to the ride. "You planning to break the rules?" he asked.

She rubbed her hands together. "Oh, yeah. We'll bump, sideswipe, and I'll come at you head-on."

He'd been warned. She was a tomboy at heart, and she was out to kick his butt. He paid for their tickets out of what remained of the twenty, then turned to her. "Is this a real game, or did you invent it?"

"My brothers created the game to let off steam when we were kids."

Great. Her family. Her rules. His loss would be quick and, no doubt, painful.

The bumper cars were metallic black with white racing stripes down the middle and silver numbers on the back. Rubber bumpers surrounded the cars. Small electric cards drew power from the floor and ceiling. The metal floor gave a flat ride. Drivers could accelerate and steer. And vibrate.

"Is your baseball cap on tight?" she asked.

"It fits okay."

She pulled her cap farther down her head, so the back rim reached nearly to her eyebrows. She tapped her foam noodle against her thigh, ready to rumble.

"Pick a car," she said.

The ride had yet to open. Twenty cars banked one wall, in numerical order. Trace looked them over. He decided on lucky number seven. Shaye chose diabolical thirteen.

She then gave him the final instructions on the game. "We move around the floor and"—she pointed her water noodle at him—"the first person to knock the baseball cap off the other person's head is the winner. You can't reset your cap. If it starts to slip, it slips."

No wonder she'd chosen a too-small hat. Hers fit snugly and would be difficult for him to tip off her head. Devious woman.

They settled into their cars and strapped on their seat belts. The bumper car was small, and he was a big man. His knees banged the steering wheel. His elbows poked out at his sides like an overgrown kid's.

Shaye slid into her car as if it were made for her.

She nodded to the operator. "Start the engines."

The cars vibrated, enough to make his cramped legs tingle. He couldn't fully straighten out his foot to accelerate. The slight press of his toe was the extent of his power. Shaye appeared to go three times as fast. The lady was on a tear.

She charged him, head lowered, like a female knight with a foam lance. She was out for blood and good at playing chicken. He swerved first. The slap of her foam noodle caught his shoulder.

He heard her laugh above the noise of the cars. She'd

released her responsibilities and was having fun. The amusement park allowed her to return to her childhood on a moment's notice. She could shift from grown-up to kid in seconds. He suddenly felt ten, though quite big for his age.

Jab! Jab! He'd foolishly let his mind wander, while Shaye was on full alert. She sideswiped him and poked the back of his neck. Her swipes were getting closer and closer to the bill on his baseball cap. He got down to business, serious now. No way would he let her win this contest.

If the lady wanted a joust, he'd give her one.

They were playing for office space.

If he lost, she would continue working from the beach.

If he won, she'd join him at Saunders Square.

He needed the win. She wasn't big on sharing. He refused to track her down every damn day for an update on the volleyball tournament.

He drove his bumper car in a wide circle, letting her come to him. He wanted her to think he was in escape mode, until she was close enough for him to disarm her.

He maneuvered cautiously and managed to get behind her. He was now a water noodle's length from her baseball cap, which faced backward.

He stretched and was able to flick the bill, but it didn't budge. He shifted on the seat and pressed the pedal flat with the side of his foot so he could get even closer. He was so damn near, he tasted victory.

He never expected her to stop short. But she did.

She let up on the accelerator, and he bumped her hard. The jolt had no effect on her, only on him. It loosened his baseball cap. The hat slipped off the back of his head and caught on his shirt collar. A slight saving grace, although he was afraid to move. He let his bumper car idle.

Shaye didn't lose any time. She circled and came up

alongside him. A one-handed, smart-ass flip of her blue noodle sent his baseball cap flying.

He couldn't believe it. He watched as the vibration of the floor captured the fallen hat and carried it beneath Shaye's car. Only the bill remained visible.

Her smile broke, and she had the balls to take a victory lap. She held her water noodle high. "Winner, winner, winner," she chanted.

"You cheated." He snatched up his cap.

"I was raised with four brothers. I learned to play dirty." She went on to park her bumper car.

He trailed behind.

The operator shut off the power, and the cars stilled. They both unbuckled and climbed out, meeting near the entrance. A line had formed, and a group of teens watched them leave. No one would ever guess that the woman walking at his side ran Barefoot William Enterprises. She looked pretty and unpretentious, yet Trace knew her ploys. She was unpredictable at best, more often outright devious.

He soon discovered Shaye couldn't even walk a straight line. She was constantly sidetracked. She stopped to talk to family and to strangers. She changed direction on him sixteen times.

After their endless walk, she finally paused in the cherry-colored doorway of The Dairy Godmother. "Do we have enough money left to buy ice cream cones?" she asked.

He jiggled the change in his pocket. "One scoop each, but I'd be willing to supplement if you want a banana split or sundae."

The air-conditioning in the ice cream parlor was as cold as a freezer. The Dairy Godmother was decorated in red and white, cheerful and inviting. The scent of fresh cream welcomed customers.

Six stools lined the short counter. The same number of booths backed the far wall. The shop was basic but busy. The parlor offered three flavors of homemade ice cream and dozens of toppings.

As family, Shaye could have cut to the front, but she took her place in line and waited her turn. Trace slipped in behind her. They still held their water noodles.

Jenna Cates from the T-shirt shop stood two people ahead of them. Her smile tipped up. "It's my sweet cousin and the sixty-dollar man."

"Are you still Three Sheets, I mean Shirts, to the Wind?" he asked.

Jenna flashed her BlackBerry, all sarcastic and smug. "I'm standing, Sixty, but I've got you captured sitting in a bumper car getting your butt kicked."

Text messaging and photographs. Obviously the operators of each ride had tracked Shaye, and word had spread that he'd suffered defeat. Twice.

A few people turned, taking an interest in their conversation. Trace closed down. There was no point in sparring with Jenna. She had blackmail photos. He broke eye contact and looked around further.

He couldn't help comparing The Dairy Godmother to Lavender's, the gourmet ice cream parlor at Saunders Shores. The differences were glaring. Lavender's catered to the discriminating palate. The specialty flavors included coconut-caramel and raspberry truffle. Those preferring sorbet selected from burnt-sugarplum, ginger-grape, and cranberry-pear.

Each dessert came in a cut crystal bowl. The portions were no bigger than a Parisian scoop, no more than two bites. Customers sat at linen-covered café tables. The lighting was soft, and French shutters were drawn against the harsh sun.

Oddly enough, Trace preferred The Dairy Godmother. He was there with Shaye, and that seemed to matter a lot. The line moved forward. He backed Shaye so closely, had they been horizontal, they would've been spooning. Her scent drifted to him, one of sunshine, Dove soap, and sexy female.

She exhaled slowly, a woman relaxed. She tugged off her baseball cap and shook out her curls. Her beaded hair band slipped, angling over her left ear.

He didn't think, only reacted. He straightened it. Her hair was shiny, soft. Her ears were double-pierced. She wore a gold post and small hoop in each one. He curved his hands over her shoulders and nudged her forward when the line progressed.

It seemed natural to touch her. She didn't turn on him, didn't demand he let her go. She did, however, blush. He watched, fascinated, as heat crept up the back of her neck and colored her cheeks.

He felt her chest vibrate, and he remembered that her cell phone rested in her cleavage. She ignored whatever call came in. Her mind was on ice cream.

He lowered his hands, but not before Jenna snapped a second picture. Shaye's cousin was photo happy. His gesture was innocent enough, but her text would make him out to be a pervert.

Trace glared at Jenna, who pulled a face, then placed her order. Another few steps and Shaye took her sweet time selecting a flavor. There were only three kinds of ice cream, yet it took her several minutes to decide.

She finally went with strawberry and added six toppings. The scoop was the size of a tennis ball. Her plastic bowl overflowed. She grabbed a spoon and started eating so fast, Trace was certain she'd have a brain freeze.

"Medium chocolate with M&Ms, chopped walnuts,

and coconut shavings," he requested. One of the employees put his order together. He left ten dollars in the tip jar by the register. The staff nodded their appreciation.

Shaye Cates stood off to the side until Trace joined her. She saw the coconut in his bowl, and her blush deepened. Heat swept all the way to her hairline. The memory of him eating coconut cream pie off her hip was still vivid. She scooted toward the door.

He caught her on the boardwalk. "You're a woman who eats on the run," he noted. "Where to now?"

"The Ferris wheel," she said. "It's quiet and a good place to talk."

He slowed. "Our business meeting?"

"I'm compromising. This is the best I can do on a Saturday."

He took it in stride. They merged with the tourists and strolled several blocks to the end of the boardwalk. Along the way, two young boys eyed their blue water noodles with interest. Shaye was about to offer them the foam toys, but Trace moved first. He collected hers and passed them to the kids. They stared wide-eyed before excitement overtook them. They hit the sand at a run. "Thank you!" echoed over their shoulders.

Shaye felt a tug at her heart. She didn't want to acknowledge his kindness to the boys, but she couldn't deny that he seemed to like children. Either that or he'd gotten tired of carrying the water toy and had simply handed it off at the first opportunity.

They arrived at the Ferris wheel as it was being loaded. Two suspended aluminum seats remained. Shaye sat next to Trace, and the operator lowered the bar across their laps. Trace always seemed to crowd her. Their shoulders brushed, and their hips and thighs bumped. It was a tight fit, with him taking most of the space. At that moment, she didn't mind, though. Snug felt peculiarly good.

The ride jerked slightly, then swept upward. The wheel lifted them high. The view was magnificent; the entire boardwalk and pier stretched out before them. Every amusement ride, arcade game, and shop was Cates owned and operated, with one exception: Nicole Archer's store.

Word had spread of Kai's interest in the woman. Whether true or false, he'd definitely spent long hours renovating her shop. Once her business was up and running, the family had witnessed him dropping off lunch and the occasional cup of coffee. Gossip had him buying a man's triple-twisted leather bracelet at The Jewelry Box. Shaye had yet to see the bracelet on his wrist. She'd be on the lookout now.

She needed to remind her cousin that Nicole belonged to Trace. The jewelry designer would only break Kai's heart if he prolonged his pursuit.

Shaye continued to be confused by Trace's occasional hot and direct stares. He shouldn't be eyeing her while he was involved with Nicole. There'd been a gentle strength in his hands when he'd straightened her hair band at the ice cream parlor. She'd felt like a couple when he curved his fingers over her shoulders and eased her forward in the line. She hadn't minded his touch. At all. That scared her. A lot.

He'd been a good sport at the carousel and bumper cars. She'd had the advantage. She'd ridden the rides all her life. She knew the technique for grabbing the brass ring and how best to knock off a competitor's baseball cap. Her brothers had taught her well.

Trace had bemoaned both losses but accepted her victories without complaint. He'd spent his twenty-dollar umpire fee on her boardwalk, then gone to his money clip for the ice cream and Ferris wheel tickets. He'd tipped big at The Dairy Godmother. His generosity was appreciated by her family.

She sighed. These were all short-lived moments without a future. He was still a Saunders, and she remained a Cates. That was a fact to face now, rather than later.

They sat in silence for three turns of the Ferris wheel. Trace finished his ice cream. Shaye had a few bites yet to go, including the toppings. She popped a pink mini-marshmallow into her mouth then a piece of waffle cone before saying, "We compromised today."

He raised an eyebrow. "How so?"

"You came to Barefoot William, and I let you stay."

"Definitely a concession on your part."

"Middle ground is hard to find."

"Cross Center Street on Monday and spend the day at Saunders Square," he invited.

Her mind scrambled with the thought. She stared off into the distance, looking for an answer. It was slow in coming.

Overhead, the sun and humidity climbed.

Along the coast, the Gulf was as smooth as glass. Sun-worshippers unfolded their nylon loungers. A few beachcombers hunted for shells. Swimmers splashed toward the sandbar.

To the east, fishermen collected on the pier.

Straight ahead, people filtered down the boardwalk. More browsed than bought. What purchases they made would barely cover the electricity for the shops.

Barefoot William needed sales. Livelihoods were stretched thin. Her family banded together to make ends meet. They rubbed two fives together in hopes of making a fifty.

She ate the last of the crushed peppermint candy, then said, "Trust me, Trace, I've got the volleyball tournament under control."

His expression was far from trusting. He shifted, and the

seat rocked. Her stomach pressed the bar. He exhaled sharply, then scrubbed his knuckles over his eleven o'clock shadow.

"If you want to take charge, take charge," he finally said. "I can live with it."

She was so startled, she choked on her candy. Trace thumped her back. Only after she caught her breath did he continue.

"But you're renting my beach, and I'll require updates. The closer our proximity, the better our communication will be. Work from Saunders Square, Shaye. I'll give you a private office and lend you my secretary, Marlene Mason. She can be our liaison."

"I've never had a liaison." She let the word roll off her tongue. It tasted like peppermint.

"Marlene is sharp and efficient." Trace recommended her strongly.

"She's also from your camp. Would she take orders from me?" she asked.

He nodded. "She's a woman full of good ideas and suggestions. She likes to organize."

Shaye wasn't a fool. The burden of organizing the volleyball tournament bore heavily down on her. The event was growing, far surpassing its original projection. She had family support, but her relatives worked long hours to survive. Everyone had a life off the boardwalk. Everyone but her.

Sleepless nights had her yawning. She needed to be at the top of her game. At the end of the day, it might be nice to have an assistant. A person to pick up the slack. Someone to keep the event on track.

His gesture was magnanimous.

She hoped there was no ulterior motive attached.

She didn't fully trust him.

"I'll give you Monday with no promise for Tuesday," she said. That was the best she could do. She would soon be crossing Center Street, a major turn of events.

He accepted her decision without argument.

She signaled to the Ferris wheel operator, and he let them off with the next turn. They climbed out and moved to the side. Trace raised his arms over his head, stretched. She heard his back crack. He'd sat confined for too long.

"Are we done?" she asked.

"Are you trying to get rid of me?"

"Now or in a few minutes." She was honest.

"I have one more errand before I head home," he told her. "Nicole sent out fancy invitations announcing her opening. I attended and saw you there. It was a huge turnout and very crowded. Customers spilled out onto the boardwalk. You avoided me. I didn't get a chance to visit with Nicole. I thought to do so today."

Shaye had thought the shop amazing. Kai had gone above and beyond in his workmanship to impress a woman who was involved with another man.

"I'm headed in that direction, too," she admitted. "I chatted briefly with Nicole at the opening, but I've yet to . . . officially welcome her." *Welcome* stuck in Shaye's throat.

They walked slowly down the boardwalk, their silence comfortable. Shaye was never chatty; she didn't need to hear herself talk. Neither did she flirt. She'd been taught to be straightforward and honest.

Trace, however, brought out the sneaky in her. He was stubborn, often unmovable. That's when she danced around him. She'd continue to do so. The tournament's success was all-important to her. Maybe she'd find an ally in his secretary, Marlene Mason. Two against one worked for her.

They soon reached The Jewelry Box. The gold door sparkled in the sunlight. One step inside, and Shaye spotted Nicole off in a corner speaking to a customer, which gave Shaye time to look around.

She knew in an instant that Kai liked Nicole Archer. Liked her a lot. Her cousin's feelings for this woman were captured in every brushstroke and light fixture. Kai had given Nicole everything she'd asked for and more. So much more.

He'd yet to submit invoices for the repairs, which meant they'd come out of his pocket. He'd paid to make Nicole happy. This was a side of her cousin that Shaye had yet to see. She found it most interesting.

She admired the setup, from the optic white mannequins draped with jewelry to the wide glass counter showcasing Nicole's more elaborate pieces. The woman was talented. Many of her designs were intricate; her choice of colors, unique.

One particular hair band caught Shaye's eye, one made with midnight-blue velvet and plaited with sterling silver. It had a Victorian quality. Shaye appreciated such period pieces. They were feminine and classy.

Nicole wrapped up her conversation and immediately crossed to them. The brunette looked beautiful in her white suit and taupe heels. Her *glow* went beyond the sparkle of her earrings and necklace. It came from an inner contentment. Happiness lit her hazel eyes.

"Trace!" Nicole hugged him first, then turned to Shaye. "So glad you both stopped by," she said, warm and sincere.

"Your shop looks great." Trace walked from front to back, doing his own inspection. "Your displays are perfect. I like the spotlights."

Nicole smiled. "Your approval means a lot."

Once again, Shaye sensed their closeness. They were a good-looking couple.

"See anything you like?" Nicole asked Shaye. "I have a pair of topaz earrings that would complement your eyes."

Trace tapped his fingers on the glass top of the display case. "Shaye's interested in the blue hair band," he said.

How did he know? The very thought that he'd caught her admiring the piece unnerved her. She cut him a sharp look, which he ignored.

"Can we take a closer look?" he asked.

"Of course." Nicole located the key and unlocked the case. She withdrew the band and handed it to Shaye. "You actually inspired the design," she said. "I noticed your hair band the day I signed the rental agreement. It had a coral rose on pale blue satin. I decided to try my hand at a new line. This is the first one I finished."

Shaye laid the hair band on her palm and was awed by the intricate work. The silver plait brought out the richness of the blue velvet. It was dressy yet could be worn to dinner or on a date.

Her heart squeezed just a little. There was no man in her life. Her days were spent working at the beach. The hair band was too pretty to be worn with a one-piece.

A glance at the price, and Shaye returned it to Nicole. Too rich for her blood. "It's lovely," she said. "I'm sure your designer bands will do well."

She caught the flicker of disappointment on Nicole's face. It was obvious she'd hoped to make a sale. Shaye, however, couldn't justify the cost. She was on a budget.

Trace didn't have a problem reaching for his money clip. Shaye soon realized that he'd buy every piece of jewelry in the store if it kept Nicole in business. He was supportive of his woman.

"Another rescue," Nicole said gratefully. "First the trade show in Las Vegas, then this shop, and now a big sale."

Shaye was confused about the trade show.

Nicole noted the crease in her brow and explained, "I met Trace at an auto expo at the convention center in Vegas. I worked there as a trade show model."

"Nicole generated a lot of traffic," Trace complimented. "She was the top spokeswoman for Porsche and boosted revenues."

Nicole looked fondly at Trace. "He bought a sports car and helped me escape one of the lowest times of my life. Mean boyfriend. Little money. He brought me to Saunders Shores and backed my business venture."

Shaye took it all in. The man was a modern-day Lancelot. She listened further as the two conversed. They seemed to speak as business associates, not as lovers.

She wondered if they were still involved. Her curiosity was for Kai, not for herself. There was no point in getting too personal. Trace would be out of her life in two and a half weeks.

"I'll wrap up the hair band," Shaye heard Nicole say.

She withdrew a sheet of sheer white tissue paper patterned with tiny silver stars. Nicole took great care in folding the paper around the band. She placed it in a shiny silver gift bag, then went on to add multicolored ribbons to the handle. The presentation was lovely. The bag was nearly as pretty as the hair band.

Two customers entered as Shaye and Trace were about to leave. Nicole gave Trace a second hug, waved to Shaye, then went to greet the new arrivals.

"I'm off." Shaye moved away from the counter.

"Don't forget your gift."

Gift? She looked at Trace and found him holding the silver bag.

"A bribe, so you'll show up next week."

"I gave you my word."

"A little motivation never hurt."

She shook a finger at him. "No, I can't accept—"

The man was quick. He looped the handle over her wrist before she realized his intention. "My gift gets us started on the right foot."

"I have nothing for you."

"Your appearance on Monday will be gift enough."

Her stubbornness took hold. "You can't buy me, Trace."

"We both want a successful tournament," he said. "Call the hair band a peace offering."

They would never know peace. A century-old feud stood between them.

He walked her to the door. "See you soon," he said. "Wear shoes."

Shaye scrunched her nose. Shoes could be a deal breaker.

She leaned against the door frame and watched him walk away, a tall, wide-shouldered man who dressed casually but still looked polished. Earlier he'd played like a kid yet didn't wear a wrinkle.

She had to admire what every woman on the boardwalk saw: Trace Saunders had sex appeal. He was hot. There was no denying it.

Six

The weekend zipped by. Monday arrived too soon. Shaye went through her closet six times to find the right outfit. Appearances meant little to her, yet Saunders Shores was all about style. She'd never cared much about fitting in, but neither did she want to look like an outsider.

She ran Barefoot William Enterprises. She had her family's respect. Even with her office at the beach.

Working with Trace was at odds with her lifestyle. She was certain he wore a suit each day. No doubt his secretary supported the image, too. The one time she'd seen his executive assistant, Martin Carson, he'd worn a tie.

Buttoned-down and stuffy would take issue with a swimsuit and flip-flops. Trace was conservative. She was unconventional. She needed a happy medium.

She blew raspberries, and an echo returned. Her Quaker parrot, Olive, mimicked her. Olive was intelligent, comical, and very social. Whenever Shaye was on her houseboat, Olive followed her from room to room. The Quaker had a wide vocabulary and could be quite vocal.

"Pick one," Olive encouraged her.

After another five minutes, Shaye narrowed her choices: either a black pantsuit or a blue blazer and tank top with skinny jeans. She'd feel more at home in the jeans, but the pantsuit gave her a more professional edge.

She held up both outfits before the full-length mirror and finally decided on the pantsuit.

"Butt looks big," squawked Olive from her bedroom perch. The parrot never lied, so her opinion mattered.

"You think so?" Shaye retrieved the jeans.

"Pretty lady." Olive stamped her approval.

Shaye couldn't help laughing. She went with Olive's choice. Her next quest was for shoes. Flip-flops outnumbered anything close-toed. She decided on a pair of cream and navy canvas espadrilles.

No makeup, but she brushed her hair. The curls had a life of their own. It was another hair-band day. She looked at the gift bag she'd yet to unpack. It stood out on her dresser, all sparkly, something to liven the dreary hours ahead. She let the bag sit a while longer and chose a band in tortoiseshell.

The weather forecast showed a possibility of rain. She didn't want to get caught in another downpour. Today she would be on a different boardwalk, one without free access to a change of clothes.

"Man boarding!" her cousin Kai called from the front ladder of her land-docked houseboat.

The vintage Horizon had once belonged to her grandfather. The hull was no longer seaworthy, but her childhood memories were stored on board. Finished in maple and decorated in summer-sand tones, the two decks combined the feel of the ocean with that of solid ground.

The houseboat had all the amenities of a home. She'd installed a hot tub on the upper deck and used the water slide as an emergency exit. The fish finder was wired for security.

Her houseboat sat on Land's End, a cul-de-sac off Houseboat Row. All the other boats were anchored along a short dock. Several of her family members preferred the Gulf over a yard; they had less to mow.

Shaye left the master bedroom and took to the center hallway. She met Kai in the galley. He surprised her with a bag of fresh Danish. Olive joined them and took refuge on her parrot swing near the sliding glass door. Her head bobbed, and she fluttered her wings, setting the swing in motion.

"Coffee?" Olive offered before Shaye could do so. Her Keurig provided individual cups.

Kai popped a Daybreak Blend into the coffeemaker, then added water. He went on to open the refrigerator and remove an orange. He peeled it.

"For my favorite girl." He offered Olive half a slice. The parrot politely took the fruit, then fanned her wings, excited by the treat.

Shaye leaned her hip against the U-curve of the counter. She crossed her arms over her chest and eyed her cousin. "Does Olive have competition for your affection?" she asked, getting straight to the point.

Kai wasn't fazed by her comment. He ran a finger over the Quaker's gray-feathered head. "Olive need not worry."

He went on to open the bakery bag and scored himself a cheese Danish. He pushed the bag toward Shaye. She selected almond-apricot. Kai poured his coffee as soon as it was ready. He set up a second cup for Shaye.

"You did an amazing renovation at The Jewelry Box," she complimented, attempting to draw him out. "I stopped by yesterday."

"I heard Trace was with you."

Word spread fast among family. "We were conducting business—"

"On the Ferris wheel."

So her life had gone viral. She wondered if there was a video of them on YouTube. "Afterward he wanted to check on Nicole. He hadn't had a chance to talk to her at the grand opening. You received an invitation, I saw you there, talking to Aunt Molly."

"The invitations were to view her shop, not a—" He caught himself, paused. He appeared inordinately relieved but didn't share why. His expression was one of prayers being answered. "You came and went in a hurry."

"The boardwalk doesn't run itself," she said. "It was business as usual." She hadn't wanted to bump into Trace. Seeing him across the room was more than enough.

She glanced at his wrist and admired his black braided leather cuff. Sterling silver domes capped the ends. A very masculine piece of jewelry.

Kai caught her stare and said, "Every shop owner needs a first sale. I was hers."

"Trace Saunders was in a buying mode yesterday, too. He bought me a hair band."

Kai's expression tightened at the mention of the Saunders name. "How serious are he and Nicole?"

"No idea," she said. "He's very protective of her—that much I know." Shaye told him about the trade show in Las Vegas as she poured her own cup of coffee, then went on to say, "Most of the family thinks you're into her, which could work in our favor. Nicole's free rental would be more acceptable if you were a couple."

"Let them believe what they will." Kai took a bite of his Danish. "I like her."

"So does Trace," she reminded him.

He sent her a self-deprecating smile. "We've been in competition for the same woman before," he said. "Trace won Crystal Smith. It's my turn."

"That was in high school," Shaye said. "And Crystal was a ditz."

"Ditz." Olive picked up a new word.

Kai sipped his coffee. "I've stayed away from The Jewelry Box for several days now."

"It's probably best to avoid someone you can't have."

"Maybe, maybe not." He was evasive.

Shaye finished her Danish and drank the last of her coffee. "I'm off to work."

"Heigh-ho, heigh-ho," came from Olive.

"Which dwarf are you today?" Kai asked her.

"Sleepy," she said. "My mind is on overload with tournament business. I can't shut it down. I'm lucky to get three hours of sleep."

She sighed. "I need to be wide awake today. Trace donated a central office for the event. I'm now working from Saunders Shores."

She glanced at her watch. It was eight-thirty. "Cage, Olive," she said. She limited her parrot's freedom when she left the houseboat.

The Quaker tilted her head and gave Shaye *the eye,* her most disagreeable look. Olive was happy where she perched and had no plans to move.

"I've got a bribe," Kai said. He stuck his hand into the Danish bag and rustled his fingers around until he caught the parrot's attention. He removed a mouse-shaped piñata filled with bird seed pellets.

"Munchies," he told Olive.

"For me?" she squawked.

He walked to the parrot's cage and hung the piñata next to the small mirror. Olive's curiosity got the better of her, and she immediately flew into her cage.

Shaye smiled. "You spoil her."

"Newspaper or piñata, Olive likes to shred." Kai closed the door to the cage and slid the lock across. "The newsstand was sold out of the *Barefoot Forum.*"

Shaye gathered her purse and laptop. Her chest felt tight and her stomach queasy. "Off to face the day."

"Kiss, kiss, love you." Olive sent Shaye on her way.

Kai followed her out.

*   *   *

Shaye walked to work. She didn't own a car. She rode a bike or hired a pedicab when covering long distances. Today she took her time. Rushing seemed ridiculous on such a beautiful morning. The full heat of the day had yet to sneak up on Barefoot William, and the breeze off the Gulf felt delightfully cool.

She stopped twice on the boardwalk, once at Brews Brothers for a second cup of coffee and at Crabby Abby's General Store for a pack of gum. She popped two sticks into her mouth. She knew she was procrastinating. She couldn't help it. She gave herself extra time with her relatives when they flagged her down to talk.

Nine o'clock rolled toward ten. She wasn't a clock-watcher. She'd often lose an hour without concern.

Tracking time was important today, though. She'd already cheated Trace out of forty minutes. She'd made a promise and planned to honor it. Once she crossed Center Street, she walked a little faster.

She soon reached Saunders Square. The midmorning sun gave the three-story windows a copper glow. She pushed through the revolving door and came to an immediate stop. Trace stood just inside, formidable, unreadable, and masculine in his light gray suit. He'd gotten a haircut and was clean shaven. She much preferred his Saturday scruff.

"I'm late." She voiced what he already knew.

"I expected you closer to noon."

"You were waiting for me?"

"I'm a patient man."

She hadn't thought him tolerant, but perhaps this was a side of him she'd yet to see. "I got sidetracked by family," she explained.

He looked at her hand. "And by gum."

The man was observant. She held up the pack. "Juicy Fruit?"

"Not now, but maybe later."

He stared at her, all penetrating and knowing. She found it hard to look away. His gaze was as pale blue-gray as a cresting wave. His cheekbones were as cut as his jaw. The corners of his mouth relaxed, as if he were ready to smile.

She thought to beat him to the smile but decided against it. There wasn't a need to be friendly. She wasn't here to forge relationships; she was here to work.

Her heart quickened as his look darkened, his stare now intimate and inappropriate in such a public place.

Against her will, her body responded. She immediately covered her chest with her laptop to conceal the puckering of her nipples. She shifted against the sudden warmth between her thighs. She was as embarrassed as she was turned on.

There was little she could hide from him. Trace knew he affected her, and he enjoyed her unease. His smile finally tipped, slow and sexy, and made her body burn.

The lobby closed in around her. A steady flow of businessmen skirted them, all in suits and carrying briefcases. A UPS driver dropped off boxes at security. Everyone nodded at Trace. She got her fair share of curious stares.

Clearing her throat, she asked, "My office?"

"On the third floor, next door to mine."

He was too close for her comfort. "You don't have something farther down the hall . . . I mean, more . . . separate?"

"Not at this time." He nodded toward the elevator. "Ready?"

She'd never be *ready*. Working from Saunders Square was as uncomfortable as wearing shoes. Her espadrilles already pinched her toes.

He placed his hand at her back and walked her across the lobby. His palm felt big against the small of her back.

She thought about shaking him off, only to realize his proprietary gesture was her invitation to be there. His familiarity guaranteed she wouldn't get bounced from the building, no matter the circumstance.

The tang of lemon furniture polish and yellow roses scented the air. The floor was so glossy, it mirrored their walk. A grouping of Haitian art brightened the walls. A painting of an island marketplace portrayed both poverty and survival.

Shaye drew in a breath and released it slowly. Today she would forego the breeze at the beach and the bake of the sun. There would be no crunching sand or coconut and banana suntan oil.

She glanced at her watch. Ten-twenty. She'd only been in the building a few minutes, and already it seemed like eight hours.

"Marlene Mason is the first person I want you to meet," Trace said as they entered the elevator. "My staff will stop by your office and introduce themselves throughout the day."

His staff? The intros weren't necessary. She was here for two short weeks. Not long enough to remember their names and get acquainted.

The elevator doors opened on the third floor, and Shaye was grateful the hallway stood empty. Trace's hand remained at her back. He nudged her forward, past his office and into hers.

She blinked, and goose bumps rose as she stood in the doorway and took it all in. There was nothing temporary about her workplace; it looked permanent.

Sunlight filtered through the wide tinted windows, casting the room in gold. The carpet was so thick, she wouldn't see her feet the entire day. Two armchairs faced each other, inviting conversation.

"Make yourself comfortable." Trace eased her inside.

Comfortable? She could barely breathe. She set her laptop and purse on a cherrywood worktable next to a healthy violet plant. A shallow candy dish held jelly beans.

Her eyes rounded as she crossed to her TrekDesk.

She'd seen them advertised but never in use. The machine was both exercise- and work-efficient.

She ran her fingers along the crescent-shaped desktop, perfectly set to her height. Atop the desk, a flat-screen computer curved into the keyboard. The manuscript holder would support books, magazines, or papers. A small printer sat on a raised stand to her right. The uphill slant of the treadmill was adjustable.

Trace stood with his hands in his pants pockets and eyed her speculatively. "You're an active woman, Shaye. I don't want you feeling cramped or claustrophobic. Here you can walk and work and still get the job done."

He gave her a moment to take it all in before adding, "You have plenty of shelving and cabinet space. I had stationery printed with your name."

She'd never owned stationery.

Yellow sticky notes delivered her messages.

She felt suddenly overwhelmed and needed to stabilize. Sunshine settled her down.

She went to the window and found the view picture-perfect. The beach was pristine and sparsely populated. There wasn't a grain of sugar sand out of place.

Bermuda-blue cabanas offered shade. Young men in white shirts and dark shorts stood in attendance. Not a single person sunbathed or utilized the white beach umbrellas. No one splashed or swam along the shoreline. It was as if they were afraid to make waves.

The volleyball tournament would soon shake things up.

She smiled to herself. Saunders Shores was about to be injected with fun in the sun.

She turned back to Trace. He looked expectant, tense,

as he awaited her verdict. He'd done so much, when she needed so little. She would've worked off a card table.

"Thank you," she said, and she meant it.

Her two words satisfied him. She heard him exhale, and the tightness in his shoulders eased. He appeared inordinately relieved that she liked her office.

Before he left, he directed her attention to a portable phone on the worktable. "All in-house lines," he told her. "Line one calls Martin. Two, Marlene. The third goes directly to me." He paused. "Settle in. I'll bring Marlene by to meet you in thirty."

She'd barely loaded her laptop when her Aunt Molly knocked on the door. The scent of sugar and cinnamon entered with her. Uncle Carl came next, followed by her cousin Jenna. A few others trickled in as well.

Her family was both concerned and curious as to her new surroundings. There were suddenly more people than chairs.

Soft laughter rose, but voices were kept low. The Cateses restrained their exuberance in the formal setting, but their consideration and affection embraced Shaye.

Trace soon returned, Marlene Mason at his side. Introductions were made. Shaye was surprised that Trace already knew everyone's name. Her relatives soon departed, and a part of Shaye left with them. Her office had lost much of its warmth.

Trace leaned against the doorjamb.

Marlene took one of the armchairs.

Shaye settled at the worktable, wanting access to her laptop.

She lived by first impressions and her intuition. They had always guided her well. She looked at Marlene first as a woman, then as a professional. Sharp-featured, the redhead presented herself in a tailored navy suit. Her dark pumps pushed her to medium height. Diamond studs were her only jewelry. Austere, Shaye thought, and all business.

"Shaye will bring you up to speed on the tournament," Trace said to Marlene. "I'll have Martin get you coffee. Black and"—he knew how Marlene liked her coffee— "Shaye?"

"Same," she said.

"I'll see you both later."

"His *later* means noon," Marlene said. "We have a lunch date." Apparently she was possessive of her boss.

Shaye let it slide. She'd planned to call Kai. They'd walk back to Molly's diner, enjoy juicy cheeseburgers and curly fries, and discuss his morning on the boardwalk. She was aware of eight needed repairs. There could easily be more.

Marlene took her time getting down to business. She openly admired Shaye's office. "This is quite a setup for a temp," she said, referring to Shaye's short stay. "Trace and Martin spent all day Sunday getting organized for your arrival."

Shaye sat quietly, although her heartbeat quickened. She hadn't expected Trace to get involved in her work space. Sunday, he should've been sailing. He was often featured in the local *Southern Shores* magazine as a winner of local regattas. "It's a great office," she agreed.

The corners of Marlene's mouth pulled tightly. "What did you do to earn so much attention?" She got personal.

"I let him ride my Ferris wheel."

The secretary's smile didn't reach her eyes. "It's good for a man to be a boy on occasion."

Shaye had enjoyed Trace's company more than she cared to admit. He'd been relaxed and proved a good loser. They hadn't been at each other's throats. They'd lived a one-day truce. Their respite just might stretch two weeks, until after the sporting event, if she were lucky.

She didn't want to talk about Trace. She preferred to

discuss the tournament. "Let's talk volleyball," she initiated. She went on to lay out her plans.

Marlene listened intently until Shaye ran out of breath and Martin arrived with their coffee. They both took a sip.

Marlene stared at Shaye over the rim of her cup, and Shaye swore she heard the woman's mind working. The secretary hadn't brought a yellow pad or jotted down a note. She must have total recall.

Marlene crossed her legs and settled deeper into the chair. She tapped her blood-red nails on the armrest. "You see the big picture but not the details," she finally said. "I've traveled with Trace and put together numerous events for the Saunders Corporation. It's the fine-tuning that pulls it all together."

They'd taken trips together. Marlene had established a closeness to her boss that Shaye would never share. While Shaye would run fast and far from an office romance, it appeared Marlene had let Trace catch her.

The man led an active sex life.

Shaye wondered how Nicole Archer handled competition.

This might be her cousin Kai's opportunity to win over the jewelry designer. The man was half in love with her already.

Shaye nodded to Marlene. "I'm interested in your suggestions."

She'd opened the door to Marlene's opinion, and the woman shot down every one of Shaye's plans, claiming them to be too small-town. Her recommended changes were considerable, and Shaye's operating budget was tight.

"Our finances are limited." She hated to admit that, but it was the truth.

Marlene wasn't fazed. "Trace has money. He'll donate to your cause."

Barefoot William wasn't a charity. Shaye didn't want his

money. Her town needed a push to get back on its feet. She was banking on the tournament's success.

"We don't need his financial assistance." She stood firm. "This isn't a sanctioned competition. My brother, Dune, is giving back to the community. All the professional players are donating their time. My family will provide the food, beverages, and souvenirs. I'm *renting*—" she stressed the fact she was paying her own way—"two hundred feet of Trace's beach."

"His beach and my expertise," Marlene said. "When you cross onto Saunders Shores, Trace becomes part of the event's success. He doesn't deal in failures."

Shaye had no plans to fall on her face, yet Marlene seemed to think she would soon take a nosedive. She wondered if Trace felt the same way.

Perhaps that was the real reason he'd brought in his so-efficient secretary. Trace saw Shaye as a liability. If so, he was damn underhanded. Shaye hoped she was wrong.

"Think about what I've said." Marlene gracefully stood and put an end to their meeting. "We'll continue our discussion this afternoon." She took off.

Shaye watched her leave. The woman had curves and a smooth walk. She presented herself well. She was competent and knowledgeable and would soon be having lunch with Trace. The garden cafés and bistros at Saunders Shores were expensive and intimate. A simple lunch on his side of the street would break Shaye's bank.

She went in search of her cell phone and found it at the bottom of her purse. She sent a text to Kai, requesting he meet her at Saunders Square in one hour. He agreed. They would backtrack to Molly's, and the walk would give them a chance to talk. She looked forward to seeing a familiar face.

Shaye shrugged off her blazer and shoes and approached the TrekDesk. She needed to clear her head. Exercise helped her think. She clocked five miles, yet her mind still remained cluttered. She could use some fresh air.

Kai arrived early, and, to both Shaye's and his surprise, Nicole Archer strolled off the elevator shortly thereafter. The jewelry designer waved and approached them as if they were old friends.

Shaye's gaze shifted between the two new arrivals. Kai stood in a gray T-shirt and jeans. His eyes narrowed and his nostrils flared at the sight of Nicole. His look was steamy.

Nicole's smile held surprising warmth, as well. She blushed beneath his stare. She looked bohemian chic in a white tunic and matching wide-leg pants. A thin gold-chain belt wrapped her waist. Her heels were cream suede. Cranberry glass and rhinestones glistened at her ears and draped in a necklace. Her bracelets were a collection of mixed metals.

Nicole turned to Shaye. "I came to check on you. The boardwalk is buzzing over you working from the enemy camp. I just learned that the Cateses and Saunders are at odds. Is this recent?" she asked.

Shaye sighed. Nicole was an innocent pawn in the rivalry between her and Trace. But Shaye had no time for explanations today. They could come at a later time. "It's century-old and a very long story" was enough for now, she hoped.

"We can take an extended lunch." Nicole showed surprising interest in their dispute.

"Who's watching your shop?" Kai asked, changing the subject.

"I hired Violet from the diner as a part-time sales associate. She has a creative eye. She'll work for me when she's not scheduled at Molly's. Today is her day off," Nicole informed them. "This next week I plan to take on two or three teenage girls. I want to put models in the store and on the boardwalk, wearing my signature white with my jewelry."

Nicole's hiring of her relatives pleased Shaye greatly. Nicole was definitely innovative. The fact that she employed family members would please the Cateses. The teenagers could use the extra money. Their allowances had been cut way back.

Nicole looked from Shaye to Kai. "Are you having lunch together?" she asked, looking hopeful that they'd invite her to join them.

Kai tensed. "Aren't you here for Trace?"

The jewelry designer shook her head. "I've no reason to see him. My mission was to check on Shaye."

Kai visibly unwound. "My cousin can take care of herself," he said.

Shaye motioned them inside her office. "Look around, and you'll see I'm doing just fine."

The two entered and openly stared.

Kai couldn't take his eyes off the TrekDesk.

Nicole caught her breath and was the first to speak. "This isn't an office designed around a feud. It's been set up with respect and reflection. Trace gave you a violet, which I know for a fact is his mother's favorite flower."

Shaye liked violets, too.

Kai shifted his stance, looking uncomfortable. His lip curled slightly. "When did you and Saunders become so chummy?"

Shaye knew the exact moment a subtle yet significant acceptance had settled between them. It had been on the Ferris wheel, when Trace handed her the tournament and a liaison and she accepted his office space.

She hoped he hadn't played her for a fool.

She remained cautious and aware of his every move.

"Trace and I aren't friends," she stressed to Kai. "We're merely two people with one goal at the moment."

Kai still looked skeptical.

Shaye was about to reassure him further when her cell phone rang. She retrieved it and looked at the incoming number. It was Uncle Chris. Chris owned Saltwater Sharkey's and had sponsored a sandlot team for as long as Shaye could remember. She hoped nothing was wrong.

"I need to take this call," she said. Shaye didn't mind Kai eavesdropping, but Nicole was a different story. This was family business.

She shot Kai a pointed look, which he acted upon. He engaged Nicole in small talk. The woman was more than willing to discuss her latest designs.

Shaye listened intently as her uncle relayed the bad news. His local bar and pool hall was financially strapped. He was forced to give up his team sponsorship. He felt awful, but she felt worse.

She disconnected and debated what to do next. Her own store, Goody Gumdrops, couldn't support two teams. It took a lot of penny-candy sales to maintain the one. She would soon be canvassing the other store owners. Surely one of her relatives could take on twelve kids for the remainder of the season. She just needed to decide whom to approach first.

"What's up?" Kai asked the second the call ended.

"You look a little pale," Nicole said, concerned.

Word of the Sharkeys' disbandment would soon spread down the boardwalk, so Shaye gave them a heads-up. "Uncle Chris can no longer support a sandlot team. We need a new sponsor."

"Oh, crap," came from Kai. He ran a hand down his face, deep in thought. "The guys at Hardware and Lumber might be an option."

"I'll also check with Jenna at Three Shirts," said Shaye.

"Let me run a list of outstanding bills," Kai said. "Maybe I could split the sponsorship with someone."

"What about me?" Nicole said so softly, they weren't sure she'd spoken.

"What about you?" asked Kai.

"I'll go halves."

Shaye was so taken aback, her jaw dropped. "Do you know anything about baseball?" she asked.

Nicole shrugged. "What I don't know, I can learn."

She looked down at her clasped hands. "I never played sports as a kid, because I worked after school. If I wasn't cleaning for my neighbors, I was doing chores at home."

She smiled at Shaye, a grateful smile. "My life has changed for the better. I now have a shop on your boardwalk. Several customers bought jewelry from me over the weekend. I'd like to give back to the community."

Shaye hadn't seen that coming. Nicole's offer to sponsor a baseball team surprised the hell out of her. Kai looked a little shocked himself.

Nicole reached over and touched Kai's arm. "Our fortune-teller gave me a reading several days ago. I think these are *the boys* Madame Aleta saw in my future."

"Who's to argue with our aunt?" Kai asked.

"Not me," said Shaye. "What are you going to call your team? I'll have new shirts printed up."

"The Jewelry Box is too girly," said Kai.

Nicole fingered her necklace. "Hook It, Cook It sounds fishy."

"Why don't you discuss the name over lunch," Shaye suggested. "You can let me know once you decide."

Kai raised an eyebrow. "I thought you and I—"

She shook her head and waved him off. "We'll talk later."

Her cousin walked out with Nicole. Over his shoulder, he winked and mouthed, "Thanks."

Now what? Shaye thought. She'd lost her lunch partner.

"Looking for me?" Trace came down the hallway toward her.

She hadn't been, but she was surprisingly glad to see him. He looked nice walking toward her. He'd taken off his sport coat and removed his tie. The top two buttons of his shirt were undone, and his sleeves were rolled to his elbows. *Informal yet hot,* came to mind.

"I just said good-bye to Kai and Nicole," she told him when he reached her.

"Nicole was here?" He looked sorry he'd missed her.

"She came for a short visit," she explained. "Nicole now knows about our family's dispute. She wanted to be sure I was treated well here at Saunders Shores."

"Interesting," Trace said. "Nicole being more concerned about you than me."

"I guess you gave her away."

Trace went very quiet. After a full minute, he flattened his palm on the wall beside her and leaned in, as if to tell her a secret. His cheek brushed hers, and his words were for her ears only. "Nicole wouldn't have survived in a boutique at Saunders Shores. She works with semiprecious gemstones. The Shores clientele prefers diamonds over cubic zirconium. She wouldn't have sold one piece of jewelry here. Though we're no longer . . . together, I didn't want her feelings hurt."

Shaye now understood. "My deception over the volleyball tournament gave you the perfect opening to put her on my boardwalk. I took her off your hands."

"Pretty much so."

"Opportunist."

"You started it."

Yes, she had. She'd finish it, too.

He eased back slightly. "Nicole is happy with her shop. I'm assuming you'll allow her to stay."

Shaye had no plans to boot the woman. Nicole Archer had woven her way into the Cateses' lives. The lady had put down roots in a very short time.

"I lost a sponsor for our sandlot league, and Nicole offered to take over the team," Shaye told him.

Trace threw back his head and laughed. It was a very deep, warm, male laugh that resonated through Shaye from the outside in. "I'll help coach if she needs assistance," he said.

"She's got Kai. They'll go halves." She gave him this information on purpose, to gauge his reaction.

He raised an eyebrow. "Kai, the man who squirted her with ketchup at the concession stand? Who then went on to tell her that she bagged popcorn like a rookie?"

"They've become friends."

Trace took it all in. His expression never changed. There was no anger or jealousy. His acceptance came easily. "She's an Archer, not a Saunders. She has no feud with the Cates family." One corner of his mouth curved. "I may have to catch a game or two."

"At your own risk," she reminded him. "My family tolerates you now, but after the tournament, your life is in your own hands."

"You're right," he agreed. "We're at odds, and you're always trying to get even."

She would always keep score with this man. That was her nature. He knew it, and so did she. Awareness was all-important. It kept her on her toes.

"Do you have plans for lunch?" he asked.

She had, but they'd disappeared with Kai. "I'm on my own," she told him.

"Me, too," he said.

"I thought you were having lunch with Marlene."

"What gave you that idea?"

She told me so, Shaye wanted to say, but she let it pass.

She shrugged, realizing Marlene's plans must have changed, as well. "My mistake."

"You're here, I'm here. . . ."

He left the sentence open-ended, letting her finish it for him. She met his gaze and then wished she hadn't. The man made her heart race. She refused to read more into his offer than was there. This was all about lunch, nothing more.

She stepped into her office and slipped on her shoes. It was too hot for her blazer. "Molly Malone's, and you're buying," she said.

"I can live with that."

Seven

Their lunches continued for ten days. Trace would show up at Shaye's office unannounced and insist she take a break. Most days the noon hour saw them at Molly Malone's Diner. Only once did he succeed in taking her someplace new. They'd enjoyed pasta at Barconi's bistro.

From daybreak to dusk, Shaye worked hard, not only on the upcoming tournament but keeping tabs on Barefoot William. Her relatives were a handful, Trace noted. They depended on Shaye, and she was dedicated to them all. He admired their closeness.

By Wednesday, Trace sensed that Shaye was tired. She had dark circles under her eyes, and her shoulders slumped, yet the moment she crossed Center Street, she shook off her shoes, and her steps seemed lighter.

She was a barefoot, free spirit who came alive in the sunshine, yet he'd coerced her to work in an office. He felt a little guilty but not enough to let her return to the beach. He believed the success of the volleyball tournament was based on Marlene's strategy.

He wanted to see Barefoot William in the black, not only for Shaye's sake but for Nicole as well. The jewelry designer seemed content. She was establishing a clientele. Her business was growing, as was her involvement with Kai Cates. Trace approved of Kai, although Kai hated him.

Kai still held a grudge from high school. Crystal Smith was their unhappily shared past.

Today was far more important. Trace returned his focus to Shaye and their stroll down the Barefoot William boardwalk. The outdoor vendors saw her coming and waved her over. She stopped and chatted with each one. The woman could eat. It soon became apparent she couldn't pass a food cart without placing an order.

Their meal this afternoon consisted of junk food and fun. They started with hot dogs, cheese fries, and slices of pizza, and ended with caramel corn, funnel cake, and fried Oreos.

The food they were unable to eat they slipped into a small wicker picnic basket purchased at Crabby Abby's.

"Snacks for later," Shaye said.

She would be munching all afternoon.

By the time they reached the end of the boardwalk, he was so full, he refused her offer of the last bite of blue cotton candy. The woman was half his size yet ate twice as much as he did. He waited for her to blow up.

He looked back over his shoulder, at the long stretch of boardwalk behind them. Their huge lunch had cost him very little, he realized. Had they dined at a Shores café, he'd have spent ten times the amount on soup and a salad.

The money didn't matter, although time spent with Shaye had become important to him. She intrigued him. She was unique, quirky, and straightforward, when she wasn't being sneaky.

He knew exactly where he stood with her. She hadn't liked him much in the beginning, but he sensed they were growing on each other, a day at a time.

There were moments when he forgot about their feud and enjoyed her company. She was easy on the eyes, and he was fascinated by the way she laughed for seemingly no reason. More often than not her laughter was directed at him. He no longer minded when she made fun of him.

"One more stop," Shaye said as they retraced their steps. "I have a surprise for you."

"No more food," he begged.

"I promise, you'll find room" was the only hint she'd give him.

They soon arrived at Goody Gumdrops, the modern-day Snack Shack. Trace was aware the original Shack had been demolished by a hurricane five years earlier. Shaye had used the insurance money to open her own shop. Kids would line up with dimes in their pockets and visions of gumdrops dancing in their heads.

A red and pink lollipop was painted on the door. She entered first, and he paused just inside to look around. The walls were peppermint striped. The overhead lights were custom-shaped as Tootsie Rolls.

Glass jars were stacked on shelves above large wooden bins of penny candy. There was so much sugar, his sweet tooth started to ache. The sign near the cash register read: ONE PIECE FOR A PENNY OR BUY BY THE POUND.

Shaye introduced the boy behind the counter as her cousin Nick. He looked athletic, Trace thought. And clean-cut.

Nick headed to the register when a cute girl close to his own age filled a small paper bag with pink rock candy and was ready to check out.

"Sweet Treat Trivia." Nick passed her a round glass bowl filled with rolled pieces of paper. "Candy over a dollar becomes half price if you answer correctly."

The girl reached in and removed a question, which she read aloud. "What candy is individually wrapped and a bright Day-Glo red with layers of various colored cinnamon?"

The question stumped her, yet she guessed anyway. "Jawbreakers."

Nick looked as disappointed as the girl. "Sorry, the answer is Atomic FireBalls. Better luck next time."

"I'll be back," she promised.

Trace vividly recalled the Sweet Treat game. He and Shaye had played years ago at the Snack Shack on the pier. His date, Crystal Smith, had suggested the game. He'd gone on to best Shaye with his knowledge of candy corn.

He watched her now as she stood on tiptoe and stretched to reach the top shelf, which held jars of his favorite candy. There were six flavors, he noted. His concentration shifted from the candy corn to her.

Shaye had one sweet body. She had slender shoulders and a sleek spine. Her butt would fit the palms of his hands perfectly. Her inner thighs were toned and would nicely grip a man's hips. He'd bet she'd make one hell of a lover.

Sex with her would be sleeping with the enemy.

His insane thought shook him. He swallowed hard. He pulled his mind back to the bins of Boston Baked Beans, Necco Wafers, and Bit O' Honeys. He started counting the wrapped morsels of salt water taffy in a jar on the counter. He went on to the alphabet to distract himself further, starting at the end and working forward: *Z, Y, X, W, V . . .*

He'd gotten to *F, E, D* by the time Shaye handed him a bag of candy corn tied with a black licorice whip. She gave him a small smile. "My treat. Enjoy."

"What, no trivia question?" he asked.

"Your candy's free."

"One question. If I lose, I'll pay double."

"You live dangerously, Trace Saunders." She passed him the bowl. He circled his fingers among the rolled paper and finally picked one. He handed it to Shaye.

She read it aloud, her expression as serious as a game-show host's. "What's a five-pack of sugary sweet liquid sealed in wax bottles, complete with its own carrying case? Most of the fun comes in chewing the wax bottles after drinking the liquid."

There was no hesitation on his part. "Root Beer Barrels."

She made a buzzer sound far louder than he felt was necessary, indicating he was wrong. "*Bottles* not *barrels*," she said. "The answer is Nik-L-Nips."

What the hell? Losing didn't sit well with him. "Go again," he requested.

"Are you sure? There's approximately two hundred pieces of candy corn in your bag, and you already owe me four dollars."

"We go triple."

"You are a gambling man," she said.

He fished out another rolled paper and passed it to her. She stretched the paper out flat. "Bazooka Bubble Gum," she said. "Name the colors on the wrapper."

Oh, crap. He'd chewed the gum as a kid but was more excited over the comic and fortune inside than the color of the wrapper. "If I'd collected one million comics, I could've sent away for a BB gun," he muttered.

Shaye shook her head. "That's what the company offered as a prize. They wanted kids to chew a lot of gum. It's not, however, the correct answer."

He gave his best guess. "White" was a standard color on most candy. "Blue" was too. The gum was pink, so he went with it. "Pink."

Her buzzer once again sounded, attracting attention from those entering the store. "Not pink but red," she corrected him. "You owe me six dollars."

He exhaled slowly. A small crowd had now gathered. He was looking bad. "You have any questions on jelly beans or candy corn?"

She smiled. "I'll go easy on you this time." She gave him a question not found in the bowl. "Over thirty-five million pounds of candy corn are produced each year. If laid end to end, what heavenly body would they circle four times?"

"The moon." He nailed it.

She nodded, and those engaged by the trivia applauded. "Happy now?" she asked.

"Winning is good." He retrieved his wallet from the back pocket of his pants and removed the money he owed her. "I pay my debts."

She hesitated, but only until a sunburned family of six came through the door. The mother and father were dragging. Their four young boys were supercharged.

Shaye watched as they searched out their favorite candies. Her expression softened. She snatched the cash from Trace's hand and crossed to the parents. She introduced herself as the owner of the shop, then awarded them each a dollar for being the fiftieth customer of the day. The parents looked surprised but grateful. The kids went nuts. Shaye pointed the children toward the sugarless candy. They were already bouncing off the walls.

Shaye was a generous woman, Trace noted. It had to take a massive amount of penny-candy sales to make ends meet. Yet instead of putting the six bucks into the register, she'd split it among a family. He admired her kindness.

He glanced at his watch and realized they'd taken a two-hour lunch. "Time to get back to work," he said.

"I'd rather take a nap."

Shaye had the look of a woman not ready to return to the office. Her sigh was long and heavy when she waved to Nick, then slipped out of Goody Gumdrops. The door didn't hit her in the ass, but it did close on Trace's foot.

She walked beside him, quiet and thoughtful. At least she was headed toward Saunders Square. Whether she'd reach the office or not was debatable. There were numerous stairs and walkways leading down to the beach. She could cut out on him at any time.

They made it to the office building without mishap. Shaye slipped on her shoes in the lobby. "Marlene will be waiting," she said on the elevator ride to the third floor. "She's scheduled a meeting and will give updates on the tournament."

They found Marlene along with two dozen Cateses gathered in the hallway. Shaye greeted everyone, comfortable in the crowd. Marlene appeared cramped.

Marlene approached Trace. "I can't work in these conditions," she stated. "We need more space."

He nodded and motioned to Shaye. "Boardroom."

Shaye went to her office and grabbed her laptop, then led her family down the hall. Marlene entered last.

Trace handed off the picnic basket to Martin and searched out a spot. He found a chair in the back, unobtrusive yet close enough to follow the meeting.

It soon became standing room only as more people arrived. The event was now only four days away. Yellow tents had been erected. The volleyball courts were measured and marked, and the nets were stretched and attached to the posts.

Trace watched as Marlene took charge, which did not surprise him. The woman was good at her job, yet apparently not the best by Cates standards.

The family favored Shaye. They deferred Marlene's suggestions to her for approval. Shaye didn't agree without a vote. Once taken, the majority ruled.

Trace was not surprised when only thirty percent of Marlene's last-minute changes passed. The Cateses knew how they wanted the tournament run and refused to add on expenses they couldn't afford. They'd already spent beyond their budget.

He knew better than to offer to pay their way. The Cates family would see it as charity. The best he could do was to offer The Sandcastle for the cocktail party to welcome the players and guests. The vote was unanimous. He would host the entertainment.

He could hand the party over to Martin, yet he chose to see to it himself. He would meet with the hotel caterer and set a menu. Shaye had worked her ass off. The least he could do was make the night memorable for her. He had the resources, and he found he liked taking part in the planning.

Between now and the tournament he needed to reveal Marlene's true role in the enterprise. He'd hedged on that to spare Shaye's pride. But guilt was pushing him to explain his decisions more fully. Shaye had put in just as many hours as the event planner. There was a slim possibility Shaye could've pulled off the pro/am without professional assistance, but he hadn't wanted to chance it. Marlene's involvement guaranteed the event's success.

He'd soon come clean.

But with his admission, Shaye would be fighting mad.

He'd have to wear his cup.

As it turned out, he never got to apologize. An unexpected knock on the boardroom door drew everyone's attention. Silence greeted the visitor as everyone stared.

Trace strained, but his view was partially blocked.

What he could see was the profile of a man, someone tall and lean with straight blond hair and a dark tan.

"Dune!" Shaye said excitedly. She slid off her chair so quickly, it teetered on two legs. She rushed to her older brother.

Her family followed, giving him a group hug.

Trace remained seated and took it all in.

Marlene, however, was nearly trampled.

"What are you doing home?" Shaye was quick to ask him. "You're two days early."

Dune held up his hand and displayed the cast on his wrist. "Scaphoid fracture. I fell on my outstretched hand at the South Beach Open. I'm here to rest and get some therapy."

He looked at Shaye and was quick to assure her, "Don't sweat the tournament. I'm going to play. I can still serve and do more damage with one hand than most players can with two."

Dune went on to scan the room, his dark gaze sharp and very curious. His frown cut deep. "Word on the board-walk indicated you were here. What's going on? Why are so many Cateses gathered in a Saunders boardroom?"

"We're planning your volleyball event," Marlene replied, raising her voice to be heard.

Dune located her, standing against the wall. Trace caught his slow smile of recognition. "Marlene Mason?"

"Hello, Beach Heat." She referred to Dune by the nick-name given him by his female fans.

Shaye's eyes rounded, and she asked what was on every-one's mind. "Dune, how do you know Marlene?"

"She owns Event Planners, based out of Miami," he said. "Her company contracts with major sporting events all over the country. She works closely with the pro beach volleyball tour."

The tables had been turned on Trace, and his gut tight-ened. Now that Marlene's identity was known, and she was no longer just one of his staffers, it was obvious he'd chosen the professional planner's expertise over Shaye's own abilities.

He'd dug himself a deep hole.

He rose and locked eyes with Shaye. Her expression punched him hard. Disbelief and disappointment drained all color from her face. Her words held a detonating anger when she asked, "She's not your secretary?" She waited for his answer.

"Marlene's her own boss," said Trace.

He watched as the big picture came together for her. She laid the blame fully on him, which he deserved. "You manipulative bastard." Her voice was as hard as her expression. "I should've known you'd double-cross me."

Panic set in, and he moved toward her. "I can explain. Give me a minute—"

"Not one second." She grabbed her laptop and shot out the door.

Her family blocked him, refusing to let him follow her. They gave Shaye time to escape the building before emptying the boardroom themselves. He got his fair share of dirty looks as they crowded the elevator.

Trace was set to take the emergency exit stairs, but Dune stopped him. "Now's not the time, dude," he advised. "My sister's damn mad. Given the mood she's in, she'd take you down in a heartbeat."

"I need to see her." He sounded desperate but didn't care.

Dune narrowed his gaze. "I've been out of town a long time," he said, "so bring me up to speed. What the hell's going on? Since when do the Cates and Saunders families gather in the same room?"

"Since the beach event," Marlene Mason said as she came to stand between them. "The tournament's out of my hands now. You two may not like each other, but you both want what's best for Shaye. So talk."

"I'm listening," said Dune.

"Make it fast," Marlene added. "I'm going to pack up, take Dune to an early dinner, then catch an evening flight home."

Dune caught her by the arm as she passed through the

door. His fingers wrapped her wrist lightly; his smile was suggestive. "Stay over, and travel tomorrow."

Marlene was easily persuaded. "I suppose I could charge Trace for another day. Our meal will be on his expense account. So will the hotel room. I'll make reservations now." And she left.

"My office," Trace suggested. "It's private."

Their conversation ran an hour. Trace gave Dune the rundown, and Dune grew so angry over Trace's distrust of his sister, his whole body shook.

Dune argued that Shaye was smart and dedicated to seeing her family through hard times. The Cateses didn't need the Saunders family in order to be successful. He told Trace to butt the hell out.

Martin Carson eventually broke them apart with cups of strong black coffee. Not long after that, Trace offered Dune Scotch from the wet bar, which the man accepted. They toasted Marlene, their one mutual friend.

It was six o'clock by the time they agreed to disagree. Nothing had been fully resolved. They were two men entrenched in a century-old feud. Their own lines in the sand were drawn as deep as their ancestors'.

Marlene came for Dune, and the two soon left. Dune's last words warned Trace to stay the hell away from his sister. Unfortunately for Dune, Trace had every intention of seeing her, once the boardwalk closed for the night. The amusement park shut down around two. That's when he'd make his move.

He hated the fact her day had ended so poorly.

The lady was pissed. She would never return to Saunders Shores, which forced him to go to her.

Go, he would. He left his office and headed home. He planned to sleep for a few hours. He needed to be alert and sharp when he met with her.

★ ★ ★

Lights flashed, and a siren blared, catching Shaye's attention. She'd been lying on a beach lounger on the upper deck of her vintage Horizon when her security system sounded. Someone had tripped the alarm.

Burglars and Peeping Toms were unknown to Houseboat Row. Yet there was always a first time. That time appeared to be tonight.

Her heart slammed inside her chest.

She fought to catch her breath.

"Stranger danger," Olive squawked. The Quaker watched way too many cop shows.

Just as quickly as the noise had sounded, it stopped. The person climbing aboard had disabled the alarm. He'd also cursed the air blue. Looking over the side, she recognized Trace Saunders not only by his voice but by his sheer size. Even in darkness, the man was larger than life. He had something in his hand. She blinked. It was the picnic basket.

Facing a robber would've been far less frightening, she realized. Here was the man who'd gotten under her skin. She'd trusted him, had come to like him, yet he'd tricked her by bringing in Marlene Mason, a professional, independent event planner, from Miami, no less.

He'd made her look bad. She felt like a fool.

"Get off my property!" she shouted down to him. "You set off my alarm. The police are on their way."

"Call and tell them you're fine!" he yelled back.

She'd never be fine around him. "I'd rather have you arrested."

"Give me five minutes."

"It's three in the morning."

"You're still up."

That was true. She hadn't been able to sleep.

She heard the rattle of her front door and knew he had entered. He hadn't asked to come on board; he'd just gone ahead and crashed her space. She would rather face him on the lower deck. The upper was her private sanctuary. A place she could meditate or sunbathe in the nude. She refused to argue where peace prevailed.

She took the stairway down, with Olive perched on her shoulder. Trace met her in the hallway. Neither spoke as she attempted to reset the alarm on the lower back deck. It beeped feebly. Trace had damaged the system.

Her cell phone rang. It was the dispatcher from the local police precinct checking on her safety. Two squad cars were on their way, which Shaye quickly diverted. She apologized for the accidental tripping of her alarm. She then turned back to Trace.

He leaned a shoulder against the wall. "Why didn't you turn me in?"

"Self-preservation," she said. "I don't need law enforcement arriving when the CEO of Saunders Shores is on my houseboat. They would misinterpret your visit."

He blew out a breath. "There would be a lot of speculation. I'd hate to have another misunderstanding between us."

He stood a good four feet from her, but Shaye could *feel* him, as if they were pressed together. The sensation left her both warm and cautious.

Moonlight now flickered through the sliding glass doors, casting enough light to bring him fully into focus. His hair was mussed and one side spiked, as if he'd run his fingers through it. His eyes shone more gray than blue. His features stood out sharply against the shadows, slashing cheekbones and a square jaw. He had dressed in commando black, from his T-shirt and sweatpants to his tennis shoes. She was surprised he hadn't painted his face.

"What's your name?" asked Olive. She was good with names and faces. Trace was new to her.

"Trace," he said easily.

"Olive," she introduced herself.

"You're smart," said Trace.

"Smarter than you."

Shaye swallowed her smile. Olive called it as she saw it. The parrot affectionately rubbed her feathered head against Shaye's cheek. *"Is he packing pepperoni?"* next passed through the parrot's beak.

Shaye felt her cheeks heat. She never knew what the Quaker would repeat. She couldn't believe Olive had taken that particular moment to air a conversation she'd recently had with her twenty-year-old cousin Abby. They'd ordered pizza, and when it arrived, Abby had commented on the delivery boy's "package." A comment Olive now shared.

Trace found the parrot's remark amusing. He grinned.

Shaye, however, wasn't laughing. She lifted her chin and said, "You've invaded my houseboat. I don't like men sneaking up on me."

"There was no sneaking," he said. "I came to visit. Your alarm announced my arrival."

"You silenced it by pulling out a wire."

"One wire, easy fix." He raised his hand. "I cleaned out the picnic basket and thought to return it."

How thoughtful. "You need to go," she said firmly.

"Good-bye," said Olive.

Trace had no intention of leaving. He set down the basket and stepped even closer. Only two feet separated them now. His gaze took her in, and she felt vulnerable and exposed. It was a warm evening, and she wore only a loose crop top and boy shorts.

Olive pecked at her hair, drawing Trace's attention.

Shaye suddenly wished she was anywhere but there. Earlier that evening she'd made the mistake of trying on the midnight-blue velvet hair band plaited with sterling silver. The band was beautiful, and she'd hoped it would lift her spirits. It had, a little. She had yet to remove it, and Trace eyed it now.

His smile was pure male ego. "Nice hair band," he said.

"I wanted to try it on once before I returned it."

His smile slipped. "There's a no-return policy at The Jewelry Box."

"Nicole will side with me, not you."

He pushed off the wall, his jaw set. "I came to apologize."

"Your actions spoke louder than words."

"You're right," he agreed. "I crossed the line and interfered in your business. Barefoot William was having a slow summer, and —"

"It's *our* slow summer, not yours."

"The tournament will give every shop a financial boost." He paused, then added, "I wanted it to be successful."

Frustration hit her hard. Olive sensed her tension and dug her nails into Shaye's shoulder. "I could have pulled it off," she swore, "but you never gave me a chance. You butted in and hired Marlene Mason, someone with a track record."

"Marlene's expertise guaranteed you a profit," he quietly pointed out. "That was my goal, for you to make money."

She caught him watching her mouth and bit down on her bottom lip. Hurt settled in her chest. "You didn't trust me."

"Marlene's gone tomorrow," he told her. "The tournament's yours again."

"It should've been mine all along, but you took it from me."

"I was looking out for you, Shaye."

"I can take care of myself."

"*Shame, shame,*" the parrot chimed in. "*He's handsome but an ass.*" And the Quaker flew off.

Oh, shit, Shaye thought. All the air left her lungs. Olive's attention span had sharpened, and her mind was clearly working overtime. The parrot's sentences were getting longer and more precise. Olive had just repeated what Shaye had muttered about Trace no more than an hour ago.

"I made a mistake, and I'm sorry," he said, his voice deep, husky, sincere.

"Too little, too late."

He flattened one hand against the wall, just above her left shoulder. She watched his face; his gaze was fixed and questioning. "Is there anything I can say to make this better?"

"Nothing at all. You're an ass."

"I'm a handsome ass, according to Olive." He shifted and was suddenly as close as the clothes on her back.

"Kiss the girl," Olive squawked from her cage.

The corner of his mouth curved. "Who am I to argue with Olive? She's smarter than me."

There was nothing smart about what came next.

Shaye knew she'd regret this kiss, but she'd wait and kick herself *after* she'd tasted him. They weren't strangers; they'd known each other all their lives, but as enemies, not friends.

It had been a long time since she'd been with a man. Trace, on the other hand, was evidently a man of many women. But she wouldn't make love with him if he was involved with someone else.

"Are you sure you're not still with Nicole?" she asked, holding her breath.

He traced her collarbone with one finger, then pressed his thumb to her full bottom lip. "Long over."

She felt a heartbeat of relief and released her breath. She would share this bit of news with Kai when she next saw him. If he didn't already know it himself. One further question lingered. "What about Marlene?"

His eyebrows pulled together, and his brow creased. "We were close in college, and when she opened her business, I hired her for several company-related events. There's nothing else between us now."

"She . . . wanted you."

"Maybe she assumed we'd pick up where we'd left off a long time ago. I wasn't interested. Besides, if she did want me, the lady's pretty fickle," he said. "She left my office for a night with Dune."

Their gazes held as he ran the back of his hand down the front of her crop top all the way to her bare belly. He stroked her navel with his thumb and fanned his fingers over her abdomen, squeezing gently.

"I want you in only your hair band." His voice was deep, rough, turned on.

He stared at her, a man of single-minded purpose. His look was so sexually charged, she nearly climaxed on the spot. The thought of having sex with him took over. She wanted to be naked with Trace Saunders.

His next move came slowly. A shift of his shoulders, and he grasped her hips. Their thighs brushed, and his sex pressed against her belly.

He took great pleasure in foreplay. The moment was seamless, timeless, as he flicked his tongue over her collarbone, then kissed the pulse point at the base of her throat. His lips slipped over her jaw, then up to her mouth.

Their first kiss was tentative, light, and far too brief. His second kiss came with intent. He parted her lips and penetrated her with his tongue. He mated with her mouth, a man of practice and experience. Her knees trembled, and she wrapped her arms around his neck. She held on tight.

He outlined her nipples through the cotton of her crop top. The tips beaded and pressed against the center of his palm. His fingers were long, the tips rough, as he edged up her shirt and snuck under. He stroked the underside of one breast, then gave equal attention to the other.

Her top came off with a slide of material. He placed a kiss over her heart before he swept a wide circle around her nipple with his tongue. His mouth closed around it, and he sucked.

Her desire deepened, erotic and enticing.

They shared an innate connection, but were they enemies or lovers?

Shaye had no idea where things would stand after tonight.

He seduced with subtlety and finesse. The combination did a number on her. Her fascination for him grew with each kiss, touch, and intake of breath.

Off came her boy shorts, and she stood naked before him. He ran his hands all over her body, taking his sweet time to learn and discover. She breathed in, breathed deeply, as he traced the sensitive crease at the top of one thigh. His fingers came near but never delved into her sex.

She was at a disadvantage, being nude while he remained fully dressed. She remedied that situation quickly.

She pulled his shirt up and over his head, and he was soon bare-chested. His sweatpants rode low. She ran her hands from his shoulders to his wrists, then stroked across his stomach. She was a sucker for muscular arms and a defined abdomen. It was evident Trace worked out. He was as cut as chiseled stone.

His body felt warm and wired for sex.

She experienced her own hot flashes.

He toed off his athletic shoes, and she went to work on the drawstring at his waistband. Only a man secured his pants with a knot; a woman tied a bow. She fumbled, fidgeted, and he took over the task. The cord loosened, and he slipped a silver packet from the side-seam pocket.

"Big Guns?" she asked as she read the name on the condom. "You came prepared?"

"I came hopeful."

His sweatpants soon dropped, and his erection rose.

He was one big man. And tanned from head to toe.

He stepped out of his sweats, and she took him in her hand. She stroked his sex until his breathing became heavy and rapid. She then sheathed him with the condom.

He lifted her easily, and she wrapped her legs about his hips. *Sex against a wall?* It proved intense, uninhibited, and a little insane. Her cheek pressed his chin, and her lips kissed his throat. Her short fingernails dug into his broad back.

His hand slid between them, his fingers seeking. He parted her folds and slipped one finger inside. She was exposed and vulnerable, damp and needy. Stimulated and electrified.

She rolled her hips, restless and ready for him. He slipped his fingers out, then entered her slowly.

She was tight.

He took his time with her.

Penetration. Pleasure. One followed the other.

He thrust, and she throbbed.

He let her adjust to his size.

Her arousal spiked, and every nerve ending in her body hummed. She moaned, unraveled, as his rhythm increased, faster, deeper, and powerfully male.

Her small breasts rose and fell. She panted softly. His heart thundered in his chest and his breath came in short pulls as he coaxed her body to climax.

Her orgasm took her out of mind and beyond time, a total surrender. Her climax lasted a long while, easing off, then returning in a rush when, seconds later, he came deep inside her.

He held her until their breathing eased. She then slid down his body, feeling every inch of him. He dropped a light kiss on her forehead, straightened her hair band. He held her loosely.

She sighed, content, until she heard herself moan.

Yet she hadn't made a sound.

The sexual moaning rose louder from the direction of the living room. *"M-Mmm, o-oh, so good."* Olive mimicked Shaye's orgasm.

Trace chuckled, and she cringed.

The parrot couldn't keep a secret.

She would soon "moan" to anyone who'd listen.

Eight

"M-*mmmm*." The low, seductive sound rolled from
Olive's beak. "*O-oh*."

Dune Cates stared at the parrot on her perch in the living room of his sister's houseboat. "Olive sounds horny,"
he said.

He caught Shaye's blush before she busied herself in
the galley. "Parrots don't get horny; they lay eggs," she reminded him. "She must have heard"—she hesitated—
"some lovemaking on a television show."

"It sounded pretty realistic."

"Reality TV."

Shaye stretched the truth on occasion, but she'd never
lied to him. Dune swore he saw her nose grow. Olive, on
the other hand, was a faithful recorder of the truth. One
time he'd belched after eating a big meal, and Olive had
burped for a week straight.

The sex sounds had him puzzled, though. Shaye wasn't
seeing anyone that he knew of.

Dune crossed to the kitchen and leaned on the counter.
He studied his sister closely. He'd offered to escort her to
the welcoming cocktail party at The Sandcastle, and she'd
accepted. Until the day before, he hadn't seen her for six
months and had arrived early so they could catch up a bit.

But so far they'd talked very little. Every conversation he'd started, she soon ended. Shaye wasn't herself tonight. He'd never seen her so anxious.

He scratched his jaw. Olive must have picked up the moaning from Shaye, he realized, and recently, too. He hadn't thought his sister seriously involved. She was particular in her relationships. She avoided one-night stands as well as long-term commitments. Her life belonged to Barefoot William. He wondered who had caught her attention.

Trace Saunders came to mind, and the thought disturbed Dune greatly. Shaye had been furious with Trace following the boardroom meeting, with no forgiveness in sight. Trace, however, had been determined to see her and apologize.

Dune had warned the man off Shaye. But, knowing Saunders, Trace hadn't listened. The man was stubborn. He owned Saunders Shores and did as he damn well pleased.

Dune hoped he hadn't done Shaye.

Love-hate relationships made strange bedfellows. Arguments often led to great make-up sex, but what future could there be for two such long-standing enemies?

Dune knew his sister would never admit to being with Trace. She was closemouthed.

The Cateses had been ready to kick Trace Saunders to the curb, following his blunder of hiring Marlene Mason. He'd hurt one of their own. They'd been prepared to minimize the event and move the tents and nets off Saunders sand. Shaye only had to give them the word. She had not.

Dune and Kai had talked them down. The tournament would continue as planned. Afterward, the line between families would again be drawn.

Dune wondered if Shaye straddled that line right now.

A few questions might get him closer to the truth. So he pushed a little. "Ready for tonight?" he asked.

"I've been ready since the moment you agreed to the tournament," she said. She continued to tidy up the galley, which was immaculate. She'd scrubbed and rinsed the sink three times. "This is a big weekend for Barefoot William."

"And for Saunders Shores," he added.

She dipped her head. "Trace doesn't need the money like we do. This event will keep our heads above water the rest of the summer."

"*Trace . . . Trace.*" Olive flew from her perch and landed on Shaye's shoulder. The parrot pecked at her hair. "*Handsome but an ass.*"

Shaye inhaled so sharply, Dune swore she'd swallow her tongue. She coughed and couldn't catch her breath. He circled the counter and patted her on the back. "Sounds like Olive's made a new friend," he said casually.

"I said his name in anger," Shaye finally managed. "Olive's a quick study."

"*M-Mmmm, big guns.*" Olive was on a roll.

Shaye put one hand over her heart and looked at the ceiling, as if in prayer. Her cheeks reddened to the color of the long-stemmed roses that decorated her coffee table. Dune had looked but hadn't seen a card.

It was obvious that Olive had eavesdropped and gotten an earful. The Quaker loved to repeat what she overheard.

He leaned a hip against the counter and crossed his arms over his chest. "Big guns," he said slowly. "Cowboys or condoms?"

"Olive likes Westerns," Shaye said. "The older shows: *Gunsmoke, Rawhide, The Rifleman.*"

"*Head 'em up, move 'em out.*" Olive mimicked the opening lyrics to the theme song for *Rawhide.*

Shaye stroked the top of the parrot's head, then rewarded her for the Western music. She reached across the counter and opened a jar of sunflower seeds. She passed the parrot one. Olive accepted it, then flew to her cage to crack the seed and eat it.

"You lucked out," Dune said.

"How so?" asked Shaye.

"Another minute, and Olive would've talked condoms."

Shaye blew him off. "I need to get dressed."

He glanced at his watch. "The invitation said beach casual." He'd worn a *Cinco de Drinko* Jose Cuervo T-shirt and black board shorts. "No need to dress to impress, unless there's someone—"

"There's no one, Dune."

Shaye couldn't fool him. He'd keep one eye on his sister and one on Trace. He'd know with their first look if they'd slept together. A part of him dreaded the truth.

Shaye was ready in no time. She looked pretty and sporty without pretense in a lavender tank top, navy shorts, and purple flip-flops. She'd worn the same clothes time and again; only the blue and silver hair band was new since his last visit. *A gift?* he wondered.

"Ready?" he asked.

She nodded. "Good luck. Tonight's all about you."

"I'll be fine," he assured her. "This isn't my first time with fans and reporters."

"Tell it like it is," Olive squawked as Shaye locked the parrot's cage and they left the houseboat.

Shannon Waite, a female reporter for *Sun Sports* magazine, cornered Dune the moment he entered the ballroom at the hotel. Shannon was good press. Dune had known her for years, and the articles she wrote were truthful, never crossing the line into favoritism or enmity.

She allowed him thirty minutes to mix and mingle, then motioned him onto the balcony. They stood by the railing overlooking the Gulf. Those who weren't partying inside The Sandcastle were doing so on the beach. Torches were lit, and a band played. The music rose to their ears.

Shaye had set the tone for the evening. Her head held high, she'd taken the initiative and approached Trace Saunders, thanking him for his hospitality. He'd nodded, and the mood mellowed.

Dune had watched them both, looking for the smallest sign they were more than acquaintances. Nothing surfaced. They were cordial but distant and now stood on opposite sides of the room. Dune felt comfortable leaving the party for a short time.

He followed Shannon outside. The reporter knew he was in demand and was quick to start her interview. "You've had an amazing season, Dune," she praised as she turned on her palm-size voice recorder. "How does it feel to be halfway through your season with six Open victories for you and your partner, Mac James?"

Dune Cates grinned. "Guess you weren't at our latest victory party."

"I was in Newport, California, covering the Junior Surf Tour," she said with regret. "I heard Mac played strip volleyball on the beach at midnight."

Dune's partner was a wild man both on and off the court. "Mac played against six women in a T-shirt and board shorts. Two missed points, and the man was naked."

"You're more conservative?"

"I prefer to have a woman undress me, not drop my own drawers."

"You and Mac are opposites, then?"

"We train, compete, and room together on the tour, but we have different lifestyles off the court."

"Being top-seeded on the men's tour makes you a target for every male player in the room," she continued. "The press gives you generous coverage, and the corporate sponsors rely on you to bring your A-game to every event. You sell the show. How do you handle the pressure? How do you let off steam?"

"I avoid too much stress," he said. "Mac lets off enough steam for both of us."

Shannon glanced at her research notes. "You have an amazing history with pro beach volleyball. There's been a major reorganization of the sport, but your past speaks for itself. You've taken the King of the Beach victory and were awarded Most Valuable Player and Best Offensive Player several years running. What's left for you this year?"

"More wins."

"You're pretty confident."

"The sun and sand are good to me."

"You're great for the sport," she said. "Female fans call you Beach Heat. I've seen the T-shirts worn in your honor."

He liked the red shirts with his caricature on the front. Woman wore him over their breasts. His face was often cuddled in their cleavage.

"You were injured recently," she commented. "How long can you continue playing in the sandbox?"

Damn, he was only thirty-five. He had lots of volleyball left in him. "I hope to have the longevity and productivity of Karch Kiraly and Sinjin Smith."

"Volleyball gods, both," said Shannon. "You've big shoes to fill."

"We play barefoot."

She smiled at him. "Ready for the 'Man Facts'?"

"Go for it."

"Female fans want to know if you wear a Speedo beneath your swim trunks."

Dune rubbed the back of his neck. A lot of guys protected their junk in case the waistband on their trunks dropped when jumping and spiking the ball. They didn't want to flash the fans in the stand. "Fans are safe" was all he'd say.

"Your ideal woman?" she asked next.

"Someone independent, intelligent, and happy. A woman who doesn't need me to define herself."

"How would she know you're crazy about her?"

"I'd think about her first."

"Is there anything better than sex?"

"Winning." It was a major high for him. "I'm very competitive. I set goals and work to achieve them."

"Do your parents still attend your tournaments?"

"There were fewer events this year than last, and they made it to each one."

"You're back in Barefoot William," she said. "Is it true your family owns the entire town?"

"We call it home."

"How long do you plan to stay?"

"One week. Then Mac and I head back to California."

"You're a workaholic," Shannon noted. "Tournament sponsors hire you for commercials. You've modeled your personal sportswear line in *GQ*. During the off-season, you're a spokesman at volleyball clinics across the country for aspiring players."

"I like to keep busy."

"What do you do on your days off?"

"Sleep in. Dine out with friends. Play cards or see a movie."

"Last question," Shannon wrapped up. "Any engagement news?"

"I'm still single."

She raised an eyebrow. "Rumors say otherwise."

Shannon was referring to Lynn Crandall, who played on the women's volleyball circuit. Lynn now hovered by the door while he conducted his interview. Media considered them a couple, and Lynn believed their press.

They'd dated for a year now, but Dune was close to ending the relationship. He planned to break the news to Lynn before word broke in the article. "I'm free and always easy," he said.

Shannon shut off her recorder. " 'Easy' works for you," she said. "I'll send a photographer to the event tomorrow. Smile pretty." And she left him to his thoughts.

His thoughts were soon interrupted by Lynn. She came to him, a woman standing six foot two to his six-six. She wore heeled sandals that brought them eye to eye.

They were the only two people on the secluded terrace. She curled her hands in the front of his T-shirt and tugged him close. "You didn't mention me in your interview," she pouted. "Shame on you."

She punished him by nipping his bottom lip, then slipping him her tongue. Her red halter dress showed a lot of skin, and her feminine heat embraced him. The lady was aroused. She tried to deepen the kiss, but Dune disengaged. He didn't believe in leading a woman on. He wasn't as into her as she was into him.

The cocktail party rocked. Trace Saunders had gone all out. The food, drinks, and music were first-class. Dune wanted to work the room, embrace family, and get reacquainted with old friends, yet Lynn wanted alone-time with him. She had him cornered now.

Tonight twenty-four top-seeded female and male players would be auctioned off as volleyball partners to the highest bidders. Fans had come from far and wide to participate in the pro/am. Players would go for big bucks. The money raised would benefit Barefoot William.

Tomorrow local commerce would thrive. The two-person teams would hit the beach and sweat volleyball. Souvenirs and sunscreen would be sold and kegs of beer drunk. Everyone would have a good time.

"You're distracted," Lynn said, breaking into his thoughts.

"I'm concentrating on the tournament," he said. "It's important to me."

"And I'm not?" Her expression tightened a fraction.

His slow response made her apprehensive. She tried to get closer, but they were already bumping hip bones. "We're good together," she said. "I love you, Dune."

He didn't love her back.

"Marry me."

Her proposal blindsided him. He breathed deeply as he prepared his answer. He tried to remember the good times before their relationship had turned stale. Those memories were few.

Lynn Crandall was a superfox. Her auburn hair, green eyes, and athletic body left men dumbstruck. Dune had done a double take on their first meeting, then gone on to date her. She'd chased him hard.

From the beginning she'd shown him her fun, sexy side. Only recently had her demands turned ugly. Her beauty only ran skin deep. He didn't do superficial.

The longer he knew her, the less he liked her. She had a love-hate relationship with his popularity. She overlooked his power to promote beach volleyball and only saw the women who crossed his path as potential hookups.

She'd gone territorial on him. She'd turned from babe to bitch in the blink of an eye, and she didn't wear jealousy well.

She had more invested in their relationship than he did. He'd never led her on, never promised more than a good time. "*I do*" was nowhere near the tip of his tongue.

Their relationship was over.

He just wished there was a way to break it to her gently. He took a step back, and her gaze narrowed as he distanced himself. "What the hell's going on?" she asked. Anger etched the corners of her mouth. The scene was about to head south.

He crossed his arms over his chest, tucked his thumbs into his armpits, and kept his cool. He needed to give her an honest answer. One she couldn't twist to her liking.

"We've had a good time, had a lot of fun," he said.

"It's only going to get better," she rushed to say. She attempted to close the gap between them, but he took hold of her shoulders, stopping her. A foot separated them, marking his space. Her lips pinched. "What the fuck, Dune?"

"I'm not ready to get married."

Her eyes flashed. "Not now or not to me?"

"Not to anyone for a long time to come."

"You bastard," she hissed. "I put my life on hold for you. I've turned down dates—"

"We were never exclusive," he quietly reminded her. "We were both free to see other people."

"Have you dated other women behind my back?"

He thought of Marlene Mason and their one-night stand. There was no need to toss that into the mix. He and Lynn had hit the end of the road. There was no reason to rile her further.

He held silent and hoped she wouldn't press. He hadn't had time to cultivate a new relationship. Between practice and his celebrity status, he worked fourteen-hour days, six days a week. Sundays he crashed, his only companion a gray Weimaraner named Ghost.

"You said you loved me," she accused.

"Sorry, never did." He hadn't spoken those words to any woman ever, outside his family.

Her face twisted, and she looked downright feral. "You're breaking up with me?"

"We were never officially together."

"You prick." She slapped him the way she spiked a volleyball. The lady had power. Her force could've dislocated his jaw.

His cheek stung, and his left ear buzzed.

He swore she'd loosened a back molar.

Her growled curses turned the air blue as she spun and stormed back into the ballroom. Her fists were clenched, and her stride was fierce. The short skirt on her halter dress swished wildly, flashing the creases between her thighs and bottom.

It was evident she wore a thong.

"Damn." Dune massaged his cheek, then slowly shifted his jaw. Nothing appeared broken, but it hurt like a son of bitch.

He glanced toward the ballroom. The French doors leading inside revealed a room packed with people. Dune recognized nearly everyone in attendance. He needed a moment alone, to clear his head, before returning inside.

By now, word would have spread that Lynn had dumped him. Dune didn't give a damn how the gossip went down. He seldom cared what people said or thought about him.

Anyone who knew him well recognized he didn't do serious. He concentrated on what he loved, and that was beach volleyball.

Those who spent time with Lynn soon realized her moods shifted with the tide. She was unpredictable at best.

Dune moved along the black wrought iron railing that wrapped the fifth-story terrace and looked out into the night. He faced north toward Barefoot William, and from what he could see, fans now packed the boardwalk. Traffic was heavy on the side streets. Car engines revved, and horns honked. The scene was festive, uninhibited, and as energized as Mardi Gras.

Overhead, a small aircraft circled, ready to land at the local airport. Shortly thereafter, a helicopter lifted off. The

Barefoot William charter chopper gave twilight tours along the coastline.

The sun split the horizon, sending fireball reds and oranges across the sand while gilding the Gulf of Mexico gold. Dusk soon diminished all color, and the edge of night flipped the timers on the city lights. The revelers seemed to glow in the dark.

Dune silenced his mind. Lynn Crandall had knocked him off his mark, and he needed to center himself. He breathed deeply, as if preparing for a match. He drew in the peace, the quiet—

The sudden rustling of tall hibiscus shrubs turned his attention toward a corner of the terrace. The outside sconce caught a flash of a dark ponytail, a bare calf, and one sandaled foot. A woman.

Material ripped, and a branch broke as she tugged her T-shirt free. She fell out of the bushes and landed flat on her ass. She shoved to her feet as fast as she had fallen. She wobbled a little.

Paparazzi? Doubtful. She didn't have a camera.

A fan? If so, she didn't rush him.

Curious, Dune crossed to her. He checked her out as she brushed herself off, then straightened. He guessed her height at five foot two, give or take an inch. Her hair was brown; her eyes, the color of evergreen. Orange reading glasses sat crookedly on her nose. Her earrings were flowers, but two different styles. One was a pink carnation, the other, a purple tulip.

She had nice skin, he noted, fair and soft-looking. Youthful. He guessed her to be twenty-two or three, too young for his taste. Her lips were full but pursed. Her body was hidden beneath an oversized *Beach Heat* T-shirt and baggy gray leggings.

She was staring at him now, not with wide-eyed admiration but rather blankly. He raised an eyebrow and waited for her to speak. Not a word was forthcoming.

He rolled his shoulders. There was only one main entrance onto the terrace. He wondered how long she'd been hiding and how much she'd heard of his conversation with Lynn Crandall.

"Who are you?" he finally asked.

She hesitated. "Sophie."

"I'm Dune Cates."

"Better known as 'prick' and 'bastard'?"

He ran one hand down his face. "You heard?"

"I was on the balcony long before you arrived," she said. "Your girlfriend ripped you a new one."

"She's not my girlfriend," he corrected. "You should've made your presence known."

"I don't like crowds."

"There were only two of us."

"That's two too many for me."

He tilted his head, looked down at her. "What were you doing in the bushes?"

"I'm clumsy." She sighed. "I tripped on a planter and took a nosedive right before you arrived." She patted her waistband. "I have an invitation. I wasn't spying on you. I was merely on the outside, looking in."

Dune wondered if she worked at the hotel or if she was employed by the Saunders Group. "The action's in the ballroom. Drinks, music, press."

"I'll move inside once the auction starts," she said.

"You plan to bid?"

"Bid and win. I want to play in the event."

He narrowed his gaze. "You're short."

"My partner will be tall."

True, all the top-ranked male players were six-two or more, and money talked at the auction. While appearances could be deceiving, Sophie didn't look rich enough to win a partner. And landing in the bushes showed her lack of coordination.

The French doors to the ballroom opened, and Mac James called out, "I heard Lynn broke up with you, dude." He chuckled. "She's hoping no one bids on you."

Dune shook his head. "Lynn will be greatly disappointed," he said. "My fans won't let me down."

"The auction starts in five," said Mac.

"I'll be right there." He looked back at Sophie. She stood in shadow, a small smile on her face. "See you inside?" he asked, including her. He was always nice to the fans. She nodded.

Sophie watched him leave. Dune hadn't remembered her, but that was to be expected. They'd met seventeen years ago, when she was seven, and he, eighteen.

She could still recall that long-ago moment. Dune Cates had made a big impression on her. It had been a Friday, and she'd been on her bike, riding home from school. Her backpack had slipped off one shoulder and knocked her off balance. She was a chubby, uncoordinated kid, and when her bike tipped, she fell hard.

Her glasses flew off, and the zipper on her backpack split. Her books skidded across the pavement.

She had so many books to gather. Her last stop of the day had been at the elementary school library. With the weekend ahead, she'd stocked up on reading material. She wasn't into sports but found a great escape in fairy tales.

A horn had honked, and a car swerved around her. She looked up and noticed she'd stopped traffic. The more she hurried, the clumsier she became. Books dropped as fast as she picked them up.

Her classmates passed her on their own bikes and snickered. She wasn't popular. She had only one close friend, whose mother picked her up each day.

No one came to help her, until Dune Cates slowed down.

She heard a motorcycle come to a stop and saw a teen-age boy dismount. He came toward her, wearing a Bare-foot William volleyball jersey, worn jeans, and beat-up Nikes. He stood over her, so very tall. She leaned way, way back to get a look at his face. His blond hair was long, and his eyes were a lion-gold. A heartbeat of seconds, and he became her first crush.

"What's your name?" he asked as he collected her books.

"Sophie," she told him.

"I'm Dune." Last names were never exchanged.

In less than a minute he replaced her books in her back-pack. He fooled with the zipper and got the teeth back on track. He then helped her to her feet.

"Nasty cut," he'd commented about the scrape on her chin.

She'd ignored the cut until it started to bleed. She touched her fingers to the sore and winced. She needed a Band-Aid.

He returned to his motorcycle, flipped open the small storage compartment behind the seat, and retrieved a wet wipe and a superhero Band-Aid. Sophie thought it was the greatest Band-Aid in the world. Dune gently applied it over her scrape after using the wipe.

"I have a sister," he said. "Shaye's a tomboy. She prefers Superman to Cinderella."

Sophie favored Snow White.

He went on to pick up her bike. He tested the front wheel to be sure it was straight after her fall. He then handed her the backpack. "Can you make it home now?" he'd asked.

She'd given him a small, shy smile. "I'm almost home." She had six blocks to go before reaching her gated com-munity.

He'd patted her on the shoulder and said good-bye, then climbed back onto his motorcycle and started the engine with a rumble. She'd watched him ride off, and a piece of her child's heart had gone with him.

It had saddened her years later to learn he was a Cates and therefore off-limits to a Saunders like herself, but she'd never forgotten his kindness.

Tonight, Dune had once again towered over her, yet she hadn't felt dwarfed. She liked his shaggy blond hair and lean face. He wore the cocky confidence of being at the top of his game, of knowing his worth and accepting his place.

Eleven years separated them, but Sophie disregarded age when it came to the heart. She'd been a fan of the man for as long as she could remember. Hero-worship came into play. She'd come to the cocktail party to catch a glimpse of him. And she had every plan to bid on him.

She drew on all her inner reserves. She didn't like crowds. She preferred solitude. Tonight she forced herself to slip inside the ballroom, even if it meant hugging the wall, which she did.

She stared in awe as the Cates and Saunders families came together for a common cause. This moment had been a hundred years in the making. This was a historic night.

She scanned the room and found Shaye Cates standing by the dolphin ice sculpture at one end of the buffet. The woman was as gorgeous as she was courageous, Sophie thought. She fought for her family and all she believed in.

Trace Saunders stood a few feet from Shaye. Sophie saw him glance at her, all hot and hungry-eyed when he believed no one was looking. Shaye would then blush, but she didn't walk away.

Sophie's romantic heart skipped a beat. They were involved. She could feel their heat clear across the room.

When had they become a couple? she wondered. Not a public couple, but two people meeting in secret.

Her stomach sank. Should her assumption prove true, Shaye and Trace would face considerable controversy. Their families wouldn't accept a marriage between these two rivals. They would have a lot to endure.

She had no time to dwell on their situation. The auctioneer mounted the dais, and the pro players gathered on his left. He went on to rattle off their names and statistics, then opened the bidding.

No player sold for less than a thousand dollars. Lynn Crandall went for two thousand and Mac James for five. The crowd was heating up, getting rowdy, in anticipation of Dune Cates. He was the hometown boy, and there were both new fans and old friends to raise each bid. He'd left behind numerous girlfriends when he'd qualified for the tour. They were all in attendance.

A few older women were eyeing him as well, all stylish cougars with unlimited funds. Sophie would have to match their bids. She inched along the wall, pushing aside the long, sheer, swagged drapes to get closer to the front.

"Dune Cates, everyone," the auctioneer called out, and Sophie focused on the man at center stage.

He made her heart race, and she didn't even know him, outside of exchanging a few words on the balcony. She wasn't foolish enough to think him perfect, but physically, he did it for her. She loved tall, athletic men.

"Three thousand." A woman near Sophie placed her bid. Dune smiled.

The brunette was far more his type than Sophie would ever be. Tanned to a berry-brown, the woman stood tall in her bikini top and short-shorts. She reminded Sophie of Lynn Crandall.

Women went nuts for Dune. They also joined forces

and combined finances to bid on him. Finally, a group of five offered seventy-five hundred.

Sophie knew what he was worth to her and how much she could spend. The room grew quiet as everyone waited for the auctioneer to close the bidding.

"Going once, going twice," said the auctioneer, all the while scanning the ballroom for a final offer.

Do or die. Sophie cleared her throat, yet her voice was more squeak than shout when she raised, "Ten thousand."

Women loudly bemoaned the fact that Dune had slipped through their fingers. Curious gazes soon settled on Sophie. She knew what they saw: someone short, her ponytail messy, her clothes a last-minute grab. It had taken two hours for her to talk herself into attending the cocktail party.

She was far from pretty, yet a cosmetologist had once told her that she had great skin. She always protected it from the sun.

The auctioneer waited several beats before rapping his gavel. "Sold!" he yelled, and he motioned Sophie toward the dais.

Necks strained, and she heard a few snickers. She didn't care. She'd set out to win Dune Cates, and she had. She hoped this wasn't the biggest mistake of her life.

She tripped over her own feet, twice, as she worked her way through the crowd. Silence held sway in the room. She heard a sharp intake of breath from near the buffet but ignored it. She wouldn't let anyone discourage her.

Dune's smile relaxed her. He reached out his hand and helped her onto the small stage. He looked at her curiously, seemingly surprised at seeing her again so soon.

"Dune Cates," the announcer said, "meet your amateur partner . . ." He held the microphone before Sophie, waiting for her name.

She licked her lips, then said, "Sophie Saunders." A

stunned silence swept the ballroom, followed by moderate applause. The quiet lasted only so long. Soon questions rose all around her.

"Isn't she Trace's sister?"

"A Cates-Saunders matchup?"

"She sure is short."

"Dune doesn't look happy."

Her name had set him off, Sophie realized. Dune was pissed. Tension rolled off him in waves. He clenched his jaw so tightly, she was certain he'd crack a back tooth.

He took her by the hand and led her off the dais. His grip was firm, and his stride was long. She could barely keep up. They had nearly reached the main entrance when her brother, Trace, stopped them cold. Sophie was not surprised to see Shaye Cates by his side.

"Hello, Sophie," said Trace. He curved his arm about her shoulders, a very protective gesture.

Eight years separated them, but he was her big brother and had always looked out for her. His expression questioned her sanity. He waited patiently for her to explain.

"I love volleyball but seldom get to play," she said. "I'm too shy, too short, and too clumsy. I was able to buy into the tournament. I bid on Dune, and we're now partners."

Dune cut her a look. "I had no idea you were a Saunders."

"My money's not good enough to support your town?" Her boldness surprised not only her, but the others, as well. She wasn't known for raising her voice. She'd never stood up to anyone, yet she refused to back down now. The tournament was all-important to her. This was her weekend with Dune.

"You spent a lot of money," said Shaye.

"It was mine to spend," Sophie justified. "My trust fund's collected a lot of dust."

"Sophie, Sophie," Trace said, unable to wrap his mind

around her bid. "Dune's injured, and you've only played volleyball twice in your life."

"That's three times, including tomorrow," she said.

"I wish you'd reconsider," said Trace. "You fly like Peter Pan."

Dune wasn't a whim. He fascinated her. He had for years. "I'm not changing my mind."

Dune grew tired of their argument. He bent toward Shaye, ignoring Trace. "Sophie won me, so bank her check," he said. "We're headed to the beach. I want to locate an empty net and see what she's got."

She had very little, Sophie knew, but she'd give it her all. Strangely, Dune still held her hand. His warmth gave her a sense of security. The man was ranked number one on the pro tour, while she was an underachiever.

Win or lose, they were partners through the double-elimination.

Dune and Sophie lost their first match beneath the mid-morning sun. It was a complete and utter disaster. They played Lynn Crandall and her partner, Bill Wesley, from Atlanta, Georgia. Bill swore he was Lynn's biggest fan.

There was no specific volleyball attire required. Lynn wore a tiny bikini, while Sophie chose an oversized *Beach Heat* T-shirt and walking shorts. She sunburned easily and needed to keep as much skin as possible covered. Trace brought her knee pads. Dune placed a *Barefoot William* baseball cap on her head to shield her eyes against the sun. Still, she squinted.

The pro/am was structured for one set and not a full match. The first team to hit twenty-one and lead by two points moved ahead in their bracket.

From the first serve, Sophie wasn't prepared for Lynn Crandall. She recognized from the outset that Lynn wasn't on the court to have fun. She was out to defeat Dune.

The woman was intense. Sophie was the weakest link, and Lynn's serves and jump spikes rained down on her. The game moved fast, and Sophie had little time to recover from each hit.

After eight straight offensive points, Sophie felt shell-shocked. Dune called a time-out. He and Lynn then met at the net, where they exchanged words. Hissing words from the sound of it. Sophie caught only bits and pieces of their conversation.

"—take it easy—" said Dune.

"—not my fault she sucks—"

"—sportsmanship. I'll stop the game."

"No mercy rule. Screw you." And Lynn returned to the baseline for her serve. She eased up for all of ten seconds.

Sophie had little time to admire Dune's play; she had to keep her mind on the game. He looked amazing in his dark sunglasses and navy board shorts, sporting his own designer logo. He had a muscular chest and strong arms. His overhand serve was powerful, precise, and pure masculine grace.

She was the "setter" on their two-person team. Pass, set, hit. She touched the volleyball second. The sequence rapidly fell apart with each of Lynn's serves.

Lynn targeted Sophie, forcing her to "dig." Sophie wasn't afraid to dive in an attempt to pass the attacked ball. She just wasn't successful. Her breasts felt bruised and her stomach flattened. She ate a lot of sand.

More than once, her hands got tangled in her baggy T-shirt. Her baseball cap continually fell off. Dune helped her up each time. He gripped her shoulders with big hands and set her straight. He patted her on the back and told her "Good try." His words kept her going.

She exhaled, and managed one solid "bump," a forearm pass, shortly thereafter. The ball had decent height, and Dune got the "kill," successfully putting it away.

The crowd rose and applauded their effort.

Boos eventually rose, growing in strength whenever Lynn slammed Sophie with the ball. Sophie found herself playing more dodgeball than volleyball. She wasn't adept at either sport.

Dune's serve was all that saved them from a skunked set. After thirty minutes, they suffered a 21–5 loss.

Their team moved to the losers' bracket.

Lynn gave her partner a high five, then sneered at Dune and Sophie. Dune glared back, but Sophie was too busy brushing off sand to respond. Her tongue felt gritty, and she needed to rinse the beach taste from her mouth. She was certain her cheeks were red and raw from being tattooed by the ball. She ran her fingers down her nose to be sure it wasn't broken. She was on the verge of a major headache.

She looked up at Dune just as he looked down at her. She noticed he supported his hurt wrist with his good hand. The corners of his mouth were drawn. She was suddenly more concerned for his injury than the sting in her cheek. "Do you need a pain pill? I have baby aspirin in my purse."

Baby aspirin? Sophie was serious, Dune Cates saw, so he swallowed his smile. "I'm fine," he assured her, even though his wrist ached like a son of a bitch.

His orthopedist had ordered therapy and rest, yet Dune refused to let Shaye and his family down. The crowd was larger than expected. The tournament would save their summer.

He now stood near the net amid a checkered play of shadows. The fans quickly dispersed, moving toward the food tents. Shaye and Trace would be monitoring crowd control.

Dune removed his sunglasses and studied Sophie. She was tough for someone so small. No matter their loss, her smile still came easily. She'd taken hit after hit when she should've ducked. Lynn Crandall had been brutal.

Sophie's baseball cap was askew, and her soft, pale complexion was marred by red blotches. Her bottom lip was slightly swollen. She had sand burn on her elbows and shins from diving for the ball. One knee pad wrapped her ankle. Her shoulders slumped, not from defeat, but from exhaustion.

"When do we play again?" she asked, pulling a face when flecks of sugar sand slipped into her mouth.

Without conscious thought, Dune brushed his thumb lightly across her lips, removing the remainder of the sand. His thumb stalled over the fullness of her lower lip. *Soft, pink, pliant,* he thought, *a kissable mouth.*

The rush of Sophie's warm breath across his palm shook him. Her eyes were wide, and she looked star-struck. That disturbed him greatly.

He lowered his hand and slapped his thigh. He was a man blessed with athletic ability, no more, no less. Yet male fans kissed his ass, and females worshiped him as a volleyball god. He couldn't control their misconceptions, but he could jar Sophie back to reality.

"Our next set is tomorrow morning at nine," he told her. "We have to work our way through the losers' bracket to play in the finals."

"The finals?" She blinked her disbelief.

"Hadn't you planned to win?" he asked.

She gave a self-deprecating laugh. "Look at me," she said. "My eyes are nearly level with the bottom of the net. I'd need wings to hit the ball over it."

"I can't make you taller," said Dune, "but I can teach you to play smarter."

Sophie sighed. "I appreciated your advice from last night, and I was able to concentrate and tune out the crowd."

They'd walked the beach after the auction. He'd steered

her toward the farthest volleyball court, seeking some privacy. People were scarce, but the seagulls were numerous, diving just offshore for their dinner.

Sophie had grown shy, and he'd coaxed her to talk. She'd admitted to hating crowds and being the center of attention, yet she'd had the guts to bid on him. He'd found that interesting.

He'd tried to ease her fears. He forewarned there would be hundreds of fans in the stands, and the cheering would get loud and very distracting. He told her to ignore the noise and keep her mind on the game.

He went over the basic rules and demonstrated a few easy moves. He'd tossed the ball to her from the opposite side of the net to test her return. The ball never made it back to him, although once it rolled underneath.

After watching Sophie play today, Dune was quick to realize that she had no background in volleyball or sports in general.

He needed to play harder, and Sophie would have to toughen up. He wanted her in fight-mode. To get there, she required practice.

The fans filtered back to the stands, looking for the best seats for the afternoon match. His tour partner, Mac James, was up next. Mac was a crowd-pleaser.

"Catch a shower and a nap, and meet me back on the beach at four," he said.

"For happy hour?" she asked.

"For setting drills."

Dune planned to recruit Mac to help Sophie prepare for tomorrow. Mac could play one side of the net, he and Sophie the other.

She gave him a small wave as she turned toward Saunders Shores. The woman was cute but uncoordinated. The sand tripped her every other step.

Nine

Four o'clock, and Sophie was prompt. Dune's chest gave an unfamiliar squeeze at her approach. He took a deep breath and squelched his pleasure in seeing her. He hadn't ever met anyone quite like Sophie Saunders.

She was a lightweight, and he felt oddly protective of her. He wouldn't let her get smacked by the volleyball again tomorrow. Fortunately, none of the other players were out for blood like Lynn Crandall.

Sophie now stood before him wearing another loose-fitting pink T-shirt and a baggy pair of khaki shorts. Her face, forearms, and calves were sunburned from only an hour on the court. She had a bruise above her right eye, and her left cheek remained red, as if she'd been slapped.

"I brought an energy drink," she said, holding up a can of Surge.

"I've got a beer," said Mac James, coming up behind her.

Dune held the volleyball. "Sophie, this is Mac," he said, introducing them. "Drinks aside, let's practice."

Sophie and Mac set their beverages at the base of one galvanized metal pole. They then came to the net.

"Are you taking us both on?" Mac asked, teasing Sophie. "Two against one."

Dune watched as his partner gave Sophie a quick hug, putting her at ease. Sophie blushed.

"I saw part of your set today," Mac continued. "One of you—and I'm not pointing fingers—needs to wear a helmet on the court."

Sophie actually grinned. "I took one too many hits to the head."

"Lynn Crandall rattled your brain, sweetheart," said Mac. "When you make the finals, it will be payback time."

"Right now, I'm hoping to make a decent showing in the losers' bracket," she said.

Dune tossed Mac the volleyball, and Mac moved six feet to the right. "For the moment, I'm going to take Dune's place and lightly toss you the ball," Mac said. "Dune will stand behind you and get you in position for the setup."

She nodded, all wide-eyed and nervous.

Dune discovered that instructing Sophie rubbed him the wrong way—or the right way, depending on your point of view. She was short, and he was forced to hunch over her. *Way* over her. The top of her head skimmed his chin. With each stretch of her arms, her shoulders brushed his chest, and her bottom bumped his thighs. Once she jumped and jarred his nuts.

Sophie stumbled, a lot. He grabbed her when she tipped forward and when she tripped over her own feet. Each time she landed flush against him. Her scent was innocent. Her hair smelled like baby shampoo. Her skin was as soft as baby lotion. Yet her body gave off a woman's heat.

His cock responded to her.

His loose board shorts grew tighter in the front.

What the hell? The women in his life were tall, tanned, and toned. Athletic. Sophie was the complete opposite. He was so distracted by her that he didn't see the ball Mac hit his way. It knocked Dune in the head. He blinked and refocused. And Mac laughed at him.

"Want to trade places?" asked Mac.

Dune looked at his partner's T-shirt, which read *Got Time for a Quickie,* and decided against the switch. "We're just fine," said Dune, his tone sharper than he'd intended.

Sophie looked over her shoulder, her expression serious. "I'm improving, right?"

"Keep thinking positive," Dune said.

She bit down on her bottom lip. "Am I ready to spike?"

"You're not quite there," Dune said, not wanting to discourage her. He had, however, seen her play. No matter how high she jumped, she'd never put the ball away.

She rested her hands on her hips, looking from one man to the other. "Am I the worst player in the pro/am?"

Mac was no help. He dodged her question by going for his beer. He leaned against the metal post, eyed Dune, and sipped slowly.

"You have the most heart, Sophie," Dune finally said. "Technique keeps the set moving, but heart wins in the end."

She thought about his answer, only to ask, "Do I embarrass you?"

Sophie was concerned about his image. He had the urge to shake her, then hold her, and tell her fan perception meant little to him. He was his own man.

"You make a good partner, Soph." Mac spoke from the sidelines. "You could've had me for five grand."

Sophie gave Mac a small smile. "Thanks."

Looking at Sophie now, Dune found she appealed to him, which made him very uneasy. He realized his reassurance was important to her. His response would make or break her spirit, so he cut Mac a look and said, "Embarrassment is having your partner hit you in the back of the head with the volleyball during match point at the Hunting Beach Championships. The discomfort continues when your partner holds up the winning trophy and tells the fans it's anatomically correct. *And,"* he stressed, *"a long-ago moment I've never been able to forget, my partner mooning the backline judge over a foot fault."*

"It wasn't a *full* moon," Mac argued.

"It was a bad moon rising," said Dune.

Sophie covered her mouth and giggled.

Dune grinned as well. "You'd never embarrass me," he told her, and he meant it. "You may not be great at volleyball, but I'm sure you're terrific at . . ." He let her fill in the blank.

After a long pause, Dune was suddenly afraid he'd set her up for a fall. Surely she was good at something.

"Reading," she said. "I devour books, often one a day."

Dune narrowed his gaze on her. He suddenly felt as if he'd met her in another time and place, but he decided that was ridiculous. She was a Saunders, and he was a Cates.

"I like to read," Mac told her.

"*Playboy* doesn't count," Sophie said, then blushed.

Mac poked his tongue inside his check. "I've been known to read more than magazines."

"He buys how-to books but has never fixed a leak, refinished a table, or built a birdhouse," Dune said.

"I'll do it all when I retire," said Mac.

Retire hung in the air between them, Dune noted. He caught Mac looking at his wrist. His partner was concerned about Dune's scaphoid fracture. There was no guarantee Dune would fully recover. A weak wrist would kill his game.

The future was not Dune's problem—not at the moment, anyway. He again focused on Sophie. "More practice?" he asked.

She was willing. Mac ducked under the net, and Dune

NO TAN LINES   207

stepped to her left. He was done wrapping his body around her. She felt too damn good for his liking. It was time to simulate an actual set. He nodded to Mac to toss the ball over the net, which he then passed to Sophie.

He was surprised by her concentration and effort. She managed to set fifteen of his fifty passes. She was so ec-static, he was afraid she'd hyperventilate.

"Dude, it's getting dark," Mac finally said.

Dusk was upon them. Dune glanced at Sophie. Her eyes were wide, her lips parted, her breathing rapid. It was time to call it quits. "We're done," he said.

Sophie wasn't certain they should stop. "Are you sure? Practice makes perfect."

"Perfection's overrated," said Mac. "I'm off. I've got a hot date and a cold beer waiting for me at the Sassy Parrot."

Parrot turned Dune's thoughts to Olive, then to Shaye. He'd wanted to keep his sister in his sights, but he had failed in his task. All his concentration centered on Sophie. He needed to locate Shaye now.

He tossed the volleyball into the air several times, while Sophie collected her energy drink from the base of the metal pole. She'd been so into their practice, she hadn't yet popped the top.

"I'll save it for tomorrow," she said, and she stuck the can in the side pocket of her khaki shorts. She looked up at him. "Any last-minute advice?"

"You might consider wearing a swimsuit," he suggested. Her clothes were baggy and hampered her movements. "There's freedom in minimal clothing."

"I don't own a suit."

That surprised him. "But you live near the beach."

She dipped her head. "I've got a fear of the ocean."

"People wade in to their waists, splash, and still have a good time. Some float on air mattresses."

"I prefer staying dry."

Sophie feared crowds and the ocean, whereas Dune had barged through life headstrong and unafraid. "You still need a suit," he insisted. "The shops are open along the boardwalk until midnight. Let me locate Shaye, and she'll go with you."

"She might not be available."

"I'll make her available." If his sister was anywhere near Trace Saunders, Dune would separate them quickly.

Sophie Saunders soon found herself in Shaye Cates's capable hands. Dune had tracked down his sister in the souvenir tent. Shaye was busy taking money, and, two tables over, Trace replenished stock. Tournament flip-flops, baseball caps, visors, and key chains sold as fast as he could lay them on the tables.

Shaye looked up and smiled. "We've sold all your 'Beach Heat' T-shirts," she told Dune. "I placed an overnight order for another five hundred. I'll meet the truck at Three Shirts at dawn."

"The event drew a bigger crowd than even I expected," Dune said, amazed by the outcome.

Shaye rubbed the back of her neck, then rolled her shoulders. "It's all thanks to you, the other players, and the fans. Everyone donated a weekend in support of Barefoot William."

She glanced at Sophie. "Are you having fun?"

Sophie scrunched her nose. "I need to buy a swimsuit."

"I volunteered you to help her," Dune said. "We're not going to move up in the brackets with Sophie getting lost in her clothes."

Shaye agreed. "You'll be more flexible wearing less."

The thought of fewer clothes made Sophie sigh. Even playing naked wouldn't help her game. But it seemed a swimsuit was inevitable.

"What are your plans for tonight?" Shaye asked Dune.

"Mostly catching up with old friends," he said. "I've been invited to a couple of parties."

"What about you, Sophie?" Shaye included her, too.

Dune looked at her, his gaze curious. "Date night?" His question sounded stiff to Sophie's ears.

Sophie shook her head. "I'll shop for a suit, then head home to a good book."

Dune appeared relieved, or maybe she read more into his expression than was actually there. The man was a sports celebrity and a Cates. She was a bookworm and a Saunders. They had the volleyball tournament between them. That was their only link.

Trace joined them. He hugged Sophie, glared at Dune, and ran his gaze over Shaye. Sophie noticed Shaye's soft blush and the slight curve of her brother's smile.

Dune also caught their exchange. His jaw set, granite-hard. "See you in the morning," he said to Sophie; then he eyed his sister. "Tomorrow's another big day. I hope you get some sleep." He hit Trace with one final shot, which Sophie didn't understand. "See you, Big Guns."

Trace went very still.

Shaye stood like a statue.

Sophie was confused. She'd never heard her brother called Big Guns. It sounded Western.

Dune and his sneer left the tent.

Shaye came around slowly. Releasing a soft breath, she said, "Let's go, Sophie. I need to stop by Goody Gum-drops first to check stock. Waves is a few doors down; the shop has great swimsuits."

"How about a trivia question for a bag of candy corn?" asked Trace.

Shaye obliged. "Chewing gum has what unique ingre-dient?" she asked.

Trace narrowed his gaze in thought. "Rubber," he said.

"Correct," Shaye said. "Your prize: a bag of patriotic candy corn, in celebration of the Fourth."

Shaye was kind, giving, and good for her brother, Sophie noted. Trace could be a little uptight at times, and Shaye brought him down to earth.

They had sweets trivia between them, a small but common bond. They also exchanged white-hot looks. Anyone in their path would be singed. Sophie was feeling quite warm at the moment herself. She was certain they also shared a bed.

Sophie caught them brushing hands as Shaye cleared the tent. They smiled over the contact.

The two women climbed onto the Saunders Shores boardwalk and blended with the fans. There were people everywhere. The party atmosphere closed around Sophie, and she was carried along by the crowd. People bumped her, and she tripped over her own feet. She felt trapped and couldn't catch her breath. Her stomach turned.

Shaye noticed her discomfort. She took Sophie by the arm and turned her toward the window of a designer shoe boutique. Shaye pressed them close to the glass. The glass felt cool even after a hot day. The reflection captured only Sophie and Shaye; those passing by were no more than a blur.

"Do you need a paper bag?" Shaye asked, concerned.

Sophie shook her head. "I don't get out much," she admitted. "One day into the weekend, and I'm already overwhelmed."

"Deep breath," said Shaye. "Another block, and I'll hail a pedicab."

"I've never ridden in one."

Shaye squeezed her shoulder. "There's a first time for everything."

"Does that first include you and my brother?" Sophie dared.

Shaye shifted uneasily, and her reflection wavered in the glass. "There's really nothing more than the tournament between us," she said.

"Maybe, maybe not," said Sophie. "I like seeing Trace relaxed and having fun. You may be a Cates, but you're good for him. He smiles a lot more now, especially when he looks at you."

"Perhaps life is treating him well."

"There are happy smiles and happily ever after smiles," Sophie said. "Trace has the latter."

Shaye blushed and blew out a breath. "You're very observant, aren't you."

"I don't mix well with others, so I've learned to observe." Sophie felt bad she'd brought up the subject. It wasn't like her to butt in where she didn't belong. "It's none of my business," she apologized.

Shaye met Sophie's gaze in the glass and came clean. "Trace and I are finding our way. We have no idea where our relationship will take us, and we're trying to be discreet." Her voice was soft, worried, and very nervous. "Your brother and I have crossed a line. We've disregarded boundaries set up more than a hundred years ago. Our families will be furious."

Sophie had never talked to anyone's reflection before and found it rather fascinating. She held Shaye's gaze in the glass. "I felt your sparks, and I think Dune did, too."

"Dune." Shaye rolled her eyes. "He's a good man, but he hates Trace. Dune's here for the weekend, but he'll be gone by midweek. He never stays long."

Dune, gone. Sophie felt a catch in her chest that had nothing to do with the crowd. "Your secret's safe with me," she said.

"Center Street may divide us," Shaye said, "but should you ever need a confidante, find me."

Sophie had never shared a secret. She liked the idea.

They stepped back into the revelry. Sophie was jostled along the boardwalk, which seemed to vibrate like an airport's moving walkway. Once they crossed into Barefoot William, Shaye located a bike taxi.

A quick stop at Goody Gumdrops, and they moved on to Waves, a small store with a large selection of swimsuits and henna tattoos. The shop was busy but not overcrowded.

Sophie flipped through the tiny bikinis and knew they weren't for her. She concentrated on the one-pieces but wondered if they had enough stretch. Shaye soon came to her rescue. She selected a cobalt blue tankini and handed it to Sophie.

Sophie went to try it on. She liked the halter top and bikini bottom. Her arms and legs were bare, and she showed only two inches of tummy.

Shaye knocked on her dressing room door, peeked in, and proclaimed the tankini perfect. Sophie changed back into her street clothes then drew Shaye to the display of henna tattoos. She felt daring and decided on an I Love Volleyball tat, depicted with a heart and picture of a volleyball. Shaye smiled, approved. Sophie planned to place the tattoo just above her left breast.

Shaye went on to purchase the suit and henna tattoo for Sophie. Sophie was both shocked and elated. Only a handful of people outside family had ever given her a gift. Shaye was generous as well as kind.

They soon returned the way they'd come. It was early yet, but Sophie found herself yawning. She accepted Shaye's hug at the corner of Center Street and Sawgrass Pass, then headed home. Tomorrow would be a day of volleyball and Dune. She had to make the most of the short time she had with the man.

★   ★   ★

Dune Cates stood outside the players' tent he shared with Mac James and scanned the crowd, looking for Sophie. Their set would start in fifty minutes, and she needed to warm up. He wanted her loose so she didn't pull a muscle.

He finally spotted her. She was the shortest person crossing the sand and was overshadowed by the fans. She wore a floppy straw hat, a green tunic, and cropped pants. She looked uncomfortably warm and out of place on the beach.

Shaye had sent him a text the previous evening: *Mission accomplished.* He'd assumed Sophie would show up in a swimsuit. She was more covered now than she'd been the previous day. Her clothes would seriously limit her play.

Her smile when she greeted him was soft and shy.

Dune knew in that moment he couldn't hold her attire against her. She looked too damn vulnerable.

"I'm here," Sophie told him.

Dune felt inordinately relieved. He held open the flap on the bright yellow tent, and Sophie slipped in. He didn't take her for a quitter, but the game had not been kind to her. She'd been hit in the face and still carried Lynn Crandall's tattoo.

They found Mac and his amateur partner sitting on folding chairs inside the tent, sipping coffee. "Ready to kick some losers'-bracket ass?" Mac asked Sophie.

"I can only hope," she said on a sigh. She looked around the tent, then asked, "Where can I change?"

Dune noticed her small wrist wallet, but that's all she'd brought with her. There was no backpack or duffle bag. "Where's your swimsuit?"

"Under my clothes."

"Don't be modest," Mac said. "Strip down, Sophie baby."

She turned all shades of red.

Dune glared at Mac. Sophie was reserved, and taking off her street clothes before two men seemed to embarrass her. This was a first for him. Most women walked into his tent with suits so skimpy, they bared both tits and ass.

Not so with Sophie Saunders. "Out," Dune said to Mac and his partner. "You play in fifteen minutes—go find your court."

Mac stood, saying, "You're pretty bossy for a loser." He winked at Sophie. "I was all set for your show."

The two exited the tent, leaving Dune and Sophie alone.

"Would you mind turning around?" she asked him.

He met her gaze and shook his head. "We're partners. You're not showing me anything I haven't seen. The women I know live in their swimsuits."

Sophie was not like any female he'd ever met. She was slow in removing her straw hat, slower still in slipping the tunic over her head. Dune stared more intently with every curve she revealed.

Her stomach was flat, and her breasts were full. He noted her newly acquired henna tattoo and smiled to himself. She supported his sport. He liked that.

He watched as she folded her top and set it on a chair. She then went on to remove her cropped pants. The pop of the snap sounded loud in the silence, as did the slide of her zipper. She eased the pants over her hips and down her legs. She straightened then, and her body left Dune speechless.

Her baggy clothes had deceived him. Never would he have thought her so shapely. She was soft, compact, and perfectly proportioned. The deep blue of her suit contrasted sharply with her pale skin.

Damn, she was hot.

Every male on the beach would soon agree with him.

She bit down on her bottom lip, more than a little fearful. He was quick to reassure her. "Nice suit."

"Shaye picked it out."

His sister had good taste in swimsuits but not in men. He'd noticed her in the stands earlier, catching a few sets. Trace sat one row above Shaye. His sister leaned back just enough so her shoulders touched his knees. Their position was not unusual or obvious, but in Dune's mind, it was far too intimate. He planned to have a long talk with Shaye before he returned to California.

He went on to instruct Sophie in a few warm-up exercises. He wanted her muscles loose and her blood pumping. She was cooperative, although clumsy. They were just finishing up when Mac and his partner reentered the tent.

"Whoa, Soph, you are net worthy, babe," Mac said, openly admiring her. "Quick set," he told Dune. "We put it away in twenty."

Dune saw the way Mac eyed Sophie; it went beyond casual interest. Dune watched along with Mac as she straightened her halter top. Her arms were raised, and she flashed a lot of belly.

"You'll need sunscreen," Mac said, crossing to his duffle bag. He selected a bottle, then eased behind Sophie. "I'll do your back."

Dune locked his jaw against telling Mac to take his hands off her. His partner stood too damn close. Mac seemed to apply the lotion in slow motion. He leaned in and playfully blew into Sophie's ear. She shifted uncomfortably, then swatted him when he placed a kiss on her neck.

"I'll do the rest," she said, and she took the sunscreen from him. She was twice as pale as usual with the white lotion on her skin.

Mac appeared let down, Dune noted. Women loved the

wild man of volleyball. Female fans stroked his ego—and anywhere else he needed stroking. It wasn't often Mac got the brush-off. Dune couldn't help smiling. Sophie wanted nothing to do with him. That pleased Dune a great deal.

She stretched a final time, wanting to be fully limber. Dune hated the fact that Mac's gaze never left her ass. Fortunately, her bikini bottom didn't floss.

"My money's on you, Soph," Mac called as they left the tent. "Kill it, babe."

Sophie's steps were slow as they crossed the sand to their court. "I feel naked," she whispered to Dune.

Her suit covered more skin than most bikinis.

Where other females flaunted their body, Sophie was self-conscious. She drew a lot of attention. She looked fresh, cute, vulnerable, Dune thought. Men felt an immediate need to protect her. Hell, he was feeling so now.

He curved his arm over her shoulders and hugged her to his side. She was the perfect height for a leaning post. She felt warm and slippery from the sunscreen. The top of her head reached his heart. The scent of her baby shampoo blended with the tropical scent of the sunscreen.

The sun did them a tremendous favor and snuck behind a cloud. Dune hoped the sun would stay hidden for the next half hour. It obliged.

They got into position, and Dune won the coin toss.

He served first. He stood at the baseline and watched as Sophie dug in her feet and wiggled her butt near the net. Such a sweet ass. Male fans whistled their appreciation. Sophie didn't understand their applause before the set even started. Dune, however, did. Sophie was a show-stopper.

They played against Ted Nathan and his partner. Ted was an aggressive rookie on the tour and out to prove himself. The female fan playing beside him depended on Ted to put the ball away.

Dune's serve racked up five quick points. He made Ted scramble. He found that protecting Sophie was his first priority. She surprised him. She played with heart and agility and was able to set up several solid hits for him.

She looked so stunned with each successful assist, he couldn't help laughing. "You're in the zone, Sophie," he praised.

She blushed through her white sunscreen.

By the grace of the volleyball gods, they eliminated Ted and his partner and went on to win the next two sets as well. They'd made the finals in the losers' bracket. They had one set yet to play.

Had this been a sanctioned double-elimination, the winners of the losers' bracket would have the opportunity to play the finalists in the championship bracket, but not so here. Shaye preferred to award trophies to both brackets. Her town, her rules. Dune was fine with her decision.

He looked at Sophie and noticed she was fading fast. She was a woman born to air-conditioning, not to the beach. The afternoon sun had come out of hiding, and it was wicked hot. He didn't want her collapsing on the court.

It was now three o'clock, and they'd been given an hour break. Sophie sat in a chair in their tent, her eyes closed and her lips parted. He wondered if she'd fallen asleep.

He was pumped and started pacing. Word had swept the tents that Mac and his partner had eliminated Lynn Crandall and Bill Wesley in the championship set. Mac had shown no mercy. Lynn and Bill had dropped into the losers' bracket.

Dune ran one hand down his face. He didn't want to face Lynn again in the double-elimination. Lynn would once again go after Sophie with a vengeance. Dune couldn't allow it.

Over the course of the hour, he'd decided winning

wasn't everything where Sophie was concerned. She was wiped out, and he didn't want to push her further. The urge to forfeit the set was a first for him. He'd never walked away from anything in his life.

Sophie came awake with a start, as if her internal alarm clock had gone off. She pressed her palms to her eyes, then patted her cheeks. "I fell asleep," she said with a shy smile.

"It's been a long day," he said.

"I'd better power up with Surge."

Dune wasn't certain the energy drink would give her the boost needed to battle Lynn Crandall. "Mac won his bracket," he told her.

It took several seconds for the ramifications to soak in. She frowned slightly. Mac's win affected them greatly. "We again face Lynn." She swallowed hard and asked, "What can we do?"

"We could forfeit, Sophie."

"I'm not a quitter."

"Neither are you an athlete." She was soft, vulnerable, and, at times, fearful. "Remember yesterday?" he asked.

She nodded. "I got creamed."

"Today could be worse." He was frank.

She took a few minutes to weigh the odds. "How's your wrist?" she asked him.

His injury had started to throb during their last set. His little finger was now numb, yet he refused to show any weakness. He would rest and get extra therapy once the weekend ended.

"It's a little sore," he admitted. "But I still have some play in me."

"So do I," she said slowly. "Let's do this."

Dune went with her decision.

He grabbed his sunglasses, then offered Sophie his hand. She took it. Her palm was small and soft and got lost in his. He tightened his fingers around hers, hoping to reassure her that, whatever happened, they were still a team. She squeezed back, and he felt the pulse in her wrist against his own. Her heart beat like a hummingbird.

The single set proved the longest thirty minutes of his life. The stands were filled, and there was standing room only. Women climbed onto men's shoulders to get a better view. A local camera crew filmed the game.

Lynn won the coin toss. She served three aces in a row, all directed at Sophie. There was something different about Sophie today, Dune noticed. Her gaze was fixed on Lynn, and she seldom blinked. Do or die, Sophie was attempting the impossible. She pushed hard, and her setups were high enough for him to put the ball away.

The score rose, and Lynn became her own worst enemy. She turned on her partner when he made a mistake. Dune saw this as a very good sign.

The rallies were short, and the kills were vicious. Dune made Bill Wesley dance. His overhead serve came down at the man's feet.

Fate took a liking to Sophie. She and Dune were ahead by one point, needing a second to win the set. However, it was her serve, and she'd yet to have the volleyball clear the net.

Dune called for a time-out and crossed to her. Sophie was flushed and sweaty and nervous. He bent down and whispered to her, "I have a trick for getting the ball over the net. Pretend someone's face is on it, someone you don't like."

"I like everybody."

She'd missed the point. Dune raised an eyebrow toward Lynn. "Wouldn't you like to get back at her for the tattoo on your cheek?"

"The mark is fading."

Where was her competitive spirit? "You're too damn nice, Sophie," he said. "I thought you wanted the trophy."

Trophy did the trick. "I've never won anything," she said.

"Get your serve over the net, and I'll land us the final point," he promised.

An angel's breath blew Sophie's serve over the net— Dune was sure of it. He wasn't an exceptionally religious man, but he knew divine help when he saw it. He'd take whatever he was given. He wanted this win for Sophie.

Across from them now, Bill stood too close to the net. His setup for Lynn was slightly off center. Lynn jumped, twisted, and smacked the ball with a damning force.

Dune sucked so much air that he swore he'd created a vortex. By all that was holy, the volleyball flew straight into the net. And time stood still.

The silence held and held, finally broken by Lynn's screech. The lady was mad. She stormed off the court and cut through the crowd, elbowing fans out of her way.

Sophie seemed stuck in the sand. She continued to stare at the volleyball that had rolled under the net and was inches from her feet. She'd yet to comprehend that they had won the set.

"It's over, Sophie." Dune came to stand beside her.

Still, her gaze held on the volleyball.

"Sophie?" He shook her shoulder.

Her breath caught, and he felt her shudder. She looked up at him and softly admitted, "I was scared. I saw the look on Lynn's face when she hit the ball. She wanted to ram it down my throat."

Lynn's expression had shown her true colors. "She was out for your front teeth," he agreed.

Sophie gave him a small, watery smile. "We won," she said.

He curved his hand about her neck and turned her toward the baseline. "Shaye's giving out the awards. It's time for us to collect."

He kept Sophie close. She was still dazed, and he understood the aftereffects. Nothing seemed real for several hours after such a triumph. Not until the next day did a player fully appreciate his win.

Mac and his partner got their fair share of applause for taking the championship bracket, but Dune and Sophie got the lion's share. The fans went nuts, not only because Dune had done right by his hometown, but for the simple reason that Sophie was shy and humble and got teary-eyed when awarded her trophy. Everyone loved her.

She became a local media darling. Cameras flashed until they both saw spots. Reporters crowded them. Dune stepped back and allowed Sophie her moment in the sun. She'd been the underdog, and such stories sold newspapers and touched hearts.

Questions were fired at her, and she couldn't answer them fast enough. Dune moved closer and picked up the slack. The interviews went on for an hour.

The reporters then dispersed to post their stories. The talk soon centered on bar-hopping and impromptu parties all along the boardwalk. A bonfire and fireworks would brighten the night sky. Mac would lead the charge for black-light volleyball and skinny-dipping. Bikinis and board shorts would be stolen by the tide.

Dune allowed the remainder of the day to wash over him. Women surrounded him, and he enjoyed their attention. He caught the swing of Sophie's ponytail as she drifted farther away from him. They'd partnered for the tournament, but she no longer had a place in his life.

He watched her walk away. She tripped over her feet on the way to their tent yet clutched her trophy tightly.

Dune detached himself, and the women bemoaned his departure. He took off after Sophie, needing to . . . what?

Ask her if she'd gotten her money's worth? Offer up a remedy for sunburn? *Good-bye* seemed so final. He had no other alternative.

There was no future in their being friends.

She was a Saunders, and he was a Cates.

He let her go.

Ten

Where the hell was Dune? Kai Cates wondered. His cousin had appointed family members to stick close to Shaye throughout the evening because he didn't want Trace Saunders within a mile of her. Kai felt that his cousin could be overbearing at times. Look at the way he'd coerced others into his scheme.

Kai had looked after Shaye for two hours now. Much of that time had been spent in Goody Gumdrops. He'd eaten Junior Mints, blue-raspberry gummy bears, and Lemonheads. He couldn't face another piece of candy. He was in need of a break.

He ran a hand down his face. He wasn't convinced that Trace and Shaye had hooked up, even though Olive had allegedly moaned the day away. The parrot had squawked *"Big Guns,"* a brand of condoms. The words might be new to her, but where she'd heard them was yet to be determined.

Dune's motives were straightforward. He thought to protect his sister not only from Trace, but from her own family as well. Grandfather Frank stood deep in tradition, and he had eyes and ears everywhere. He'd yet to question or comment on the situation, though. He was waiting for the final proof.

Any day, at any time, he could call Shaye onto the carpet for sleeping with the enemy and question her loyalty to her own family. If she was seeing a Saunders, there would be consequences.

Kai exhaled sharply. He knew if Trace wanted Shaye that he'd come for her. No Cates could keep him away. Kai felt the same about Nicole Archer. Tonight was their night, and nothing would stand in his way. Only his word to Dune held him up now. He was about to renege on a promise.

Hoping he wouldn't regret it, he headed over to Shaye and tapped her on the shoulder. "Take a walk?" he asked.

And Shaye agreed. She seemed content to stroll the boardwalk and pier. The fireworks lit up the sky and cast a sparkle over the waves. Shouts and laughter echoed from the beach.

Couples had paired up, and Barefoot William was breathing heavily. He glanced at his watch for the tenth time and saw Shaye smile. "What's so funny?" he asked.

She leaned against the railing on the boardwalk and looked out over the sand. "You're babysitting me when you'd rather be with Nicole."

Shit. "It was that obvious?" he asked.

"You don't wear cologne for me," she said softly, sounding tired. "Trust me, Kai, I won't be seeing Trace tonight or any other night for that matter. Our lives are complicated, and we're giving each other space. You can leave in good conscience."

"Dune will kill me if I leave you alone."

"I'll stand right here until he shows up."

"Promise?" he asked. Dune would be angry should Kai desert her. But, damn, ever since Shaye had told him that Trace and Nicole were no longer a couple, his desire to see her stole his common sense.

They'd both missed the cocktail party. Her shop had been overrun with customers, and he'd been called to

Molly Malone's Diner to repair a refrigeration coil. Tonight they were hoping to make up for lost time.

Shaye nudged him. "Go be with Nicole."

He did so, but not without second thoughts. He'd taken twenty steps when he glanced over his shoulder in hopes she'd kept her word.

There was no sign of Shaye.

The space she'd occupied stood empty. He quickly scanned the boardwalk, looking for a blonde in a yellow tank top. Nothing. What did catch his eye was a tall, broad-shouldered man with dark hair stepping from the shadows and almost instantly blending with the crowd. Son of a bitch.

Trace Saunders, possibly, but Kai couldn't be sure.

If it was, Shaye had put one over on him to be with Trace. His cousin was sneaky, but it had been a long time since she'd played him. He'd forgotten how good she was.

He took out his cell phone and sent Dune a text.

Dune would have strong words for Kai tomorrow.

Kai didn't much care. Tonight it was all about him and Nicole. His stride was purposeful as he dodged townies and rowdies along with street musicians, jugglers, and pedicabs. The carousel spun, and the line for the Ferris wheel wound like a maze.

He wished Barefoot William saw this much action year-round. This weekend was one in a million. The Cateses were grateful to Shaye and Dune. Kai would soon be celebrating their good fortune with Nicole.

Nicole saw Kai a moment before he noticed her. He looked so handsome, her heart quickened. His hair was brushed back, and his cheekbones cut sharp. She liked her men lean. He wore clean-cut slacks, an open-collar shirt, and loafers without socks.

Her eyes moved lower, and she grinned when he reached her. "No tool belt?" she teased.

"No work tonight. I'm here to play."

Nicole was ready to fool around, too.

"Have you been waiting long?" he asked.

"Only a few minutes," she said, when in actuality she'd arrived thirty minutes early, so as not to be late. "The fireworks inspired me to design a collection of rings with lots of flare."

He took her hand. "Rings are good."

"You're better," she said.

He shot her a sexy look that said he liked her honesty. She was not one for games. Directness worked best. She went after what she wanted, and she desired Kai.

A subtle breeze kicked up, billowing her white halter-top dress. Kai watched the material flutter wide like angel wings; his eyes were on her thighs. She felt an instant warmth between her legs, and her thong went damp. Just from his look. She heated even more.

"Where to?" he asked. "You name it, we'll claim it."

They stood in the neutral zone, Nicole knew. Barefoot William stretched north, and Saunders Shores ran south. The Cates boardwalk rocked, loud and wild, while the Saunders side was subdued.

She gave Kai his choice. "Do you prefer the money crowd or free and easy?" she asked.

"You decide, wherever you're the most comfortable."

The man was tough to pin down. The only time she'd moved in the big-money set was when she worked the classy trade conventions as a model. She'd met Trace at a car show. She was posing on a revolving turntable in a tight black silk dress next to a silver Porsche Carrera GT, a big smile and bright lights in her eyes when he spotted her.

By the end of the convention, Trace had opted to buy the car—but only if she came with it. Dinner turned into a whirlwind affair that left them both breathless. When it ended, Trace insisted that she continue living in a suite at The Sandcastle until she got on her feet.

"How about a walk on the beach followed by a drink in my room at the hotel?" she suggested.

"Works for me," he agreed.

Kai knew she lived at The Sandcastle rent free while she was house hunting. She needed a place of her own. She'd narrowed her choices to two homes, both in Barefoot William.

She wanted to live near her shop and her sandlot base-ball team. She had big plans for the Topaz Tarpon, a name she and Kai had debated to death. He'd finally given in, but only after they'd argued nose to nose and she'd kissed him to get her way. She wanted more than a kiss tonight.

She could still picture him renovating her shop, his bare chest, low-slung jeans, and all those rippling muscles. He'd look amazing naked.

He took her hand then, as casually as if they'd been a lifelong couple. They walked along the shore. She slipped off her high-heeled white sandals and looped the ties over one wrist while Kai waded through the foamy crest in his loafers. He didn't mind getting damp.

Nicole breathed in and sighed deeply. She never tired of the beach. The last of the fireworks shot across the night sky, and the darkened Gulf shimmered orange, red, and gold. The torches along the Saunders boardwalk cast min-imal light. They walked slowly, encased in deep shadows.

This was true intimacy, she thought. Two people wrapped in darkness, comfortable with their silence, their bodies brushing, sidestepping the bigger waves.

Beside her, Kai cut his gaze toward the designer bou-tiques, upscale and pricey. He kicked some sand, then slowed. "Do you miss Trace?" he asked.

"You know our history," she said. "We were friends with benefits. He helped me escape Las Vegas, and I will always be grateful. We didn't have much in common. He's Champagne and caviar, and I'm peanut butter and jelly."

She smiled at him. "I'm here with you and have never been happier. I own The Jewelry Box, enjoy psychic readings by Madame Aleta, I'm sponsoring a sandlot team, and I—"

He raised an eyebrow, waiting for her to finish.

"Have a few close friends."

"What if one of those friends wanted to be more?"

"How much more?"

"Heat-your-sheets more."

"I'd have to give it some thought."

"You have three blocks to make up your mind."

"Then what?"

"I'll make it up for you."

He kissed her then, capturing her surprise on his lips. He feathered her mouth with soft kisses that made her sigh. Her breath caught in her throat when he held her around the waist with his strong hands, rubbing his palms up and down her back with long, light strokes.

Her heart raced when he pressed his lips harder against hers. She dropped her high-heeled sandals onto the wet shore and arched her body toward his, pressing her breasts against his hard chest.

The Gulf swirled around their feet as she stood on tiptoe, flushed and aroused. He was all male. She responded to his strength, his scent, his body. The bulge beneath his zipper gave him away. He wanted her.

He deepened the kiss, his tongue mating with hers. He tasted of lemon and raspberry and a hint of mint. She slid her arms around his neck, and he squeezed her waist. A heady warmth flowed through her.

She wanted his kiss to go on and on—

Splash!

A surge of water rushed over her feet and up her bare

legs. She broke the kiss first, jumping from side to side as a second wave crashed around them. Horrified, she looked down at the puffy circle of her white silk dress holding her captive until the wave rolled back out to sea. Standing on the wet shore, she tugged at her skirt, now hugging her hips and bare legs like silken seaweed.

"Where did those waves come from?" she asked, scouring the soggy sand for her sandals. Gone. Snatched by the tide.

"A lucky break for me," Kai said. Paying no attention to his pants soaked up to the knees, he wasted no time in making his move. He scooped her up in his arms.

"Put me down," she said halfheartedly. "I can walk."

"The hotel is only two blocks," he said, cutting across the sand toward the boardwalk. "What's your room number?"

Kai Cates was one happy man.

Nothing turned him on more than having a beautiful woman in his arms, all slick and wet. Nicole clutched him tightly, and every curve of her luscious body pressed into him. She made his groin ache. He was so hard, he could barely walk. The hotel seemed a mile away.

He noticed several stares from the valets when he stomped his loafers outside the main doors, but he didn't want to track sand onto the terra-cotta tiles and Persian rugs. Nicole wiggled her bare feet, and he found her violet-painted toes sexy.

The doorman let them in, and the raised-eyebrow look from the concierge followed them to the elevator, but no one said a word. Discretion was key to a guest's privacy at The Sandcastle.

They kissed until they were both out of breath on the ride to the tenth floor. Kai felt her up and smiled against her mouth when he located her card key in her ample cleavage. She had beautiful breasts, high and creamy with lush brown nipples that he caught a glimpse of. Their full-ness spilled over his palm.

They left the elevator, and his loafers sank into the beige carpet as he carried her down the hallway. He shoved the key card into the lock. The door buzzed, and the green light lit up. He kicked the door open wide.

Silence invited them in. The suite was large—a sitting room and bedroom were separated by a frosted sliding door. Expensive leather furniture formed a crescent around an entertainment center. A bouquet of tea roses and assorted glossy magazines decorated a low coffee table. The lighting was subdued.

A glance toward the bedroom, and he noticed the queen-size bed was turned down. A gift box of Godiva chocolates sat on her pillow. Two bottles of Perrier were available on her nightstand.

He dropped a light kiss onto her brow, then brushed his cheek against her hair. It smelled like the sea air with just enough jasmine to make him moan.

His moan made her shiver. Her breath warmed his neck when she said, "We need to get out of these wet clothes."

He set her down slowly, not wanting to let her go.

She bit down on her bottom lip, then asked, "Towel or bathrobe?"

"Shower and skin."

He put his arms around her and lowered her halter top, cupping full breasts enclosed in filmy lace. The dreamy look on her face told him she liked his touch, and that pleased him immensely.

Kai was as aware of Nicole's hands sliding down the zipper on his trousers as he was of his eager fingers unhooking her bra. Off came the see-through lace, and out spilled her breasts as fast as his erection made an appearance through the opening in his pants.

A slight shift of her hips, and her silk dress shimmied to

the floor. Damn, she was beautiful. She did justice to her thong. The white lace curved and cut in all the right places. It exposed and enticed and made his fingers itch. His palms began to sweat.

In one quick movement, he slid her silky thong down her thighs, then worked his hands back up her long, shapely legs. His fingers lingered over her Brazilian wax. She sighed, aroused. Her hips swayed, and her heat enticed.

He savored her beauty. She stood before him in only her jewelry. A rhinestone floating heart pendant rested between her breasts, sparkling against her pale, smooth skin. Her wavy silver bracelets complemented her narrow wrists, and her long, slender fingers glistened with stacked rings.

He toed off his loafers and removed his shirt, pants, and Calvin's in record time. He grabbed a condom out of his wallet and clutched it in his fist. He kicked his clothes aside and returned his full attention to Nicole.

The lighting cast a romantic glow on her voluptuous body; her naked silhouette was outlined on the walls painted in ocean colors. Her eyes dilated, and her lips parted. "Ready to scrub my back?" she asked.

He didn't believe in making a lady wait. He picked her up in his arms and carried her into the luxurious bathroom with its gold and marble fixtures. Frosted double glass doors inlaid with an artful seashell design opened into a shower built big enough for two. Nicole shot him a look that told him he was to leave no seashell unturned.

They stepped inside, and he set the condom in a soap dish. He turned the fancy knob engraved with *The Sandcastle* logo. Warm water sprayed down on their nude bodies from directly overhead. Tiny but powerful built-in water jets covered the ceiling, splattering them with a refreshing waterfall shower. An outdoor paradise indoors.

The hand-held shower massager would also add to their pleasure. He had plans for that shortly.

He went on to cup her breasts, pulling on her nipples, then licking them. His tongue played with the hard buds until she could stand it no longer. She threw her head back, and her whole body trembled.

Kai knew she was his for the taking, but he wanted more than release. He wanted to appreciate every inch of her. He did so, slowly, and with great dedication.

He filled his palms with rain-forest liquid soap and worked his hands all over her body. He lathered her breasts and gently dotted her hard nipples with clusters of translucent bubbles.

She soaped his chest and ran her fingers through his chest hair, tracing her way down to his groin. She thumbed his navel, teased the hollow on one hip.

He pulled her closer and parted her thighs. He probed her sex with one finger, then two, and her body pulsed against his palm. She shivered in spite of the steamy, hot water.

His breath was ragged as her climax neared.

She brought him to the edge, too. The pendant from her necklace pressed into his chest, leaving the imprint of a tiny heart over his own. Her wavy bracelets drifted over his cock with each stroke of her hand. The slide of silver against skin did him in. He was a goner.

He couldn't hold back any longer.

He wanted this woman, *now*.

He slipped on his condom and backed her against the wall. She gasped as he glided into her, only to groan moments later when he opted for the hand-held massager. High-powered and pulsating, the water beat where their bodies joined, heightening their release.

Nicole climaxed first.

She clutched his back and moaned her satisfaction.

Kai followed, his hips pumping until the end.

His sigh was deep, his body, sated. He returned the shower massager to its wall casing, then held Nicole close.

They were squeaky clean and physically spent when they emerged from the shower a few minutes later. They wrapped each other in guest bathrobes and moved toward the sitting room.

Their clothes littered the floor, and they both took a moment to straighten up. Afterward, she went to the minibar for a bottle of wine, an assortment of cheese and crackers, and a cluster of green grapes. She spread the food on the low coffee table.

He took her hand and drew her down beside him on the plush green leather sofa. He stretched out at one end, and she curled her feet under her and leaned back against him. He slipped his arms beneath her breasts. She felt soft and warm and womanly. He liked her curves.

"We need to talk baseball," he said, kissing the soft spot just below her ear. "Our team is number one and will soon play Southern Trust from Saunders Shores in the all-star challenge."

"Are we any good?" she asked.

"We need to be better," he said. "I'm going to schedule additional practices. I want you at the park, too. The boys think you're hot. They fall all over themselves to get a hit when you're cheering them on."

"They liked their dog tags," she said.

Kai smiled against her hair. She'd designed brass tags with the boys' names and their position on the team, along with the word *Winner* on the back. "You gave them team spirit," he said. "No boy has taken his tag off even to shower."

"How can we beat Southern Trust?" she asked.

"Prayer." He was honest. "It won't be easy. We've never won the summer challenge. In the past we've faced a shutout and the mercy rule that ends the game if one team leads by ten runs."

"That's awful," she said, appalled. "We can't let that happen this year. I want my boys to win."

"So does Shaye," he said, smiling. "She's competitive and cheers until she's hoarse."

"Our team will do just fine," Nicole said, so positive, Kai believed her. "I'm more worried about Shaye and Trace. I'd hoped they would connect after the volleyball tournament. But they seem so distant."

Distant? Doubtful, Kai thought. He was fond of his cousin, but she'd become secretive recently. He wondered what went on behind closed doors at her houseboat.

Trace Saunders nuzzled Shaye Cates's neck. Her skin was amazingly soft. They lay entwined on her double bed. A blue cotton sheet covered their hips. The curtains were drawn against a full moon. Privacy was of the utmost importance to these two. A summer-breeze-scented votive candle burned on the bedside nightstand. The top drawer was open, and the box of twenty-four condoms was down to the last two.

It had been a sexually charged week.

They couldn't get enough of each other.

Trace now lay on his back with Shaye curved against him. Her hair was still damp from their shower. He breathed in her scent, Dove soap and woman. "I like you next to me," he said.

She smiled against his midnight stubble. "I like a man who keeps me in hair bands. Have I thanked you for the red velvet with the filigree bow?"

"You thanked me twice," he said. Their night had been arousing and hot. She now rested her head on his shoulder, and he stroked her arm. "But feel free to do so again."

"Again is good," she agreed, skimming her hand across

his chest and down his abdomen. She dipped a fingertip into his navel, then gently pressed her palm into his stomach, stretching her fingers south.

Trace liked the way she touched him. He was barely able to concentrate as Shaye stroked his cock.

She kissed his right pectoral, then flicked her tongue over his nipple. The moist heat of her mouth did him in. He rolled her under him so fast that she gasped.

He settled over her. Her belly cradled his sex, and her nipples pressed against his chest. She clutched his shoulders and softened into him. Heat flashed across her face, and her body warmed. Her mouth tempted, grazing his, and she parted her lips, welcoming his tongue.

He lusted for this woman.

Her skin was silken, her flesh sensitized.

Her gaze was passion-glazed.

He kissed her with promise and possession, holding nothing back. He made love to her, aware she was his future. He wanted no other.

Her touch was intimate and knowing. She traced the lines and dips of his defined ribs, then went on to circle his sex. The short strokes of her fingers matched the mating rhythm of his tongue.

He took a heartbeat of seconds to locate and fit his condom, then returned to her. His hands moved over her breasts and down until they rested on her thighs. He slowly parted them and, without pausing, pushed inside her. She took him deep. They fit perfectly.

Her breathing came faster.

His chest rose and fell quickly.

She arched as his thrusts grew hurried.

His hips pumped, and her thighs tightened.

He felt her heart beat against his chest, rapid and wild.

His own pulse raged, raw and out of control.

His muscles stood out beneath her hands. She gripped

his back as if she'd never let go. The crescent curve of her nails marked him as hers.

Pleasure took them both to a new level, where intensity and satisfaction collided. He took her closer and closer to orgasm, until her desire crested. He clutched her hips, and he came in a pulsing rush.

He gave her one last kiss before rolling onto his back. Minutes passed as he waited for his heart to calm and his breathing to slow. His focus took even longer. The white-hot flash behind his eyelids had been blinding.

He exhaled his satisfaction. He'd had good sex, even great sex, but never like this. Shaye engaged his mind as much as his body. He was committed to her.

He finally rose and rid himself of the condom. He returned to find her under the sheet, hiding from him.

He shook his head. She knew he wanted to talk, so she ducked to avoid him. He would force her to listen.

Shaye felt the sheet slide down her body and made a mad grab for it. Trace was far quicker and whipped it beyond her reach. He wanted her exposed and vulnerable.

He slid in beside her, drawing her close.

She warmed to his body.

She knew what was coming next. They faced a repeat of the same conversation they'd had the past three days. Her chest squeezed.

"I want you to stay at my place tonight," he said.

"I'm not ready for that yet."

He drew a deep, patient breath and said, "Sleeping only at your houseboat shows a lack of commitment on your part."

"I'm comfortable here."

"Here is easy," he said. "I understand your concern, but you're thinking of your relatives and not us."

"They wouldn't be happy." *Furious* was more like it. She

bit down on her lower lip and tried to delay the inevitable one more night. "This is all moving too fast."

"We've been thirty-two years in the making," he reminded her. "We've known each other all our lives."

"I never liked you until recently."

He had the nerve to smile. "I took an interest in you at the Snack Shack years ago. Even though you were so prickly and mean to me. You gave me stale candy, and I chipped a tooth."

"I'd hoped to send you to the dentist."

"That night was the start of us," he said. "The way I see it, we need to make up for lost time."

She pressed her palm to his chest, right over his heart. "Don't rush me, Trace."

"I know you, Shaye, and you procrastinate. We'd stay like this forever if I didn't push you."

She scrunched her nose. "Is that so bad?"

"It could get a whole lot better."

She sighed. "There's no natural course to the future for us. We're so very different."

Trace rolled onto his side and raised himself up on his elbow. As he looked down at her, his hair was mussed, and he was in need of a shave. He looked rough-and-tumble and incredibly handsome. The sharp slant of his jaw and thinning of his lips told her that he was serious. Very serious.

"We're more alike than you think," he said. "It's time for a heart-to-heart, Shaye."

She squirmed against him. "Can't we at least put on some clothes?"

"Not for this chat."

"Bare my body, bare my soul?"

"Exactly," he said, not cutting her any slack.

She ran her hand over his shoulder and down his arm.

She took his hand. "We need more than great sex between us."

He agreed. "Compatibility goes beyond chemistry. It's what we create together that connects us. We challenge each other, communicate, and negotiate. I've met my match in you."

"I've come to trust you," she could honestly say.

"You've stopped being sneaky."

She bit down on her bottom lip. "But relationships take work, and we're both so busy."

"We could set a time to be home each day, stick to it, and unwind together."

The concept sounded good. "We both love our families," she went on to say, "but they don't like each other."

"We may not be able to change them, but we can respect each other's commitments to our families."

"I can be outspoken."

"No argument there," he said. "You're novel, interesting, and totally yourself."

"We laugh when we're together."

"I laugh *with* you, and you laugh *at* me."

"You're the mature one."

"Not when I'm at the amusement park. Then I'm ten again." He kissed her brow. "You're competitive, but I don't mind losing to you. Someday I want a rematch at baseball caps and bumper cars."

She'd win again. He'd be a good sport. She liked so much about him. "You're logical," she said. He offset her tendency to jump into situations feetfirst, then second-guess herself.

"You're spontaneous, which keeps life interesting."

"Am I smart enough for you?" she wondered out loud. "You spent four years at Florida State, and I went to a junior college. You took off for New York City, only to return when your father had his accident. Any regrets about living here?"

He shook his head. "I love the way you think," he assured her. "You're intuitive and imaginative. You do the daily crossword in ink."

He ran his thumb lightly over her cheek, then across her lips. His touch was soft and soothing. "Saunders Shores is where I belong. I only have to return to the city every three months for a corporate board meeting. We could travel together. You'd love Coney Island."

"Money." She hesitated, then went on to point out the obvious. "You're loaded, Trace. I fight most days to stay afloat."

Their finances didn't seem to concern him. "I want to take care of you, Shaye, but you're independent as hell. I respect that. I'll help you budget, and, if necessary, we'll clip coupons together."

She couldn't help herself; she laughed *at* him. "I can't envision you buying two for the price of one or getting excited over fifty cents off any product."

"I do what's necessary at any given time."

She pulled a face. "You drive a Porsche, and I take pedicabs."

"We both reach our destination."

"I go barefoot for days at a time."

"Haven't you noticed?" he asked. "I'm wearing shoes less." He'd kicked off his Sperry Top-Siders when he'd arrived. The pair sat inside the door.

"You like candy corn and jelly beans," she mused aloud, counting off what they had in common. "And I have a candy store."

"We both like coconut cream pie."

His words made Shaye blush as she recalled his scooping the filling off her hip. The incident seemed a lifetime ago.

He nudged her gently. "Hopefully children are in our future."

She'd love to make babies with this man. "You could take our kids sailing, and I could teach them to paddle a canoe." Her success in a canoe was minimal, but she didn't share that fact. She tipped over more than she paddled. Her children would wear life jackets.

"There's the sandlot league, too."

His mention of the league reminded her of the all-star challenge. "We'll soon be seated on opposing bleachers during the July game."

"I'm hoping to coach your nephew Jeff before the play-off," he said. "I want to give him a few more pointers."

Her heart warmed. Trace was a kind, considerate man. "Thank you," she said. "The rules put him on the field for one inning if he wants to bat. He'll play third base."

"I'll be sure he's ready."

She poked him in the chest. "What do you do when you're not working?"

"I jog, golf, and play the occasional video game."

She could get on board with all three. "I like scary movies," she said, "ones where I put a pillow over my face and scream."

"That made the hairs on the back of my neck stand on end," he said. "I appreciate the warning."

"TV shows?" She didn't want to fight him for the remote. "I like *Castle* and *The Mentalist*—you?"

"*NCIS, Criminal Minds,* and *Hawaii Five-O.*"

"Books?" came next. "I prefer spy and psychological thrillers."

"Biographies and nonfiction business and finance for me."

No surprises there. She raised an eyebrow. "What's on your iPod?"

"Sophie keeps me in music," he said easily. "She loves

the opera and classical music. I'm listening to *The Best of Andrea Bocelli* at the moment."

"I'm blasting Cyndi Lauper. 'Girls just wanna have fun,' " she sang the lyric.

"You have enough fun for ten people."

They both exhaled at the same time, then grinned at each other. So far, so good, she thought. "I cook, but not often."

"I like to grill."

She had one pet peeve. "Would you change which end of the toothpaste tube you squeeze, if it was important to me?" She was methodic, always squeezing from the bottom and rolling the tube forward. Quirky, perhaps, but that was her way.

He nodded, agreeable. "I'm fine with the toothpaste and promise to rinse the sink after I shave. I'll put the toilet seat down and give you full control of the toilet paper. It's your call if the sheets roll over or under."

She had one final thought. "Maybe we should get a reading from Madame Aleta." In Shaye's world, psychic validation was important.

"Maybe we should trust our own feelings."

"Maybe . . ." She made no promise. If she walked past her aunt's shop, she just might stop in.

Trace read her mind and rolled his eyes at her. "She'll tell you what we both know," he said. "Nothing will ever be perfect between us, we won't even come close, but perfection is overrated."

He pressed a gentle kiss to her lips. "I love you, Shaye Cates. I want you as my best friend as well as my lover. I have every intention of marrying you."

Her eyes rounded. "Is that a proposal?"

"I'm making it official."

"I'll think about it."

"You have until morning," he said.

"I could use some convincing."

"We're down to one condom."

"Then we'll have to get creative."

Trace had lots of ideas.

Afterward they fell asleep in each other's arms.

"Rise and shine," Olive squawked. She'd left her cage and now flew into the master bedroom to perch on the nautical carved headboard. She cocked her feathered head. *"Morning, Big Guns. M-mmm."*

Shaye couldn't help grinning. The Quaker always called Trace Big Guns, adding a moan. Fortunately he didn't seem to mind. He merely shook his head.

"Feed me," the parrot requested.

Trace stretched, yawned, and said, "I'm hungry, too."

"I have eggs, toast, strawberries, and sunflower seeds," she said.

"I'll take the first three."

"Seeds," came from Olive.

Shaye eased out of bed. A night of sex was great, but she was more than a little sore. Trace was a big man, and she'd stretched muscles she never knew she had. He made her shiver and gasp, and she nearly lost consciousness. Sleep was overrated.

She quickly showered, dressed, and moved to the galley. Olive was served first in her cage, a slice of strawberry and six sunflower seeds. *"Yummy,"* she thanked Shaye.

Scrambled eggs and rye toast brought Trace to the small café table. Shaye set a bowl of berries in the center and went on to pull the shades against the morning sun. Had she been alone, she would have left them open so she could appreciate the sunrise. But the sight of a Saunders sitting at her breakfast table would draw serious stares should anyone pass by.

Trace wore a black polo and jeans, casual attire for him. She'd offered him closet space, and he now used a few hangers. She liked him laid-back and relaxed.

He ate slowly, eyeing her the entire time. She shifted in her chair, squirming a little. His stare was hot, sexy, and required an answer to his late-night question: *would she marry him?*

She let him sweat until they were on their second cup of coffee. "Yes," she said, looking at him over the rim of her cup.

He smiled, equally relieved and satisfied. "Let's set a date—how about two weeks from today?" he suggested.

Her heart skipped a beat, and her words ran together. "Why so soon? That doesn't give me much time. I have a lot to do."

"Very little, actually, if I know you," he said. He reached for her hand and slid his fingers through hers. "It will be an informal wedding. We'll get married on the beach. I doubt you'll even wear shoes."

"What about invitations?" she asked, sounding panicky. "A reception?"

"Meet with my assistant, Martin," he said. "He has countless connections. Tell him what you want, and he'll make it happen."

"I want you," she said, the words rising from the bottom of her heart.

He brought her hand to his lips and kissed her palm. "Right back at you, Shaye Cates."

She ate the last of her toast before saying, "We'll need to tell our families, and that won't be easy. A hundred years of mistrust won't vanish overnight."

"Not everyone will be happy," he agreed. "Let's start by talking to my parents, then we'll meet with your grandfather. Hopefully someone will give his blessing."

"What if no one does?" That was her greatest fear.

"Then it's up to us," he said. He leaned back in his chair and grew thoughtful. "Do we let history dictate our future, or do we set our own destiny?"

She didn't have an answer for him.

Eleven

The family visits did not go well.

Shaye had been aware of her own family's grudge against the Saunders clan all her life, yet not until she faced Trace's parents did she fully understand their own aversion to her relatives. It was definitely two-sided.

The hour in their company was tense and eye-opening. Brandt and Maya didn't mince words. The four of them met in a living room so large that Shaye could've gotten lost rounding the crescent-shaped couch.

The view from the floor-to-ceiling windows showcased the yacht harbor, a tennis court, and tiered landscaping with manicured hedges and exotic flowers. The view was pristine and perfect, lifted straight from *Town and Country* magazine.

They were served iced tea in tall crystal glasses etched with an *S*. Finger sandwiches and thin slices of a tropical fruit pie were served on a sterling silver tray. The food was artfully arranged, in a look-but-don't-eat display.

Shaye went with iced tea, as did Trace.

The food sat untouched.

His parents were stiffly polite and spoke directly to their son. Shaye felt invisible. They reminded him that his heritage had been established when Evan Saunders brought commerce to the Gulf Coast. His ancestor had been a de-

veloper with foresight. Saunders Shores had grown, pros-
pered, and was listed by *Forbes* as the wealthiest resort
community in the country.

They went on to note that Barefoot William was still
nothing more than a fishing village with outdoor amuse-
ments.

They recognized that the volleyball tournament had
benefited the town but didn't see the effects as long last-
ing. They stressed that their beach was closed to a future
rental.

His father firmly stated that a merger between the two
families would be a win for the Cateses but detrimental to
them. Barefoot William would prove a financial drain on
Saunders Shores.

Shaye and Trace left his family home with stilted good-
byes. Maya pleaded with Trace to reconsider the marriage.
He told his mother the wedding would proceed as planned.
They'd receive an invitation shortly. It was their choice
whether to attend or not.

He wrapped his arm about Shaye's shoulders during the
walk from the house to his sports car. His strength and
warmth shored up her confidence.

"Your parents don't like me much," she told him as he
opened the passenger door on his Porsche and she lowered
herself into a buttery soft leather seat that molded to her
bottom.

"You're a Cates," he said, being logical and practical and
the perfect man to ease her mind. "We've gone from enemies to getting married in a very short time," he reminded her. "We've kept our relationship secret. My folks
weren't even aware we were seeing each other until
today."

"Surprise, surprise," Shaye said as she fastened her seat
belt. "I saw the shock on their faces firsthand."

They drove for twenty minutes, soon turning down a

rural winding road that led to her Grandfather Frank's stilt home. He lived ten miles from the beach, preferring to distance himself from the tourist trade.

The older man took their news while seated on a porch swing overlooking a small orange orchard. He was a widower of twenty years and as close to Shaye as her own father.

Her parents had begun traveling as soon as their children graduated from high school. During their frequent absences, she had gravitated toward her granddad, and he'd become her confidant and moral compass.

Her grandfather had taught her to play cribbage and bridge. He beat her at horseshoes. He was the only person she knew who still had a phonograph and played vinyl records. He loved listening to Sinatra. As a kid, Shaye memorized the lyrics to "Fly Me to the Moon" and "The Way You Look Tonight."

They both loved Barefoot William and treated the town like a relative. That was their strongest bond.

Grandfather Frank had offered them freshly squeezed orange juice and cranberry-orange muffins, which they both declined. Shaye clutched the wicker arms on her fan-backed chair as she spoke of her future with Trace.

Her granddad listened with his head bent, shoulders slumped, and his expression pained. He seemed to age ten years before her eyes. He did not take the news well. He was obviously skeptical and disheartened that his granddaughter would even consider a Cates-Saunders marriage. Had she lost her mind?

What hit Shaye the hardest was when he turned and fixed her with a piercing look. "Are you really willing to give up Barefoot William for this man?" he asked sternly, making it clear that, as far as he was concerned, there was no middle ground. His question felt like a physical punch.

She wasn't an emotional woman, yet at that moment

she was so upset, she couldn't answer. She forced back tears.

When they left her grandfather, Trace offered to return her to the houseboat. Once there, he held her tightly as she gave way to emotion.

"Shh, shh," he soothed. "We can work through the family theatrics, Shaye. You'll see, all of this will sort itself out with time."

Shaye wanted to believe him, but a part of her knew the life she now lived had come to an end. Her heart broke with the thought. She felt beaten down and off balance and needed to be alone.

"Time—you're right. I need a few days to sort through my feelings. Can you give me that, Trace? Just until the all-star challenge?" she pleaded.

Shaye could tell he wasn't happy to leave her, but in the end, he respected her wishes, leaving her to pace the length of her houseboat as she tried to work out which was more awful, alienating her family or losing Trace.

"Marry me, Shaye," Olive mimicked in a deep, masculine voice. She sounded exactly like Trace. The Quaker walked her perch and flapped her wings as Shaye prepared for the all-star challenge. *"Marry me, marry me."*

"Olive, please, not now," said Shaye.

"Please and thank you," the parrot squawked.

Shaye rubbed the back of her neck. She'd spent the last few days looking at her choices from every angle. Being an adult wasn't all it was cracked up to be. Making grown-up decisions was often terrifying.

Family was all-important to her, yet Trace filled a place in her heart that had been empty far too long. In the end, she'd realized she didn't want to live without him. He was all that mattered.

He challenged her and made her crazy.

She wanted to punch him most days.

But there was no way she could live without him.

Even if it meant sacrifice.

They might not live happily ever after among relatives and friends, but being happy with each other meant just as much.

She showered and dressed in a *Topaz Tarpon* T-shirt, jeans washed white at the knees, and a pair of *Barefoot William* flip-flops. She grabbed a pack of throat lozenges, in case she got hoarse from cheering.

She drew Olive to her cage with a slice of fresh peach. *"Yum, m-mm,"* the parrot said with a throaty moan.

Shaye needed to remember to close her bedroom door when Trace and she made love. Olive had heard too much.

She caught a ride with Kai and Nicole to the ballpark. Kai was calm, while Nicole fluttered like a mother hen. She hoped their boys would perform well, but, more important, she wanted them to have a good time. Win or lose, the team would enjoy pizza and ice cream after the game.

The parking lot was packed, and the walk to Saunders Field was slow. The recreational facility was large by Barefoot William standards. The scent of freshly mowed grass on the warm, summer breeze promised an exciting evening of youth baseball. They passed the visitors' locker room, and Shaye fell in behind the Tarpons. She caught bits of their conversation.

"—*five* urinals—"

"—private lockers with combination locks—"

"—showers—"

"—feels like the World Series."

The kids were excited and awed. Their own Gulf Field

was old and in need of an overhaul. It had withstood forty seasons of baseball. The scoreboard had cracked so much that the final score was no longer visible. The fencing dipped, and the bleachers sagged. They'd run out of chalk to mark the baselines.

No matter the condition of their park, their team spirit could not be denied. They were there to play their hearts out.

Nicole and Kai headed for the dugout. Shaye watched as the team clustered around Nicole, waiting for her pre-game pep talk. They all adored her. She would be the first crush for several of them. Kai didn't mind; he couldn't take his gaze off her either.

Nicole looked sporty in her *Topaz Tarpon* T-shirt, white walking shorts, and white Keds. She wore as much jewelry to the ballpark as she did in her shop. Every piece glistened beneath the bright outdoor lights.

The Cateses sat on the northern bleachers, and many of the parents gathered along the first-baseline fence. Moms and dads encouraged and inspired their kids during warm-ups.

Shaye climbed up the bleachers, searching for a seat. Word had spread she was involved with Trace Saunders. Most of those in attendance weren't pleased with her decision. Disapproval hung heavy in the air. The silence spoke loudly. Few could meet her eye. Those who did looked at her as if they no longer knew her.

Her heart squeezed, and her stomach hurt. She felt suddenly alone among the hundreds in attendance. Her legs were shaky by the time she reached the seventh row. No one scooted over and offered her a seat, not until Molly and Violet did so at the very top. Even their smiles were reserved.

Once she was seated, Molly leaned over and whispered, "History runs deep, Shaye. I love and respect you, but I just can't support your decision when it comes to Trace. None of us can. Sorry."

Shaye found it difficult to swallow. Her throat felt dry and swollen closed. She wasn't certain she could even cheer. The fun of the game seemed sucked out of her.

Somehow Trace sensed her sadness from the opposite side of the ball field. He left his family to find her. She caught him jogging up the bleachers as if he couldn't reach her fast enough. He was well dressed for a kids' baseball game. He stood out in his green collared polo, navy shorts, and Nikes.

Gazes narrowed, and jaws locked all around her. A few people got up and changed seats. Trace squeezed in beside her. They became joined at the hip.

"Cold shoulder?" he asked, keeping his voice low.

"Total freeze-out. How about you?" she whispered back.

"I got a hug from Sophie and a high five from Martin but otherwise was ignored."

Shaye felt as bad for Trace as she did for herself. She offered her support. She laced her fingers with his and held on tightly. He squeezed her hand. He understood. They sat quietly and let the rivalry between their towns play out.

A flip of a coin, and Southern Trust was first to bat. Umpires had been recruited from another county. No partiality would be shown on the field.

The Barefoot William team was physically smaller than their opposition. Only Brick Cates stood out. He'd gone through a major growth spurt. He looked fifteen instead of twelve.

The teams were evenly paired in pitching but not in hitting. Southern Trust deployed only their best players, while the Topaz Tarpon kids rotated with each inning. No one warmed the Barefoot William bench. Even her nephew Jeff, who was not at the same level as his team-mates, received equal respect.

Southern Trust loaded the scoreboard with five runs by the end of the first inning. They'd managed four singles and a home run. They walked the walk and talked trash. The Tarpon players ignored them and kept their minds on the game.

Southern Trust pitched six innings of no-hit ball. The Tarpon couldn't catch a break. Even their young power hitters struck out. It was an ego-bruising walk back to the dugout.

The seventh-inning stretch gave the players a breather. Then the game progressed with intensity. Southern Trust had more skill and talent, but Topaz Tarpon was scrappy.

The Cateses raised their voices when the Tarpon caught a break and started a short rally. The team landed runners on first and second. Jeff was next to bat. Everyone at the park was aware of his limitations and expected little from him. Most important, they didn't want him to get hurt.

"Easy out," the first baseman called to the pitcher.

"Maybe not as easy as he thinks," said Trace. "Jeff's started strength training, and I watched him stretch before the game. He's loose and pain-free. Given the right pitch, he has more than a sacrifice bunt in him."

The Cateses were all on their feet, clapping, stomping, and willing Jeff to do well. The boy looked calm and focused.

The catcher for Southern Trust motioned to the infield to expect a bunt. The players closed the gaps. The pitcher got cocky. He placed a curveball across home plate for a strike. A fastball followed. The pitch clipped the right corner of the plate and forced Jeff to jump back. He stumbled and nearly fell down. Ball one.

Balls two and three were called in succession. The pitcher's temper lit, and the boy glared at the umpire.

"Bad calls, Mr. Magoo." The first baseman's disrespectful jeer drew his team's laughter.

The pitcher's face heated with his next windup and follow-through. He released the ball in anger. The pitch went wild.

Jeff saw it coming right for him, as did everyone else at the park. He couldn't move out of the way fast enough. The fastball slammed him in the hip. Cowhide against bone made for one loud pop.

"Damn, that had to hurt," Trace muttered.

Shaye felt Jeff's pain as if it were her own.

The force knocked Jeff down. He sat on the ground, as stunned as everyone in the stands. The umpire called a time-out. Nicole ran from the dugout and reached Jeff first. Kai was close behind.

Nicole was one irate coach. She went toe-to-toe with the Southern Trust coach, demanding he control his players. There'd been no reason for his pitcher to throw like a lunatic.

The Tarpon emptied their dugout and stormed home plate. The kids circled Jeff. They clenched their fists and kicked dirt until the umpire broke them up. The ump called the pitch an accident, which drew boos and hisses from the Cates bleachers.

Jeff pushed to his feet and went on to take his base. The baseline stretched long for him. He had a slight limp and now a bruised hip. Brick Cates was next at bat. The bases were loaded.

"That's one big kid," Trace noted.

"He looks like a bully but has the heart of a teddy bear," said Shaye. "He'll knock one out of the park for Jeff."

The pitcher took Brick to full count, three balls and two strikes, before the boy airmailed the ball all the way to the beach. The home run added four runs to the Tarpon score. Jeff pumped his arm when he crossed home.

Brick jumped on the bag so hard that he disengaged the anchor. It took the umpire several minutes to reset home plate.

Only one run now separated the teams.

Saunders Shores grew subdued, while Barefoot William went nuts. The Cateses grabbed and hugged one another. Shaye caught an enthusiastic hug before her second cousin realized she had hold of her. Emma quickly let her go.

Throughout the excitement, Trace stood with his arm about her shoulders. He didn't care who saw them together. They'd gone public. They were a couple. He watched the game with an impartial eye.

Shaye relaxed and got into the spirit of the game. These were her cousins, and she had every right to cheer for them. She made up for lost time. She cupped her hands to her mouth like a megaphone and encouraged them loudly. Kai looked up into the stands and gave her a thumb's-up.

Kai kept his players in line. They capitalized on their opponents' mistakes and minimized their own. The youthful batters refrained from reaching for the fence and delivered solid line drives.

The outfield ran and dived for those uncatchable fly balls, which somehow landed in their gloves. Through it all, elbows and chins were scraped. The center fielder sprained his ankle.

Nicole was both nurse and coach. She wrapped the center fielder's ankle with an Ace bandage, then handed out Band-Aids, even for the tiniest scratch. The players stood before her, small in stature yet with warrior hearts. She made each one feel ten feet tall.

Top of the ninth and the score remained 5–4 in favor of Southern Trust. This was the closet game ever to be played between the towns. Parents, family, and friends sat on the edge of their seats, holding their breath and silently praying.

Jeff played third base in his rotation on defense.

He looked uneasy, positioned a foot off the bag.

Shaye and Trace soon shifted their vantage point. They left the stands and moved to the fence along the third base-line. They picked a spot near Jeff. There, Trace attempted to fire him up. Jeff gave him a nervous smile and nodded. He rubbed his hip, then bent slightly at the waist, ready to attack any ball hit his way.

Three pop-ups came within his range.

Fortunately two went foul.

The third dropped between third and short. The short-stop called for the ball. The shortstop scooped it up and threw to first. The umpire called the runner out. The shortstop gave Jeff a high-five, awarding Jeff equal credit for the play.

Shaye's chest squeezed as the inning moved in slow mo-tion. Each hit, each catch, seemed to last forever. The Topaz Tarpon finally closed out the inning, holding Southern Trust to a one-run lead.

Jeff was in the final lineup to bat.

Shaye fidgeted until Trace took her hand. "He'll be fine," he said. "This is his chance to shine."

They changed spots once again, moving along the fence, finding room near the Tarpon dugout. They were now in clear view of the action. Nicole's voice rose, calm and reassuring, as she told each boy he was a superstar. Win or lose, she was incredibly proud of her team.

The boys were pumped and promised her the trophy.

Everyone held their collective breath when the first two batters went down swinging. The pitcher looked smug. He had a strong mound presence for someone so young. The outfielders smirked, only to be caught off guard when the next hitter powered the ball into right field. He landed a double. He took a long lead off second base.

Jeff now crossed to home plate. He appeared decisive,

positive, a boy out to prove that, no matter his size or disability, he was worth his place on the team.

He tapped the head of his bat on the bag as if he owned it.

The pitcher curled his lip.

"Third out," shouted the first baseman.

"Third, third," resonated from the outfield.

Shaye ignored their chant and crossed her fingers.

"A little faith," Trace said. "Jeff's going to hit."

She hoped so. The pitcher took him to two strikes, and the Saunders bleachers began to empty. They believed the game was over.

They were wrong.

"Shoulders—keep them even," Trace said under his breath as he clutched the fence.

Jeff batted right. Shaye knew her nephew's scoliosis raised his left shoulder slightly higher than his right. That was to his disadvantage. She watched as Jeff drew in a deep breath, shelved his pain, and by the grace of God lifted his right arm. The new slant to his stance was suddenly as solid as any normal kid's.

She saw Trace smile, and her heart warmed.

He'd given Jeff a chance to hit.

The pitcher threw a fastball for ball one, then followed with a changeup. The unexpected off-speed pitch sailed waist-high across the plate. Another batter would've taken it as ball two. Not Jeff. It was the perfect height for him.

"Now!" shouted Trace, willing the boy to swing.

Bat and ball connected, and Jeff knocked the ball just over the pitcher's head. The shortstop botched the catch, and the runner advanced to third. Jeff pushed himself and reached first base safely. It was the longest sixty feet he'd ever jogged.

The Topaz Tarpon were at two outs with a runner on third, within scoring distance.

The cheering grew so loud, it could be heard in the next county, possibly all the way to the state capital.

Brick Cates stood just off home plate and took a practice swing. Shaye overheard Kai instruct the young slugger to be smart, to wait for his pitch, and not to reach for any ball.

The Tarpon's fastest runner was on third. A solid single from Brick, and the kid would score. The game would then be tied. A tie would be spectacular. Barefoot William would rejoice for a year.

A win against a team literally out of their league would be cause for a parade, maybe even fireworks.

The game sat on Brick's shoulders, and fortunately they were wide. He took his time, finally smacking a fastball into left. The outfielder reacted quickly and relayed the ball to third. There was no point in firing the ball home. The runner had already crossed the plate.

The scoreboard numbers flipped, reflecting a 5–5 tie.

The third baseman spotted Jeff sneaking into second. He fired the ball, expecting Jeff to be tagged out. Jeff refused to go down easily. He turned back toward first and suddenly faced a rundown.

Three infielders came after him, including the pitcher. Jeff ran forward, backward, then hopped aside. He didn't stand a chance, but that didn't stop him from trying.

The ball was passed a dozen times before the pitcher ended the taunting series of exchanges. He rushed Jeff, and, instead of a sportsman's tag, he shoved him. Hard. Jeff flew into the first baseman, who then collided with the shortstop. They all hit the ground, a sprawl of arms and legs.

Two of the three players rose.

One boy spat and wiped his mouth with the back of his hand. He'd taken a mouthful of dirt.

The other held his arm close to his body.

Jeff remained flat on his back.

A shocked silence hovered over the field.

Shaye grabbed hold of Trace's arm. "Is he okay?"

He strained to see. "I can't tell," he said. "He's lying still."

The Southern Trust team stepped back when the umpires, coaches, and Tarpon players crossed the field and gathered close.

"Go see what's going on," Shaye said. "Jump the fence— it's quicker."

Trace didn't hesitate. He cleared it in a second.

Concern pressed in the center of her chest, and she could barely catch her breath. Jeff was special. She'd vowed to somehow find the money to help pay for the corrective surgery to his spine. His parents didn't have health insurance and had put it off too long.

She clutched the fence so hard that the metal wire left an imprint on her palms. Jeff was slow to rise. Trace and Kai helped him up. The boy favored one ankle. He was unable to put any weight on his right foot.

Shaye was certain the ankle was broken.

She heard sirens in the distance and was relieved when an ambulance parked near the Topaz Tarpon dugout. Two paramedics carrying a stretcher crossed the field.

Jeff refused their assistance.

He said something to Kai, Trace, and the home plate umpire that didn't carry to Shaye. A debate followed. The umpire turned to the Southern Trust players and asked several questions. Ones Shaye still couldn't hear. She grew more and more frustrated.

A heated intensity rolled off the baseline. The opposition argued and frowned. They weren't happy. The pitcher threw down his glove, cursed.

The umpire finally nodded to Jeff, then returned to

home plate. Trace and Kai looked worried but honored whatever request Jeff might have made. Trace bent, retrieved the boy's baseball cap from the ground, and passed it to him. Jeff put on his cap and dusted himself off.

He motioned to Brick and Derek, his closest friends on the team. The two kids supported him as he hopped on one foot. The three boys rounded second, then third, and headed home. Jeff's face reflected his pain. He was deathly pale, and his lips were pinched.

Brick and Derek released Jeff ten feet from the bag. Jeff panted and hopped; he was a player out to score. He managed to keep his balance as he crossed home plate. He raised his arms in victory.

The umpire shouted, *"Safe!"*

Silence held as family and fans looked at one another, awaiting an explanation. No one understood the umpire's call.

The umpire quickly cleared up their confusion. He raised his voice and said, "The pitcher shoved Jeff Cates but never officially tagged him. The run stands."

The scoreboard flashed, one number flipped, and the five became a six. The Topaz Tarpon had won the all-star challenge.

No one cheered louder than a supportive family, Shaye thought, as laughter and shouts echoed on the night air. This was the first time she'd stood aside and watched the joy and happiness unfold. It was explosive. The Cateses knew how to love and praise their own. Smiles stretched from ear to ear, and bear hugs left everyone breathless.

Their excitement was short-lived. Then their concern for Jeff took top priority. People soon emptied the bleachers and moved onto the field.

Jeff stood on one foot, supported by his two best friends. He looked ready to pass out. The emergency personnel took over and got him into the ambulance. The Southern Trust player with the injured shoulder was also taken to the hospital.

Shaye heard Nicole promise Jeff she'd meet him there. Jeff wanted the team to celebrate without him. No one would hear of such nonsense. There'd be no partying until Jeff could take part.

She leaned heavily against the fence as her family took off for the hospital. She wanted to go with them, but now was not the time. She'd only make them uncomfortable. All their concentration needed to be on Jeff.

Trace found Shaye standing in the same spot he'd left her. She stared after the ambulance, her expression sad. He put his arms around her and hugged her close.

"Jeff will be fine," he assured her. "He's the hero of the night. Winning will carry him through his surgery and recovery. I'm pretty sure he broke his ankle."

She sighed, soft and wistful. Her cheek rested over his heart. "I may not be able to see him for a day or two," she said. "Not until family clears out and he's up for my company."

"I doubt Nicole will leave his bedside," he said. "She was pretty shaken up when Jeff got hurt."

"Getting injured is a big part of sports," she said. "Jeff is a kid we all wanted to protect."

"Look how strong he was tonight."

"He didn't give up during the rundown."

"He was smart enough to realize he hadn't been tagged by the ball," said Trace. "He came through for Barefoot William."

"We won." She smiled against his chest.

"It was a good game." He bent to look into her eyes. "What about us? You promised me an answer tonight."

"I haven't given up either," she said, smiling up at him.

"Whatever my family thinks, you and I are a team. I love you, Trace."

He picked her up and whirled her around, a man pleased by her decision. "We could have a small victory party all our own."

"My place or yours?" She left it up to him.

He wanted to bring her into his world, to share his home and see if she could adjust. But Trace realized tonight was not the time. Her life had been turned upside down by family. She was now on the outside looking in.

A sense of familiarity would bring her the most comfort. "The houseboat and Olive," he finally said. "I'm hoping if I talk really sweetly to your parrot and bribe her with sunflower seeds that she'll stop calling me Big Guns."

Shaye leaned back and laughed. "Good luck with that."

Trace kept Shaye busy over the next few days. They decided to take a long weekend, and neither went to work. Instead they relaxed, something they hadn't done for a long, long time. They watched television, listened to music, danced, played board games, and made love. They connected on so many levels. He'd never felt closer to another women.

He spent time with Olive, coaxing her to call him Trace. He had little success. The parrot was fixated on Big Guns, followed by a whole lot of moaning.

His assistant, Martin Carson, came to the houseboat and helped plan their wedding. Shaye put him in charge of invitations and the reception. Trace could tell by her expression that she didn't expect a soul to show. She went very small-scale.

He found a few tasks to occupy his time. He painted the railing on the upper deck of the Horizon a dark blue, while Shaye went on a cleaning streak. She dusted, mopped, and washed windows. She also sorted through every drawer and cupboard, working her way to her bedroom closet.

He located her late one afternoon seated cross-legged on the floor in her bedroom, unpacking a box of framed vintage photographs. He dropped down beside her. "These are amazing," he said, picking up a black-and-white photo of the pier under construction.

"Uncle Dave preserved the town's history," she said while admiring a picture of the carousel.

He held up the largest of the photos. "Barefoot William was an infant back then. There were only three shops on the boardwalk."

She passed him another photo, one with a dozen big boats scattered offshore. "We were once a commercial fishing village."

He removed the last remaining photograph from the box and stared with an intensity that drew Shaye's attention.

"What's wrong?" she asked. "You look like you've seen a ghost."

Trace tapped his finger on the glass of the framed photo. "Who's this man?"

She took a look. "My great-great-great-grandfather William Cates, the founder of Barefoot William."

He shook his head. "Unbelievable." He then pointed to the dot in the distance. "I have this same photo. That dot is Evan Saunders, William's archenemy. A lone photographer must have captured them from different angles."

Her breath caught as she ran one finger along the framed edge. "This reveals so much, then. The men never agreed on town growth or development, but at twilight they shared the beach, the Gulf."

He nodded. "They had fishing in common."

"Too bad their disagreements caused such a rivalry between families."

"A hundred years is a long time to carry a grudge," he agreed.

"We're the first to break from the past," she said. "It's not going to be easy."

"Nothing worthwhile ever is." He placed a light, reassuring kiss on her lips, then, tongue-in-cheek, suggested, "We could always start our own town."

She smiled, liking the idea.

They repacked the photos and shoved the box back into her closet. They both stood. She brushed her hands against her thighs, at a loss what to do next. She'd run out of projects.

"Are you ready to visit Jeff?" he asked.

"I think so," she said slowly. "Molly sent me a text. Surgery repaired his broken ankle. He'll remain in the hospital until tomorrow. Then he goes home."

Trace pulled the car keys from his pocket. "I'm ready, if you're ready."

She collected her wallet off her dresser. "On the way, I want to stop and buy a new baseball glove. The one Jeff uses now should've been thrown away two years ago."

Trace drove her to a local sporting goods store, where she purchased the best infielder mitt money could buy. He next stopped at Helium City and bought a giant sports "walking" balloon.

Bobbie Baseball stood four feet high and was three feet around. He was white with black stitching. He wore a small baseball cap and was designed with a smiley face, accordion arms and legs, and wide, flat, cardboard feet. One light push. and Bobbie managed a short walk.

Their gifts in hand, they proceeded to the hospital. Bobbie Baseball sat next to Shaye on the front seat, bouncy and distracting. Trace parked his Porsche in the visitors' lot. They walked two blocks to the entrance.

They located Jeff on the fifth floor. They glanced inside

and found his room momentarily quiet and family-free. Trace nudged Bobbie in ahead of them.

They both smiled when Jeff caught sight of the baseball balloon and laughed. They entered a moment later, just in time to prevent Bobbie from walking into a wall. They positioned the balloon at the end of Jeff's bed.

Two patients occupied the room. Both boys had undergone surgery. Jeff's roommate was Landon Davis from Saunders South. Landon had dislocated his shoulder during the rundown play.

They both had casts.

Each cast had a hundred signatures in Magic Marker.

Trace crossed to Landon and shook the boy's hand. Landon's father was an attorney. His firm rented office space at Saunders Square.

He next looked at Jeff and said, "Hello, hero."

Jeff's smile was wide and proud.

Shaye came up beside him. She nodded to Landon and gently patted his good shoulder. She then hugged Jeff so hard, he wheezed. "How are you feeling?" she asked him.

"I'm bionic," Jeff said. "A pin, plate, and four screws are holding my ankle together. Once I've healed and the hardware's removed, I get to keep it."

She went on to admire all the names on his cast. Many were people she didn't recognize. "Who are Barry Royce and Thomas Caine?" she asked, confused.

"Players for Southern Trust," he told her.

Trace noticed Shaye's surprise. She squinted, read further. "What about Kyle Young and Rosalind Taylor?"

"Classmates of Landon's," Jeff said. "Anyone who's come to visit has signed both our casts. Even the pitcher, Rich Gaffney, wrote his name and a message down by my toes."

She scanned Rich's words: *Wait until next year.*

The rivalry would continue. "It's great you've made new friends," she said.

"Friends only for my hospital stay," said Jeff.

Trace understood. The boys were recovering together now, but once they left the hospital, their association would end. They lived on two different sides of Center Street.

The only time Barefoot William and Saunders South came together was for the summer all-star challenge. Once a year was all either could handle.

He was touched by the depth of emotion between Shaye and Jeff when she presented him with his new leather infielder glove. Tears banked her eyes when her nephew whooped and slipped his hand inside. He pounded the pocket with his fist. It fit perfectly.

"I want to become a great fielder," Jeff said. "I'll need to play catch to break in my glove."

"You'll have to soften the leather, too," Landon advised. "I'd use saddle soap or mink oil."

"Brick uses his dad's foam shaving cream," Jeff said. "Derek goes with Vasoline."

He was so excited over his glove that he forgot Shaye and Trace were still in the room. Within minutes Nicole and Kai arrived. Jeff showed off his glove to an apprecia-tive audience.

The boys began to rehash the ball game, and the adults moved to the hallway, where they had an opportunity to talk.

"The boardwalk's not the same without you," Kai was quick to tell Shaye. "Molly's so worried about your wed-ding, her cooking has suffered. I ordered a meat loaf sand-wich and cup of soup for lunch yesterday and was served a chicken pot pie."

"Same here," said Nicole. "Molly burned the bacon on

my BLT and gave me mashed potatoes instead of French fries. Her regular customers are being kind and overlooking her mistakes."

"Jenna at Three Shirts hasn't placed an order since the volleyball tournament," Kai continued. "You've always helped her with stock and inventory. She's down to sale items only."

"How's Eden doing? Is she open for business?" Shaye asked.

"She's moved in, and I hung the sign for Old Tyme Portraits just this morning," said Kai. "I'm helping her get organized. She'd hoped for your approval on the life-size cardboard cutouts before she started taking pictures. She spent more than she should on camera equipment."

"Goody Gumdrops?" she next asked, concerned about her own shop.

"You've trained Nick well," said Kai. "Our cousin knows the business inside and out. He's even making bank deposits."

Shaye appeared relieved.

"Madame Aleta keeps muttering, 'This, too, will pass,'" said Nicole.

The fortune-teller was no doubt right, Trace thought. However, he knew the difficulties Shaye faced. One such problem would be their wedding. They hadn't received a single RSVP from either family. The bridal party itself had yet to be decided. It was going to be tricky to find two people to stand up for them.

Shaye now breathed deeply as she asked Nicole, "Will you be my maid of honor?" Her voice sounded hollow, but if Nicole noticed, she didn't let on.

Nicole's excitement spilled over. She grabbed Shaye and gave her a big hug. "It would be an honor."

Shaye nudged Trace, and he went along with her earlier

suggestion. He met Kai man to man, eye to eye. "I need a best man."

Kai looked as if he'd rather poke a fork into his own eye. He took a long time to answer, a full minute according to the clock hanging on the wall of the nurses' station. Trace wasn't certain he'd agree.

Kai ran one hand down his face and exhaled sharply. "I may not approve of Shaye's decision, but she's always been crazy. Only for *her*," he stressed, "will I stand up at your wedding."

"Thank you." Shaye's voice broke.

Trace pulled her to him and lent her his strength.

She was the strongest woman he knew, yet the lack of family support left her vulnerable. She'd lived her life embraced by many. Now only Kai stood by her side.

He knew that her love for Barefoot William would never die, no matter her future. He would do everything in his power to make her happy for the rest of their lives.

Ten days later, the barefoot bride and groom stood on the beach at twilight. The sky was a swirl of purple and gold. A faint breeze cooled the air.

The groom stood on the sand in a light brown suit.

The bride wore a white sundress and an ivory satin hair band sprinkled with diamond dust, a wedding gift from her maid of honor.

Something old was their past.

Something new lay in their future.

Something borrowed was Trace's ancestral photograph of Evan Saunders on the shore at twilight. Shaye clutched both his and her framed photos, feeling the heartbeat of a hundred years against her breast.

Something blue rose at high tide, when the turquoise Gulf washed over their feet.

A judge from the Saunders courthouse married them.
Nicole stood to her right.
Kai was on Trace's left.
No one else would attend their wedding.
It was a strangely solitary moment.

Pain shot beneath Shaye's breastbone as she slowly turned her back on the empty stretch of sand and boardwalk and looked out over the ocean. She released a slow breath.

She'd made the right decision.
She loved Trace Saunders.

He held her hand through the ceremony. He brought her warmth, strength, and security. When he looked down at her, she knew he loved her, too.

They exchanged rings, plain gold bands. Shaye had gone with simplicity; their lives were complicated enough.

Their wedding ended with the traditional kiss, a promise of tomorrow. Trace would see her through the good times and the bad. And she, him. They'd survived a century-old feud and lived to tell about it. They would have countless stories to share with their grandchildren.

Where they would go and what they would do was yet to be decided. Whatever happened, they'd face it together. As Trace's strong arms held her, Shaye felt a surge of unreasonable joy. She was home.

"We have company," Nicole whispered to Shaye.

Full of wonder, Shaye turned. There on the beach, a small crowd had silently assembled to witness the ceremony. Through teary eyes she spotted numerous family members and friends gathered behind them on the sand. Not everyone, but a significant number had defied tradition to share in her happiness, and the warm smiles on their faces meant more to her than she ever could have imagined.

Those who touched her most were the young sandlot

players. The boys wore their team T-shirts and jeans. Jeff leaned on his crutches between his best friend, Brick, and his hospital roommate, Landon Davis.

Madame Aleta was the first to come forward, soon followed by Molly, Jenna, and Violet. Sophie Saunders hesitated until Shaye waved her over. Sophie hugged her the hardest.

As they offered their congratulations, Shaye was so choked up, she could barely breathe. Nicole passed her a dainty lace hanky to blot her tears.

Trace pointed to the boardwalk. Standing fifty feet apart, but still in attendance, stood his parents and her grandfather. There was stiffness in their shoulders and an uncompromising look to their features.

They'd refused to give their blessings, yet at the end of the day, they'd overseen the union of a Cates and a Saunders without hysterics or disruption.

It was the start of a new era for both sides.

"It's going to be okay, isn't it?" Shaye sought her husband's reassurance.

"Better than okay," he promised. "If our ancestors could fish and share a beach at twilight, then our families can find common ground, too."

Her smile curved. "They won't want to miss out on our children."

"Babies are good," he agreed.

"I like big families."

"We can start our own sandlot team."

"It's time to get Olive a friend, too."

Trace rolled his eyes. "Two moaning parrots in the house?"

"That's right, Big Guns."

Did you miss the last in the series, SWEET SPOT?

Score

James "Law" Lawless is the star second baseman for the Richmond Rogues, the wildest group of free swingers ever to barnstorm their way through the big leagues. So when he hooks up with a seductive stranger at a costume party, it feels like he just hit the winning run of the World Series.

Extra Innings

Catherine "Cat" May was the hot number in that skimpy Wonder Woman costume. But she's not about to let Law know it—especially after he hires her to help him expand his off-the-field business empire. But how's she going to keep her identity secret when his every touch urges her to make him her very own . . .

Home Run Hero

Hallow Days of May
Club Haunt
Midnight

Orange strobe lights. Pumpkin-scented incense.
    Glow-in-the-dark spider webs.
Evil-faced jack-o'-lanterns.
Ouija board and tarot cards.
Inhibitions were left at the door, along with the cover charge. The adult Halloween costumes guaranteed anonymity. Everyone wore a mask.
Pheromones heated the crowded club and sweat trickled down chests and between thighs. Anticipated sex throbbed to Michael Jackson's "Thriller."
Captain America stood against the wall and took it all in. On the dance floor, Darth Vader fondled Scarlett O'Hara. At the corner of the bat-shaped bar, a sexy skeleton stroked Jesse James's revolver. The outlaw was cocked.
A well-oiled Tin Man felt up Dorothy beneath an exit sign. Her red heels clicked as he kissed her back to Kansas.
In a darkened corner, Zorro twisted more than the fringe on the flapper's costume. Behind the buffet, a zombie unwrapped an Egyptian mummy down to her thong.
It was a night to get laid.

Captain America shifted, adjusted his patriotic body suit, a replica of the original American flag motif. His blue mask had an "A" centered on his forehead, and gold polyfoam wings clipped his shoulders. His red boots reached his knees. His red gloves cleared his elbows. He was armed with an indestructible shield that could be thrown as a weapon.

"This is one hell of a party." The Incredible Hulk handed the Captain a Samuel Adams. "I'm glad you wanted to check out the club. Haunt has investment potential."

Captain America nodded his agreement. The renovated warehouse sat on a prime piece of real estate in downtown Richmond. Its notorious adult Halloween parties drew celebrities, athletes, models, and executives. The waiting line wrapped an entire city block every single night. Customers sold their souls to the Devil at the door to enter. "I meet with Driscoll Financial tomorrow," the Captain reminded Hulk. "My offer will have been presented to Dan Hatton and I hope to close on Haunt."

Hatton was the present owner of the club. He'd recently suffered a stroke. The man had worked hard all his life, and on his eightieth birthday, his heart had warned him to slow down. As a result, he'd begun selling off his holdings, starting with Club Haunt.

The hot property was a diversified venture for Captain America. If all went well, he would soon own the trendy night club of secret identities. His adrenaline rushed at the prospect.

Midnight, and the music built. The sounds became darker, kinkier, more suggestive. Haunt pulsed, and bodies ground against one another. The air vibrated, and the sexual tension pumped to orgasm.

Hulk took a long pull on his beer, then caught the eye of a Victorian vampire. She flashed her fangs at him. "Lady wants to bite." Hulk grinned.

The Captain watched as the mean, green fighting machine in the torn purple pants sauntered toward the gothic-looking woman in a tight black leather bustier and flowing skirt. Her auburn hair fell to her waist and her blood red fingernails were as long and sharp as her fangs. Her white face powder gave her an eerie glow.

Captain America's testicles tightened. The vamp wouldn't have been his first choice for a hookup. She looked damn scary. The Hulk, however, liked the dark side.

An enormous T-Rex lumbered past, and the sweep of his thick, spiky tail tripped a dozen people in his wake. Only Wonder Woman avoided the collision. Agile and sleek, her red satin cape swung wide as she hopped over the tail and landed lightly on the balls of her feet.

The Captain stared at the woman in the red leotard with a blue bottom patterned with white stars. He noted their costumes were quite similar, even though he was an Avenger and she fought for the Justice League.

He admired her endless legs, a hint of pale hip bone, and the slight dip of her belly. The heels of her knee-high red and white vinyl boots added five inches to her height. She proved a true Amazon princess, and one fine DC comic book heroine.

Wonder Woman had curves. High, full breasts and one hell of a nice ass. A wide gold belt cinched her waist and two silver cuff bracelets banded each wrist.

A sparkly golden headband contained her dark curls and a red-winged mask hid half her face. She tapped her Lasso of Truth against her thigh in time to the music.

The Captain liked what he saw. He handed his empty bottle of beer to a cocktail waitress, then elbowed through the crowd. There was no direct path to Wonder Woman. He was stopped twice, once by a flirty, cotton-headed female q-tip and a second time by a Barbie doll in a cellophane box. While both women drew his smile, it was

Wonder Woman who held his interest. He pushed forward, filled with purpose and intrigue.

Wonder Woman was partied out. It was time to call it a night. She had a big day at work tomorrow. Her boss had suggested she attend the club in costume to evaluate its market value. The warehouse was worth its asking price. Haunt had an unidentifiable sexual mystique no amount of publicity could buy. It was the hot spot of the city. From what she'd witnessed, the club was a gold mine. Her boss had a client ready to invest. According to her audit team, Haunt turned a solid profit. Her recommendation was to buy quickly. The club showed no signs of slowing down.

The nightly Halloween celebrations masked reality. People gravitated and gyrated to the unknown. Wonder Woman had lost two boyfriends to Haunt. They'd both entered the club monogamous and left for a ménage.

Anonymity turned partiers into players. She wasn't a fan of the place.

The club's cardinal rule forbade sex on the premises, but what happened in the parking lot stayed in the parking lot. While this wasn't her personal playground of choice, those around her were having a hell of a good time.

Wonder Woman stifled a yawn. She wanted to get out of her costume. The brown wig had begun to itch and the curls had lost their bounce. The bra cups on her leotard squeezed her breasts like a bustier, doubling her cup size. The blue bottom was as skimpy as a pair of bikini panties. She was totally out of her element.

The crush of the crowd made her claustrophobic and the noise level was deafening. Her eyes burned from the candle smoke and her lungs demanded fresh air. She was exhausted from turning down the advances of amorous costumed characters. Bozo the Clown's big floppy feet had stepped all over her boots when requesting a dance. Gumby had twisted his body around her like a pretzel.

Rising on tip-toe, she scanned the room. The warehouse was enormous, and there was no immediate sign of a black-and-red Lady Bug. She and her friend Carla had agreed that should they get separated, each would find her own way home. The Lady Bug had hoped to get lucky, and she'd had her eye on Daffy Duck.

Wonder Woman turned to leave, only to run smack into Captain America. *Could the man stand any closer?* His proximity smothered her.

All sound in the club receded, and it was only the two of them in a sea of costumes. Stillness, stark and indefinable, embraced them both until someone jostled her elbow and all the noise crashed back. Instinctively, she raised her indestructible bracelets to ward him off.

Behind his mask, daredevil dark eyes gleamed at her and his lips curved in a slow, sexy smile. "No need to defend yourself against me, babe, we're both superheroes on the side of justice," his voice was deep yet distorted against the background noise.

Wonder Woman swallowed hard. She was certain she'd need protection against this man, he was one fine Avenger. She couldn't fully see his face, yet she instinctively knew he'd be handsome. No doubt too handsome for his own good.

There was no padding to his costume, his body suit fit like a second skin. He was six feet of broad shoulders and ripped muscle. Tight spandex cupped his groin, leaving little to her imagination. Captain America leaned in, his power raw and tangible. His cologne elicited desire and passion, an orgasm in a bottle. "Are you here alone or in the company of Superman and Batman?" he asked.

Alone made her available. While the pulse of the club

had gotten under her skin, she wasn't looking for a one-night stand. Not even with a Marvel comic book hero who'd mastered the martial arts and was known for his intelligence, strength, and super reaction times.

"The members of the Justice League are always close by," she raised her voice above the music, letting him assume the trinity was in attendance. "Are you here with the Avengers?"

"Only the Incredible Hulk," he stated. "He hooked up with a blood sucker."

The Victorian vampire. Wonder Woman had noticed the vamp circling the crowd, looking for her next victim. The Hulk would get fanged.

The Captain's gaze narrowed and his jaw shifted. "Are you a regular?" he wanted to know.

He wondered if she was a serial dater; if she slept around. "This is my virgin haunt," she strained her voice to be heard. "How about you?" She roped his arm tightly with her Lasso of Truth, so he could not lie.

"First time for me too," he said.

"You're not into nightly costumes?"

His gaze glittered behind his mask. "Only if my woman wanted to dress up privately for me in the bedroom."

Her lasso went slack. She could imagine a very naughty nurse stripping for this man, as well as the hot, sweaty sex that would follow. He'd have satin sheets and skilled hands. He was satisfaction guaranteed.

She blushed, and desperately hoped it was too dark in the club for Captain America to witness her embarrassment.

His grin punched dimples, and her whole body flushed. The man was a mind reader.

"Have you eaten?" He nodded toward the buffet. "There's chicken witch fingers, miniature bat burgers, and Bloody Marys."

"I've had dinner." Her throat was so raw from shouting, she now sounded like Minnie Mouse. She'd soothe the scratchiness later with a cup of tea and honey.

The music soon turned eerie and hauntingly slow. The floor reverberated with a deep, sexual bass. Goose bumps skated down her spine. All around her couples compressed and kissed as if it was New Year's Eve.

Boldly, the Captain propped his shield against the wall. His hands now free, he made his move and drew her body flush against his. Her booted heels raised her to his height. Her palms splayed across his chest, as solid as armor plate. Her lasso dangled dangerously near his groin.

She inhaled their closeness.

They shared air, breath, and heat. The darkness captured and seduced; their intimacy was compelling. Her heart slammed hard and her stomach shimmied. He consumed her.

The man was physical perfection. For one hot moment, she savored the superhero. They swayed together, their attraction dominant. Her inhibitions slid down her legs like a pair of silk panties.

She could handle one dance before she sneaked into the crowd and out the side door. She'd hail a cab and disappear into the night. Too bad she didn't have her invisible plane.

Beneath the orange strobe lighting, Captain America's strong hands now spanned her waist, then worked higher. He brushed the underside of her breasts and her nipples tightened in response. She ached to be touched further.

His warm breath fanned her cheek, a forewarning of his kiss. He claimed her mouth like a conquering hero. The man was all touch, tongue, and temptation. His stubble scraped the soft curve of her chin.

He stroked down her ribs, thumbed her navel.

He squeezed her hips with sexual urgency.

She sighed, and he swallowed the sound.

Wild currents built as she wound her arms tightly around his neck. Her fingers dug into his back.

He grabbed her bottom and their bodies grafted. The spandex made them fluid and seamless as they simulated sex.

She rolled her hips to feel him fully, and his bulge confirmed him super-sized. Friction sparked, and their chemistry shot through the roof. Desire zinged between her legs. She went damp for him.

Time swelled, and his kisses deepened. He bit her lower lip, sucked her tongue. The moments seemed surreal. Caped in darkness and anonymity, they groaned and grew impatient. She clawed his shoulders and he stroked the crease of her ass. The rhythm of the night overtook them. They dry humped, harder, faster, all control lost to her wetness and his rigid inches.

Her skin stretched, taut yet tender.

His erection strained.

His heart seemed to beat in her breast. They were as close to being one as two people could get without being naked. Sensations fogged her brain. His desire branded her. There was no delaying the inevitable.

The intensity was insane.

So crazy, she climaxed.

She came apart in his arms on the dance floor.

Spasms of release left her body liquid, and shame soon cleared her head. *What had she done?*

She'd humped a comic book hero at a club known for anonymous pleasure. He'd teased her and turned her on. She'd let herself be taken. She'd fallen to the darkness and decadence and one erect Avenger.

This was so not her. She needed to leave.

Hand-to-hand combat was Wonder Woman's specialty, and a strong elbow to the Captain's ribs freed her. She forced long, deep breaths into her lungs, clutched the golden lasso protectively to her chest.

His brow furrowed beneath his mask as sex fuzzed his brain. She hated to be his buzz kill, but her night ended right here, right now.

She backed away from him, one step, then two.

His gaze held surprise and hunger. He spread his hands wide, openly confused by her departure. She couldn't explain her feelings, how she'd foolishly lost herself in him. She'd walked the dark side and experienced the sexual mystique of Haunt. Instead of satisfaction, she felt hollow and numb. And incredibly easy.

Humiliated, she turned toward the exit. King Kong provided the perfect cover and she darted behind him. She pushed past a Chicago gangster and a samurai warrior. A glance over her shoulder, and there was no sign of Captain America. She picked up her pace, moved faster through the crowd.

A whirling, twirling ballerina knocked the Lasso of Truth off her wrist. It whipped beneath the feet of a dancing bear. Wonder Woman didn't stop to pick it up, it would only cost her time.

The side exit was in view. A final dash and she cleared the dance door. The bouncer flagged down a cab.

She was gone.

Captain America caught the taillights of her taxi. He imagined her taking off in her invisible plane. A cleared runway, trays in an upright position, and her hanging onto a bag of peanuts. She'd fly full throttle into the night sky. Far away from him.

His gut wrenched over his inability to stop her. He and his overactive libido owed her an apology, yet she'd run off while he'd been bone hard and unable to give chase.

On his way to the exit, Little Bo Beep had snagged him with her pink staff and requested a dance. He'd waved her off. A nun in full habit had invited him to sin. Had he not met Wonder Woman, he might have taken the nun up on her offer.

The heroine had hit him low and left him hard. He wasn't a man to bring a woman to orgasm on the dance floor. He preferred his privacy. Yet she'd gone off on him, a woman with a short sexual fuse. He'd absorbed her climax, then her uncertainty. She seemed to hate herself for letting go.

He flat didn't understand.

They'd been damn good together.

A part of him hoped she wasn't a tease. Or a good girl gone bad for the night. He liked his women stable and sane.

He reentered the club and was immediately propositioned by Olive Oyl and an Indian maiden. He chose to go home alone. His desire for the Amazon Princess held strong.

Head down, he crossed the dance floor. A golden rope was being kicked about by the dancers, and it nearly tripped him. He bent and retrieved the Lasso of Truth. Her scent lingered on the golden lariat, patchouli and spice.

His smile shaped slowly. His life had taken a turn for the better. Wonder Woman had lost a part of her costume. He'd have his administrative assistant contact every Halloween shop in Richmond until he located the customer who'd returned her suit without the lariat.

He'd soon know her true identity.

He had every plan to see her again. If the lasso fit, she'd be forced to tell the truth. He wouldn't let her run a second time.